The New Collection of
Short Stories

The New Collection of
Short Stories

Andrew G Riddell

THE NEW COLLECTION OF SHORT STORIES

iUniverse books may be ordered through booksellers or by contacting:

iUniverse
1663 Liberty Drive
Bloomington, IN 47403
www.iuniverse.com
844-349-9409

ISBN: 978-1-6632-4852-7 (sc)
ISBN: 978-1-6632-4858-9 (e)

Library of Congress Control Number: 2023908751

Print information available on the last page.

iUniverse rev. date: 05/15/2023

Contents

I would like to thank my publishers

Dedication

To mom. Without whom financial assistance this work would not have been possible.

Acknowledgements

To whom it may concern:

These stories were written with the authors own effort and with no other influence. It was inspired by the love I had in humanity and my fellow human beings. I owe a special thanks to my mother for her financial support, and a special thanks to the girls of the Canadian National Institute for the Blind, without whom this work would not be possible. I would also like to thank the girls of Starbucks, and the Loyalist Retirement Residence. I might add, that the royalties of this book shall be donated to this charity for their usefulness and help, as well as my mothers in the writing of this manuscript. I'd also like to thank the following people: Fallon Veltri, Dana Blais, and Taryn Montague, whom without this work would not have been possible. Melanie Mason, Brittany Fletcher, Jocelyn Evans, Elizabeth Majentyi, Mary Bell, Ray and Marlene Dortono, the people of CNIB, the baristas at Starbucks, Kim Pilot, Karen Harpwood, John Gardiner, Mike Kirby, Dan and Dave Riddell, the girls of the Loyalist, and sister Nadine Matthews and family. Half of these stories were written while I was legally blind.

A Note from the Author

My earliest recollections are a black and white TV with all the modern conveniences. One morning, my mother got us up and showed us a herd of deer running between the neighbor's house and across the street. My buddies showed up about half an hour later and we followed them to an open field. We hid behind an old log, I was five. The leaders jumped over us. To this day we still can't believe that happened. It was like a dream to us.

My father used to watch a movie called "On the Waterfront" with Marion Brando. It was about a laborer whose employees they looked up to. They were involved in a strike where he was beaten up and refused to be beaten and walked back to work. The rest of the crew followed him. The lesson to be learned here is that mt father is a labor man. It is important to stand up for what you believe in.

In grade 9, there was a TV program called "Welcome back Kotter". The teacher reminded us of Mr. Kotter. His name was Walley Row. Then there was "Happy Days" where we met at the 'rendezvous' after school. My friend had a souped up '57 Chevy that could do the ¼ mile in 7 seconds. We used to go to the A&W drive in for Mama and Papa burgers. The girls looked nice in their hot pants.

Grade 12 came and a bunch of us decided to help rehabilitate x drug addicts. The teachers got out cooperation and they trained us. They even got us a room to work out of. Two years later I moved to Vancouver and worked in a drug rehabilitation center for a while. One night, I witnessed a heroine overdose that would not be the last one either. That was around the same time I was taking a therapy for a personality change. My friends thought it was odd that I didn't go with them. That's when I found myself. I didn't know what I wanted to do with my life, so I travelled to the east coast. I had hitched all across Canada alone.

"People weave in lonely thought, for I have to care, I will regret, having spent time enough to share" was a poem I wrote because I was always alone. I was always reading literature and wrote many poems. My thinking went to eastern mysticism. I studied a higher level of martial arts and became quite thorough in it. I still am.

Years later I met a Spanish writer named Angel Mila, who had written 14 books in the Spanish tongue, 2 of which is till have. One was on Astro Projection. The masters of Kung Fu believe in similar levels of consciousness, prayer, meditation, and exercise. I learned from reliable sources that it was not all that normal thinking, and also had little experience in similar levels of thinking (Jack Nicholson's, I'm OK, You're OK). I don't relate to Jack Nicholson. The movie 'Easy Rider' is easier to relate to in his day in age with the amount of drug use going on. In the National Football League, there was a couple of incidences similarly that were made to that level. Marriage of NFL players with charges of domestic violence. The study shows anger among marriage partners is up. Anger results in assault chargers which is why people study martial arts.

A few years ago, the news hut international legislation of hate crimes of men and women verbally charged. People all over the world are being accused as sexual perverts and facing criminal chargers. The fact that people come to live in an age where truth is replaced by trust. Black criminal what is the world coming to. What will be replaced by trust.

So then I decided to settle down and work for a living. I was living at my girlfriend in a city not far from my hometown. I took a job doing manual labor. I had to tear down a vault that was used for refrigeration purposes. It had Styrofoam wall panels that had to be torn out as well. All I had to use was a crowbar. It was an invigorating experience, all the self-control I could gather. You'd be amazed what you can do when you put your mind to it. I then had to tear out the door frame to the vault which was tight shut. I ended up using a jack hammer and lifting it above my waist. That's not the last time I did that experience. As a young boy I was a skinny kid. But soon put on a few pounds from added work and exercise. That was the beginning of my chance of having a family life. My girlfriend had a family of five daughters.

Honor and virtue not to mention moral principles are going out like an old fade. I became a published writer in 2010, 9 years ago. I took interest in martial arts and have read a few books studying and practicing some of moves. One book in particular on mastering King Fu states that many artists become poets, writers and philosophers. I published two novels, and have recently began publishing my third with the difficulty that occurred in 2020 with 'COVID', the stress and challenges of daily life is being questioned by most. The fact that someone can deal with it, and survival may be a surprise to most people, but to me it's a way of life. We all receive our rewards in life whether it be good or bad, ''God knows the intent of the heart.'' Whether we chose to follow him or not is our own choice. His will is whether we stand aside or pick up our sword and fight.

The Author

November 2022

Introduction

The 1970's movie Kung Fu, starring David Carradine was a story about a dynasty of masters who thought it wise to hand down the wisdom to a younger generation. An American boy was interviewed and asked to snatch the seed from the master's hand. If he was fast enough in which he was, he was accepted. He was trained to be a master and when he was old and mature enough, he took a pilgrimage. An attack on the dynasty occurred and one day as the old man walked down the road he sensed and awareness of a warrior going by because he was blind as a result of old age. He grabbed a spear and blindly killed him. They pursued the aged master and executed him.

Intrigue

She had short curly light blonde hair that covered her head radiantly in a mad sort of way, two rosy rouge covered cheeks rounding into a deceivingly sly smile. A fortune teller working out of her own tent content in the cotton candy pathway amidst the smell of fresh pop corn. As she chanted her hands waving freely as if some magic was causing the round red rubber balloon tiny at first then extending into an over inflated pop.

The fortune teller was one exhibit amongst many in this traveling carnival that was in some city miles from someplace they called home.

The screams from the roller coaster mixed with the sounds of the exhibits pop guns and shouts of numerous Carney bums broke the air waves as a lady's scream is muffled leaving a corpse amidst the crowd as they gather around horrified.

"It was an older man in a trench coat," one bystander observed.

"He had a knife," someone shouted.

"Someone call the police."

Three days earlier, it had been raining all afternoon. An operator of one of the target exhibits poured out the remainder of the bourbon into a glass.

"When is the pay off?" he asked the blonde fortune teller who was sharing a tent with him on this dark, damp, dismal afternoon. She was sitting in a maroon colored cot next to the door watching it rain in torrents as the mud began to thicken. A flash of lightning and then a crack of thunder.

"Next week," she answered him. "It's to be an even split," she warned.

"I won't share my half of the split with no one else you hear," he shouted. He was exceedingly drunk. He was not himself when he was drunk and she knew it.

"What makes you think I'd cheat?" she screeched. She was sober and quick enough to duck as he threw the bottle at her barely missing the mark. He then lay back passing out on his cot.

"Anyone home?" a familiar voice shouted outside the tent. Another flash of lightning and crack of thunder. The blonde opened the flap and there stood a man with a plastic covering his head. "Can we talk?"

"Go ahead," the blonde said. "He's passed out. Come in out of the rain."

"The information is to be delivered at the stroke of midnight on the 24th," he explained after entering the damp tent and standing at the door.

"And the payoff."

"That's to be done after the information is delivered," the man demanded. She nodded as she understood. "You know where to go?" he asked.

"Yes"

"Good," he then turned and walked out again into the mud and rain.

In 24 hours the storm clouds cleared and the skies opened up bringing sunny, warm weather. The carnival became a maize of people celebrating the good weather and the candy floss, candy apples, pop corn, and many exhilarating exhibits the carnival had to offer. A clown bending long balloons into animal shapes and handing them to children walked over towards the fortune teller's tent. He bent three long balloons into a yellow dog and smiled changing his sad expression into joy as he handed the balloon to the blonde teller. She frowned and accepted the gift as Rodger, the shooting galley attendant, noticed this became frustrated turned and continued setting up the targets in a fit of jealousy.

A warm breeze picked up carrying the smell of the carnival everywhere as the sun began to set a red haze formed on the horizon mixed with the smog that accumulated from the bustling city. It was the 23 of August a little over 24 hours before the informative was to deliver the information. As the lights of the pathways, illuminating the Carney strips displaying the various exhibits, exchanging tokens for food and stuffed animals, the dim light became a halo with sand flies buzzing.

Rodger woke and looked around him. It was pitch black as the drip, drip, of runoff water could be heard outside he could feel the throbbing in his head. His mouth tasted dry, like sandpaper. He struggled to get to the refrigerator in the trailer to quench his thirst with a soda. As he opened the trailer door he noticed Betty sprawled out on the bed in a provocative way. She was a light sleeper and upon hearing Rodger enter suddenly woke. Scratching his sandy colored hair and rubbing his skinny rear end, Rodger spoke.

"Why didn't you tell me the rain stopped?" he asked grabbing a soda and un- screwing the lid.

"It was late and I didn't think it was important."

"Did the contact show," he asked.

"Yes" Betty exclaimed.

"What did he say?"

"I'm to give him the information tomorrow night at midnight," she explained.

"Where?"

"The shelter at a trolley connection somewhere off of Remy Street."

The ground was still damp from the evening rain as a dark figure in a grey trench coat approached the rear of the trailer quietly and listened.

The SS Rothchild was a global freighter that was bound for the Port of Charlottetown carrying illegal contraband. Cocaine which is a by-product of cocoa was being smuggled into the country from some foreign soil by a handful of smugglers that were run by one man. It was to be distributed by contacts throughout the city. The code number which was the number of the ship, was the information that was to be given at the trolley depot on the 24th of August. The payoff would be great giving Betty and Rodger enough money for a few years maybe giving them a chance to get out of the carnival

Betty left the carnival at 10 o'clock and caught a street car. After transferring streetcars she left the car and crossed Remy Street with a slight gallop. She had to meet her contact at the trolley depot which was in a rural neighbor hood at the edge of the city.

'That shouldn't be too hard to find,' she thought 'All I have to do is find a railway track.' She walked a couple of blocks looking for a railway sign. She new the depot was somewhere on Remy Street and after walking a couple of blocks she found the shelter. It was 11.40 PM, twenty minutes before she would meet her contact.

At 11.45PM the trolley pulled into the depot to load and unload passengers. It was scheduled to leave again at midnight. A gentleman wearing a dark blue suite got off the trolley. He was wearing a derby and was receiving the assistance of a cane. Upon noticing Betty he approached. There was no one else under the medal shelter so he was free to say what he pleased discreetly.

"Do you have the information?" he asked.

"Yes, it's the SSRothchild7462851," Betty explained handing him the information.

"Thank you, here's the address," he said handing her a piece of paper. He then climbed back on the trolley. A dark stranger in a grey trench coat saw her leave, remaining hidden from the light at the rear of the shelter.

After returning to the carnival Betty entered the one room trailer. Rodger was asleep on the bed. She poured herself a drink from a fresh bottle of bourbon and then left through the door to sit on her cot in the tent(which was attached to the trailer). A short time later Rodger walked out, stretching, asked her drowsily, "When is the payoff?"

"The 2nd day in September," Betty explained. "I've got the address written down."

"Did the contact show?"

"Of course."

"Did any one see you?" Rodger asked looking somewhat concerned.

"I don't think so. Maybe the trolley car driver," she explained. "Why"

"I hope for your sake nobody did. Someone in the crowd was stabbed tonight, Betty."

"Really. Are you sure?"

"The cops were here and everything," Rodger explained.

Betty looked away from Rodger as if in a trance and starred into nothingness. Rodger poured himself a drink.

"What did he look like?" she finally asked.

"Who?"

"The man that was killed?"

"Male, about forty, co caisson, about 5 ft. 11inches, wearing dark slacks, sports coat and white shirt," Rodger said as he described what he heard.

The next morning was sunny and brilliant as the carnival slowly came to life.

Someone began snooping around asking questions about what went on the previous evening. The smell of bacon cooking was in the air as the detective took out his notebook and began jotting down notes. Water on the tents and grass soon dried up as the dew from the previous evening disappeared leaving the stale smell of pop corn and cotton candy.

"Anyone home?" the detective shouted after knocking on the trailer door. Betty and Rodger were late sleepers and were just waking up as they heard the knock.

"Can I help you?" Rodger asked after he opened the door.

"Like to ask you a few questions," he said after he showed him his badge.

"Just a minute," Rodger demanded closing the door and grabbing his shirt. He gave Betty a warning with a keep quiet finger over his mouth and a few facial expressions.

Rodger closed the trailer door and joined the detective on one of the cots. "Where were you at 7.45 PM last evening?" the detective asked.

The detective was professional looking with light brown hair that was clean but un-kept, that he kept covered with a grey fedora. He wore a white shirt, no tie and light blue sports coat.

"I was working behind the booth like I do every evening," Rodger explained.

The man jotted this in his note book then asked, "You didn't happen to notice a tall man in a grey trench coat wearing a black fedora, did you?"

"No"

"Anyone of that description in the last 24 hours?" he again asked.

"No"

"Do you live alone here?"

"Yes"

"What's your name?" he asked.

"Rodger" The detective also wrote this in his note book.

"Thank you, you've been a great help," he said upon getting up to leave.

The detective entered the canteen tent and bought himself a cup of coffee. He had already eaten although the smell of bacon and eggs was tempting. "Any luck?" the Carney asked.

"No, no leads," was all he said. He took a moment to sip his coffee in deep contemplation. Then said, "You know, it's hard to believe someone like that can live alone in such a large trailer." He was referring to Rodger. After some discussion the detective not only found out that Rodger didn't live alone but that his mistress the fortune teller was not at her booth later the previous evening.

So Rodger and Betty were closely watched for the next few days. He watched when they came and went, when they work, and when they eat and sleep. No one knew when the detective was watching because he was always in the shadows. So far there was nothing suspicious going on.

On the second day of September he noticed Betty leave. He decided to follow her where she went to a secluded coffee shop. He watched as a suspicious looking character in an expensive suite order two coffees, then handed her a package. He then got up to leave and was followed by the detective.

The next day Rodger and Betty were hustled down to the nearest precinct. The reason for the arrest was suspicion in laundering money in narcotics.

"They followed him to an abandoned warehouse where they made the biggest cocaine bust this town has ever seen," Reno the officer on duty explained while the two were being interrogated.

Caught in A Dilemma

Chapter 1

The wind continued relentlessly as the old man unlatched the squeaky gate leading to the front entrance. The fence wasn't too high. He could have stepped over it but he was getting on in years. The entrance was overgrown, the wisterias having long ago choked everything living leaving only that which was touched by human hands.

He withdrew his keys upon approaching the front door. With much effort he unlocked the door as the wind blew against it. It took all his effort to hold it from flying out of his hands. Closing the door everything suddenly became still.

Discarding his cane in the corner he waddled over to the table and dropped his parcels. Hanging his shattered coat on the hook, he waddled over to the wood stove and opened the oven door. Fetching a nearby log he threw it in and lit a match. The stove soon had a roaring fire inside. Persevering, the old man fetched an iron kettle and placed it on the stove.

Suddenly there was a knock on the door. Making his way, he opened it and held it tight as the wind blew against it. There was a gentleman in dark clothing holding onto his bowler hat.

"Who are you?" he asked holding the door, preventing the wind from blowing it out of his hands.

"I'm the coroner," the gentleman explained, raising his voice above the sound of the storm, "I'm sorry to say Mr. Abernathy I have some bad news."

The old man became impatient. He persisted, "What is it, what is it?"

"Your daughter drowned in the river last week. She left you as executer of her estate."

The coroner paused and there was a moment of silence between him and the old man. They became aware of the sound of the wind whistling. It was a frightening sound as memories of his little girl flashed through the old man's mind, grief began to overtake him.

The coroner began to explain, "I understand it's a tragedy Mr. Abernathy but this business must be taken care of. Call me when you're ready to talk." He then handed the old man his card. "Good day," he said tipping his hat turned and walked away.

The next day was Tuesday and the village was a metropolis of activity as the old man weaved his way through the congestion of bodies on his journey to the address that was written on the card. The ringing of bells could be heard as the solid oak, office, door squeaked open then shut again, the bells being used as a door alarm. The old man walked up to the huge oak desk.

Mr. Abernathy recognized the clean shaven gentleman, who according to the card was named Mr. Peacock, with neat, dark, hair, looking out over a pair of spectacles. He had a serious look on his humorless face that gave the impression that he was about to demand something. It was an expression without feeling or gender. His black suite was modest but clean.

"Good day. What can I do for you?" Mr. Peacock asked.

The old man took the card out and presented it to him.

"Yes of course, please step this way," the coroner stated as Mr. Abernathy waddled into another comfortable well lit room that was just to the left side of the entrance. There was another desk and two chairs as well as a good collection of old books, a small end table, and a coal oil lamp. The gentleman asked him to have a seat as he sat behind another oak desk and replaced his spectacles on his nose. Looking at a piece of paper he paused and then asked, "Was Louisa Anne Melbourne you're only child, Mr. Abernathy?"

The old man hesitated stumbling with words then mumbled, "Ye yes, she was. Why?" Mr. Abernathy was an inquisitive old man, always curious, yet never letting his guard down. He wore an old worn out shirt that he had washed only a week before. His trousers were worn too, covering an old, dusty pair of brown shoes. His hair was mostly grey but unkempt and as he said this an expression changed on his aged face to a confused, distaste.

"It appears that Mrs. Melbourne was quite well off," the coroner observed from the paper without looking above his glasses. "Are you the only surviving relation?"

"Ye yes, I think so," the old man stated. The thought made him a little delusional.

"Might I ask what happened to Mr. Melbourne?"

The old man hesitated, slowly continuing. "I don't know."

"May I offer you a little advice. According to this document, Louisa is leaving you as sole heir of her estate. I might add that she is also making you guardian of her only child. This is a huge responsibility. I find it odd that you're faced with this responsibility and you don't even know what happened to her husband," Mr. Peacock stated looking at him over his square wire spectacles.

The old man hesitated, "Yes, well we've been out of touch for some time."

"Do you accept the responsibility of guardianship of her boy?"

"I accept," the old man blurted focused but unsure what to do.

"Then sign here," Mr. Peacock offered presenting Mr. Abernathy with the document and a pen. "Of course you understand there's a charge for doing the paperwork?"

Mr. Abernathy reluctantly signed the piece of paper.

"My creditors will be in touch to get you're banking information," the gentleman concluded.

The old man closed the withered, battered, door, and stored his cane as usual in the corner. He hung up his warm, worn out coat on the hook.

Throwing another log in the stove he closed the oven door as it already had enough embers from the morning's meal. He threw the kettle on with the intent to make tea. A short while later as he sat in his chair, savoring his tea, loneliness began to overtake his thoughts. Memories began to come back.

He dreamed of a bright sunny day while Lilly was still alive. There was a cottage by a lake and he saw a young man with his shirt off, wiping the sweat from his brow. A little girl came running only to be caught in her father's arms, his wife strolling, (umbrella in hand,) in a long white and pink cotton dress.

He didn't notice as the time passed tears began to swell in his eyes.

The days changed to weeks when the old man got a knock on the door. Upon answering it he found a little boy with a suitcase, well dressed, about ten years old, wearing a clean blue shirt and trousers, and a small tweed cap. His face was freckled and he had light brown hair.

The little boy looked up at Mr. Abernathy and shouted, "I'm Louisa's son, Mathew." Confused as to what to do, Mr.

Abernathy, scratching his head mumbled, "Yes of course, come in."

The inside of the house was an assembly of furniture, an old wing chair which was Mr. Abernathy's favorite, a table and four wooden chairs assembled in the kitchen or pantry, the main piece of furniture being the stove. There was a large wooden box where he kept the firewood, a small battered coffee table and a kerosene lamp. Two other soft chairs decorated the room. The house had one main bedroom but next to it was a large storage closet that was big enough for a small bed. The furniture's condition was rustic but for the old man it was home. The well and the outhouse were out back as well as a shed where he kept firewood.

In frustration Mr. Abernathy waddled over to the corner and picked out a log, opening the oven door he threw it in. Struggling to put his shoes on he grabbed the kettle and headed for the door. Looking around he noticed Mathew standing in the middle of the room.

"Sit down and make yourself comfortable. I won't be long," Mr. Abernathy explained as he took the kettle to the well to fill it.

He returned with a full kettle and found Mathew sitting on one of the soft chairs. "I hope you'll join me in a cup of tea," Mr. Abernathy offered.

"Yes," he mumbled.

"I was hoping you would," he replied, "We have a few things to discuss."

Mathew's grandfather handed him a cup of piping hot tea and then settled comfortably in his brown wing chair. It was mid October, the air was getting cool as the bushes and trees began to shed their fall colors. His cottage was in a rural neighborhood along the Thames on the outskirts of London.

There was a pause as the two people savored their tea.

"Who told you to come here?" he finally asked.

"The adoption agency," Mathew stated. "They told me you would be taking care of me."

"Do you go to school?"

"Yes"

"How old are you?" he asked.

"Ten"

"I only have the one bedroom but there is a small room off to the right side that'll fit a mattress. The outhouse is out back behind the wood shed. When I take a bath I do it in the river but there's a wash basin in the kitchen. Any questions?" he concluded.

Mathew shook his head.

"I should be in touch with the bank in a few days so maybe there'll be a little more to eat around here," the old man stated, looking around, "Until then you can sleep with me."

Mr. Abernathy noticed as Mathew played with his tea how lost the little boy looked staying in his own little world. He was obviously grieving his mother. Louisa had been married to a sailor before he lost his life at sea. She worked as a laundry woman as a means to help bring up her boy. Her husband left them a substantial amount of money.

"Do you have any friends?" his grandfather asked.

"Yes"

"Louisa must have had friends? Louisa and I never kept in touch as you already know. I never knew she had a son. When my wife died I stopped taking care of Louisa and didn't know she and her husband had married until I ran into her by accident," the old man explained.

Mathew remained silent. Do to his good upbringing he had learned through experience that listening and respecting ones elders was important.

"Are you hungry?" he asked.

"I haven't eaten since breakfast," Mathew stated his stomach telling his mouth what to answer. It was 1.30 pm when Mathew knocked on the old man's door and his last meal had been at the orphanage.

He had some dried cereal and fruit, a few crackers and some honey to offer him. He knew he would need more food.

"I think we should go into the village," the old man said. "We can get food there. I have to do some banking anyway."

Mr. Abernathy and Mathew weaved their way through the horde of people doing business on the main street of the village. It took them the better part of the afternoon to get there due to his grandfather's slow walking. They arrived at the community bank just in time as it was about to close for the day. The tiny village was a suburb of London.

Much to his surprise he had some funding to fall back on. Before all the shops closed, he and Mathew paid a visit to Mr. Peacock's office. He gave him his banking information and Mr. Peacock warned him that he would be in touch.

Mathew and the old man walked into a small café and sat down at a square wooden table. The table was covered with a blue checkered table cloth and had a glass vase in the middle with a small bouquet of purple violets.

The waitress came to take their order. A kerchief tied her sandy colored hair back as she stood with pencil and paper in hand. She wore a long cream colored, ankle length dress with a red and white lacey apron.

"The special tonight is steak and kidney pie, but we do have some leftover lamb," she exclaimed. "My name is Greta, but you can call me Molly."

"Just don't call me late for dinner," Mathew smiled cynically and said.

"They used to call me Ike," the old man warned.

"Well pleased to meet you," Molly demanded offering Ike her hand in friendship. "Now, what's you're pleasure?"

"I think I'll have some of that lamb," Mr. Abernathy stated.

Molly made a scratch on the piece of paper and then looked at Mathew.

"I'll have the steak and kidney pie, Maim'"

The time seemed to pass as Mathew and the old man waited for their dinner. There was a coo coo clock on the wall that chimed when it turned six. A little bird came out and shouted "coo coo, coo coo."

"Your mother must have known a lot of influential people," grandfather mused after a long period of silence.

"Yes she was quite well known," Mathew reminisced. "She had many friends."

"Did she know a man named Abercrombie?" Ike asked out of curiosity. Mathew thought he could detect fear in the old man's voice. Ike was uncomfortable at the sound of 'Abercrombie.'

"That name sounds familiar," Mathew again reminisced. "Yes it seems to me I've heard that name." Mathew was a bright child, working his way through primary with exceptional ability. He was a leader at home and at school.

The waitress finally came with their dinner.

"Eat quickly Mathew I'd like to buy some provisions before we go home," the old man warned savoring his lamb. They ate with relish enjoying a much needed home cooked meal.

"I know where I heard that name," Mathew remembering the conversation they had had earlier.

"I'm listening"

"He was a friend of moms. There was a rumor going around that he was into some shady dealings," Mathew warned.

Ike recalled from memory purchasing his property and the trouble he had had with the creditors. Abercrombie was a ruthless businessman threatening to throw him out if he missed any of his mortgage payments. Ike had learned from the school of hard knocks that there are no free handouts. You get what you pay for in life.

The old man paid the waitress generously and he and Mathew left the café', only to pick up some provisions at some of the local establishments before they closed. They took as much as they could carry and then wandered home.

Ike Abernathy had bought porridge, biscuits, dried fruit, fresh bread, and it was cool enough that he bought fresh mutton. That would keep them going for a while. To add to this he bought a couple of bars of soap. Soap was affordable nowadays as they had recently opened soap factories in London.

Twig light was falling on the suburban village as Ike Abernathy and Mathew wandered up the walkway to the threshold of their urban 19 century cottage. He fidgeted with his key before opening the battered, front door.

Chapter 2

It was a good arrangement for some time; Mathew slept on the mattress in the little closet, and went to school faithfully each day, the school being within walking distance. It was a relief for Mathew to chop wood for the stove; the weather was becoming cooler as the days grew closer to Christmas. On Saturday they would walk to the village and get provisions for the coming week.

One day a short time later Ike walked into the bank, and to his surprise they asked him to sign some forms as a settlement for his inheritance. He discovered he and Mathew would be able to live comfortably for some time.

Mathew found the arrangement comfortable. He didn't mind chopping wood, and his grandfather cooked most of the meals. His duty was to take care of himself and get an education. He had the ambition to learn so he learned to chop wood and clean up after himself. The only thing he didn't like was going outside to the outhouse. It was alright in the warm weather but the weather was getting cool. Winter was approaching.

Ike's days where consumed with making sure there was enough to eat. It wasn't a difficult duty just time consuming. It took all his time fetching the ingredients to make the meals. One good thing about the arrangement was a friend of Louisa's that used to work with her, now came regularly to do all of their laundry. It was a social life that was unfamiliar to Ike Abernathy.

"I won't have this batch done till Thursday," Carol said as she gathered all of their clothes in a clothe laundry bag, after leaving the fresh linen on a soft chair. "I brought some fresh potatoes to go into you're stew. I usually get paid by the load although I will take an IOU. Do you have any cash?"

"No," Ike explained.

"I've written it out on this here paper, see." She showed Ike the piece of paper. "'I Ike Abernathy owe Carol Lombardi 5 shillings for washing my laundry.' Now just sign here," Carol demanded.

Ike signed the paper.

"And I expect full payment at the end of each month too," she concluded.

Ike Abernathy retired after twenty years of work on the docks of London. One morning he was routinely unloading a ship when a bail crushed his leg. Luckily for him he escaped with only a fractured leg but it created a limp that he would have for the remainder of his days. For Ike it was a lonely time not having Lily to support. Louisa was grown and eventually drifted away and took care of herself. Ike had some savings to fall back on but until Louisa died he was dangerously close to running out of funds.

Ike was returning from the village one day when he ran into David Abercrombie.

"Well Ike, do you figure on paying your mortgage this month?" he demanded with a cynical smile, half thinking that maybe he could. It was not always convenient to make payments for Ike but he eventually did. It was just that he got behind on a few payments and David Abercrombie was not shy,(being the shrewd business man that he was), to tell him what he felt.

"Why yes," Ike exclaimed much to David's surprise, "Come by tomorrow and I'll have it for you."

The next day Mr. Abercrombie came around to see if Ike had the payment for the mortgage. As he approached the front gate Ike had a second look as he was returning from the well and spotted Abercrombie. "You know you could do a little work on this place Ike," cynically Abercrombie warned, "It is going to be yours some day."

He was shocked to find that he had all the papers and they were ready to be signed for the sole ownership of the property. As Ike showed him the deed David Abercrombie said, "So you've decided to be dishonest in your old age. Surely you don't expect me to believe this is honest money?"

"I can prove it if you like."

As he signed the deed he exclaimed, "I didn't think you had it in you Ike."

Later Ike felt there was call for a celebration. Mathew got home from school and Ike decided they would go to the village for dinner. The dinning establishment was around the corner of the main business district. It was on a quiet little street away from all the hustle and bustle of the main business district.

As they entered the lighting was soft. There were only a few customers as they made their way to a secluded table. The table was covered with a clean white table cloth. In the centre was a bouquet of violets.

They didn't have to wait long, Molly brought a dinner menu and warned, "The special is stew, Ike, but I don't think you'll like it. The mutton is fresh."

Ike's memory was not that sharp due to his age. "What did you say your name was?" he asked.

"You can call me Molly."

Ike decided to have a bit of spiced rum with his meal and he ordered Mathew a new drink that was the talk of the town, ice cream soda.

Mathew continued to go to school and Ike continued to take care of the two of them for some time. One day Ike decided it was time to buy Mathew some new clothes. So Saturday they walked to the village and began going through the shops. Ike bought himself a new pair of clothes and did the same for Mathew. He also bought some new overcoats for the two of them and to top it off bought a new cap.

Ike decided the two of them should drop in and pay a visit to Carol Lombardi afterwards so he could pay her in full. Mathew knew the address so they had no trouble finding the place.

Winding up their day by starting out for Carol's, they ran into David Abercrombie.

"Where you off to in such a hurry, Ike?" he asked from his horse and buggy.

"I don't know that it's any of your business Abercrombie?" Ike shouted.

"Ok, just trying to be friendly," David explained cracking the whip. "Some day you're going to need a friend, Ike."

Ike found it odd that Abercrombie was trying to be overly friendly with them. He had no reason to act differently and having known the type of man he was, Ike didn't think he was being unreasonable. David Abercrombie was a mystery that was yet to be solved. The fact that Louisa had drowned in the Thames and having a dark relationship with the man gave reason for suspicion. It was not just him that was involved here but Mathew as well. If it did turn out that it was Abercrombie that drowned her, Ike would be sure to get even.

Mathew found the address.

Knocking on the weathered door Carol answered.

"I come to pay my IOU's," Ike warned pulling out a bag of coins.

"That'll be 5 shillings, and I'll rip up the IOU's," which

she did after receiving the money. "I'll be by on Thursday, Rudy has an extra turnip. I'll bring it for the stew," she said. She closed the door leaving Mathew and his grandfather alone.

The weather turned nasty that February and Ike unfortunately came down with the grip. Carol came around for their laundry as usual on Thursday.

"You all right Ike? You don't look so good." Carol asked.

"I think I've a bit of the grip," he stated. He had a slight fever and wrapped himself in some blankets.

"I'll get some medicine from a friend of mine. He's a friend of David Abercrombie. Ever heard of him?" her curiosity getting the best of her. She was completely unaware that Ike knew who he was.

"Where did you hear the name David Abercrombie?" continuing their conversation.

"You hear these things through people."

It seemed to be falling into place for Ike. Sooner or later the truth would come out and he'd find out just who this Abercrombie was. The more he heard the name Abercrombie the more suspicious he became.

Carol went to the well to fill the kettle and made Ike a hot cup of tea. She then threw a couple more logs in the stove. It warmed Ike's heart to have someone care for him. He hadn't had someone take care of him since Lily died.

Ike Abernathy got over the grip in a few days. Carol brought some hot soup.

Ike's and Mathew's relationship continued to grow. The days changed to months and the months to years as Mathew came to appreciate Ike like the father he never had. He would come home and tell Ike what he had learned in school and the old man would sit and listen with astonishment.

Mathew had other friends as well. He met children in the school yard as well as hanging out on his days off. Most of his friends liked Ike although their relationship didn't last long. Mathew's friends were taken out of school and ordered to work in factories so their families could eat.

Ike's finances were getting low too and with the cost of things being so high he felt it may pay to take Mathew out of school. But Mathew's future was bright and the old man didn't want to screw it up for his only descendant.,

One day Mathew came home from school and approached his grandfather with a new ambition.

"I think I'd like to work in the salt mines, grandfather," he explained. In late nineteenth century England employers didn't have an age limitation for boys like Mathew. When you were old enough you went to work.

The old man looked up surprised. "We could use the money. Maybe fix this place up."

It was not that much of a shock to Ike that Mathew wanted to start work. Education was not one of Ike's stronger traits. He decided not to discourage him if he didn't want to get an education. It might also improve their quality of life.

"Why the salt mines?" he asked.

"It's clean, the pay's good," Mathew confessed.

"But it's hard work," grandfather warned.

"That I'm not afraid of. Besides every body works now days," he explained.

Mathew was entering puberty now and was beginning to fill out physically. He was a few inches taller and had put on a few pounds. He had a full head of messy brown hair and he was losing most of his baby fat. He was achieving a handsome complexion with the evidence of being a man.

Salt works were a popular place to work although they were becoming obsolete with the use of brine. Brine was becoming more useful as a way of obtaining salt. It was easier and more efficient. The mines had become huge institutions being used as dinning and entertainment establishments mostly for the elite. In early eighteenth and nineteenth century the governments put a tax on salt it being such a commodity with everyone as young as eight required to buy a certain amount of salt per year thus the saying, (worth your weight in salt.)

The next day instead of going to school, Mathew went to the village and caught a train which took him to Cheshire. He would have just enough time to apply for the job and take the 3.15 back to the little village. He should be home in time for dinner. As he approached the front gate the sign stood prominently like a threshold over the entrance. It read 'Cheshire Salt Works' like the entrance to paradise.

A gentleman came walking by the front office and seemed to be in a bit of a hurry didn't notice Mathew. Mathew flagged him down.

"Can you tell me where they do the hiring?" Mathew asked.

The man pointed his finger directing him to a door at the side of the building.

He walked into the office and approached the desk where the personnel manager. sat. The office employee was moderately dressed in grey and cream colored pants and slacks. He sat behind a wooden desk which had stacks of papers. There was a coal oil lamp hanging above the desk that was giving light to the dim room. In the corner was a small stove to give heat. Mathew warmed his hands as he stood in front of the desk.

Mathew was dressed in a white cotton shirt and wore a grey tweed cap. His bottom was covered with a pair of black knickers with cream colored socks that came to his knees, accompanied by a pair of leather shoes. To cover his shirt and keep him warm he wore a navy blue jacket.

"Looking for work?" the gentleman asked getting right to the point.

"Yes," Mathew replied.

"When can you start?"

"Tomorrow," he insisted.

"Fill out this form. You can write can't you?" the gentleman asked. Mathew nodded and took the form. "Be here at eight tomorrow morning."

That night while they ate dinner Ike asked him, "What do you want to do with your life, Mathew?"

"I don't know. I'm too young to make a decision like that now. It seems that that's what people do is work for a living and it's important to eat. I think I'll eventually get married some day," the boy explained.

"Now don't take work too seriously. You have the rest of your life to work. Besides a boy your age shouldn't be made to work in a factory, he should be out chasing girls," Ike explained.

Mathew looked at his grandfather and something inside him began to ignite. He remained silent and was overcome with a sense of contentment. 'There'd be time for women', he thought. 'For what he knew about them he was a little reluctant to learn more.'

Ike Abernathy and Mathew were sitting in the café one Saturday night having a bite to eat. The café was mostly empty but for a few people when suddenly the door swung open and in walked two men. It wasn't an unusual circumstance other than the fact that one of the men was David Abercrombie. They sat a few tables away and Abercrombie looked like he had been drinking. He gave Ike a dirty look.

"Got nothing better to do with your time but to spend it with innocent children?" he mumbled loud enough for Ike and Mathew to hear but low enough to make like it was a conversation between him and the man he was with.

Ike's anger began to build but he was smart enough to suppress it. Molly was close and walked up to their table.

"Don't mind him he's drunk. Everybody knows what he does on the side," she whispered.

Ike was confused. "What?" throwing his hands in the air and preparing himself for what was to come.

"Child trafficking," she again whispered then asked loudly changing the subject. "Can I get you two anything else?"

Mathew was getting a lot of hours now working up to twelve hours a day. He had the night off and he thought it good to spend it out doing something. Ike needed to get out too. Mathew paid the bill as he and his grandfather got up to walk out.

Abercrombie got up and blocked Ike and Mathew from getting to the door. He was angry and drunk. His hair was messy and he was sweating profusely. He looked demonic like.

"Mathew's going with me. I could get a good price for him on the docks. He'd pay good money on the plantations or as a servant boy in some rich palace," Abercrombie slurred in a threatening tone of voice.

In actuality boys that were captured off the streets of London and sold into slavery often ended up delivering newspapers on the streets of cities like New York or as shoe shine boys or even worse, working for some money launderer as a pick pocket.

'So that was it' Ike thought. 'Abercrombie wanted Mathew as a slave boy. May be it was him who drowned Louisa in the river after all. He had to find out.'

"Mathew's going with me," Ike said not budging an inch.

Abercrombie was too drunk to put up any resistance so he backed down. Ike had his cane to protect him. They made their way to the door.

Chapter 3

Ike locked the door to his urban nineteenth century cottage one morning in early April. It had been raining through the night but had stopped a few hours later and it was still overcast and dull. Ike was on his way to the village hoping to stir up some dirt about Abercrombie from some of the locals. As he waddled along depending on his cane for support the thought occurred to him that this man Abercrombie was an influential citizen. Ike might make a few enemies.

He waddled into the popular dining establishment later that morning and sat at a clean table. He was prepared to order a cup of tea to get some information about Abercrombie. Molly came with the tea.

"Say Molly, you know this Abercrombie quite well don't you?" he asked opening up the conversation.

"Well I just learn what I hear in here," she exclaimed.

"You said child trafficking. What did you mean?"

"They take children off the street and make slaves of them. It's an underground organization that makes money," she explained.

"Along with every thing else that he's into, he owns real estate as well," Ike warned.

"As long as he pays his bill, I've got no quarrel with him," Molly stated.

"Thanks Molly," he said. "Does he have any contacts? I know he associates with a man named Roscoe. I don't know what his first name is. They do business together. He must be just as shady as him."

Fear became apparent on Molly's face. "I've got a lot of work to do," Molly explained in a fit of terror as she grabbed her apron and held it in her hands. "Excuse Me". She then walked quickly back into the kitchen.

Next he went to see Carol Lombardi. She wasn't so pleased to see him.

"What did I do now Ike? Don't tell me I forgot to press your shirts?" she asked looking rather guilty.

"I don't owe you any money do I?" he was quick to react, relieving the tension between them.

"9 shillings"

"You know a man named Abercrombie, am I correct?" Ike took out a bag of coins.

"Yes why?" she asked. She wore a long plain white dress that was acknowledging her plump body in a embarrassing sort of way. Her complexion was fair with light brown hair that was wound around and tied on top. Ike handed her the coins.

"What do you know about him?" he asked.

"I know he knew a man who was charged with breaking and entry not long ago." Ike's bushy eyebrows went up as if something caught his interest. "….happened a short time ago. They threw him in Newgate. He left a wife and two children."

"What was his name?"

"Dougal"

"Thanks you've been a great help," Ike reminded her.

"I don't know about you but I like to keep my nose clean. There's a lot of crime in this area," Carol concluded. "I hear there is a killer around that stock's prostitutes."

Ike left and made his way to the closest taxi stand. There was one waiting just around the corner. He wasn't dressed like a gentleman but with the money Mathew made and his inheritance he could afford it. As he opened the coach door he motioned to the driver, "Newgate Prison, please" He then climbed in.

The driver cracked the crop and grabbed the rains as the work horses began to walk. The cab made its way to Newgate Street and Old Bailey and Ike climbed out. Giving the driver 2 guineas he stopped to reflect at this awesome site for a moment. It towered above him like an historical icon turning back the pages in history as if reopening stories forever forgotten in time.

He climbed the steps to the ancient doors and entered. As he waddled up to the main desk he became thankful that he had never been thrown in here. He heard stories about the ancient prison. A poor man was not allowed privileges once convicted and was likely to die here. There were a number of ways for a poor man to die in 1800 but for Ike prison was not the most pleasant.

The clerk was a round little man about medium height with round wire spectacles and long but scruffy red hair. He was clean shaven and had bushy eyebrows.

"Can you help me?" Ike asked.

"You name it," the clerk said.

"Is there a man named Dougal that was incarcerated here?

"One moment please," the clerk stated as he began looking through the records and a few moments later after he completed his search he said, "Yes, it appears as though a James Dougal was sentenced to30 months, 6&1/2 weeks ago."

"He left a wife and two children right?"

"That's correct," the clerk again stated.

"…any news of their whereabouts?"

"I have the address here if you like?" the clerk explained.

"Would you write it down, please?"

Thinking that the old man couldn't mean any harm the clerk wrote it on a slip and handed it to Ike. "You don't look like a criminal to me,´ he said.

"Thanks, you've been a great help," Ike concluded and walked out.

The next day was overcast with a misty fog. Ike was getting his exercise walking and he caught a cab again to the address written on the paper. It was a well developed residential neighborhood in London, where a row of narrow, tightly packed, duplexes were separated by only a few feet. He found the address only by chance when a delivery boy was delivering food. There were many doors but only a few numbers on them. Ike knocked on one of them.

"Can I help you?" an eight year old boy asked answering the door. A woman's voice could be heard from the inside.

"Who is it John?" She came to the door wiping her hands on her apron.

"Sorry to hear about your misfortunes, maim," Ike stated. "I was wondering if I could ask you a few questions about your husband?"

"Who do you work for, Scotland Yard?" she asked a little hesitant to give out information.

"I assure you my intentions are honorable," Ike explained. "I'm interested in a man named Abercrombie."

"That no good scoundrel. He's the reason Jimmy's in Newgate. If I can stir up enough dirt to get him convicted it would be a pleasure," the woman explained. "…as long as you don't work for Scotland Yard."

"Of course not," Ike warned her. "What connection did your husband have with this man?"

"Abercrombie was the man he worked for. I don't know exactly what type of work it was although he did own property. He never told me what he did," the woman explained reluctantly keeping herself in front of the door preventing Ike from entering. "My husband never brought him around. As a matter of fact I never even met him."

"Do your children go to school?"

"What business is that of yours?" she screeched. "Jimmy don't want me giving no information about his kids."

"Did he know a man named Roscoe?"

Fear became apparent as the woman got a hold and backed into the doorway. She grabbed the door and began closing it. "I'm sorry I can't answer any more questions."

'That was the second person that showed fear at the name Roscoe. This Roscoe must be just as bad as Abercrombie if not worse' Ike thought as he waved another taxi down and climbed in. "Union station," he proclaimed.

Ike Abernathy was considering asking around to see why everyone feared this man in the meantime he would find out where Abercrombie lived. He was sure he had an office somewhere. He decided to try the post office. He found Abercrombie's address to be 151 Cheapside Street.

Knowing Abercrombie's address was not necessarily the answer to what Ike was looking for. He still needed information about him that might be difficult to obtain but he still wanted to investigate. If he had a business office somewhere it would be easy.

He found the address by visiting the local Cheapside Precinct and asking one of the Bobbies. It began to drizzle as he walked along the Avenue he used his umbrella for protection. The address was only a few blocks away. He stood down the street from the address as the light rain fell and observed if anyone was coming or going. After about a quarter of an hour he decided to call it a day. He had accomplished a lot and he decided to wait for it to be clearer to do more.

David Abercrombie's address was a five story structure above a butcher shop. It was in a flat up on the third story. St. Paul's Cathedral was only a few blocks away. Ike would have his work cut out for him questioning the number of people that did business here.

The next day was a bright sunny spring day. He casually found the butcher shop that was the habitat of Abercrombie. His observations from across the street told him that it was a busy little business as he bought a pretzel from one of the local street venders. People seemed to flow in and out as this lucrative establishment catered to its local cliental. He stood there for some time watching if something shady was going on.

He finally gathered the nerve to approach the butcher who seemed to know nothing of who he was talking about. Years of experience working on the London docks and dealing with the likes of guys like Abercrombie told him the man was probably lying. As a young man with a family Ike had taken a few hard knocks.

"I find it hard to imagine you have a man living above you and you don't know who he is," the old man gathered the nerve to say.

"Sometimes it's good not to know too much," the butch warned him. "You might find yourself hanging from a meat hook."

The warning was all the information Ike needed. From here on it would be a battle of wits. He was sorry he had done business with Abercrombie in the past and very thankful that he got out of it. It would be a bit of a challenge because he was getting on in years and was tiring. His only reward was his grandson and he wanted to keep him out of this if at all possible.

That night Ike made a leg of mutton for him and Mathew. He served it with boiled potatoes and fresh asparagus. He even had mint tea.

Ike told Mathew about the research Ike had done on Abercrombie. "Do you remember anything about him when you lived with your mother?" he asked hoping that he might learn something more about the man.

"I recall one evening when my mother had to make a delivery to someone with a name that sounded like Abercrombie. She was told she could find him at a place called, 'The Rendezvous'. I distinctly remember that night because I wanted her for something but she was out late," Mathew recollected savoring another piece of mutton.

The next day it rained. Ike stayed warm and dry by the stove. The following day he again went to the post office where he found the address.

Chelsea was where he found a business called 'the Rendezvous'. It was a London coffee house or tavern, being established for many years by local cliental interested in lively conversation, good food and a variety of drinks.

Ike found the people there friendly as well as entertaining and he suddenly realized it would be a great place to find the information he needed. He had to be careful not to be too pushy, it would only give him a bad name. He began making conversation with a man named John.

John was a coal miner and it showed from the coal dust on his skin and clothing. He liked to come here for a dram of whisky on his days off. Like Ike, he was a bit of a loner but made pleasant conversation with anyone that was willing.

"Is the food good here?" Ike asked at a loss for something better to say.

"Not bad if you're lucky enough not to get a cigar butt in your soup," the gentleman stated with a grin. "They get fresh fish here from the Grand Banks."

Ike having worked the docks knew what John was talking about. He was curious to see if John knew something about child trafficking being careful not to 'let the cat out of the bag'.

'It'd be good to know if there was someway to hire servant help for this rich friend of mine; say a child?' Ike asked.

"That I couldn't say," John warned.

"Yes they're forcing children to work too soon," Ike demanded eager to change the subject. "Were you born in London?" He felt the conversation refreshing.

"Lived 'ere all my life," John explained unsure as to whether to talk to this stranger, he knew nothing about. He suddenly let his guard down. "I come 'ere to get me some lovin'."

"What do you mean?"

"'hores", he again explained.

It was a bit of a blow for Ike Abernathy finding out that "the Rendezvous' was a 'den of iniquity'. He found it hard to visualize that Louisa could be a 'lady of the night.' He would simply not accept it. Deep down he knew that this would possibly explain how his daughter had ended up in the river. He had to know more. He also knew he would have a hard time telling Mathew. It had been a bit of an adventure for Ike narrowing all possible evidence to the Rendezvous but unfortunately for him the truth was being revealed. It was not until he passed a newspaper stand on his commute that he read the headlines, 'Another Victim of Jack the Ripper.'

THE END

The Future

The world was deteriorating more every day. Mankind was aware of the deterioration and was resolving some of the problems but his determination to provide for his own needs had more priority, and the earth was slowly falling away. Eco systems were deteriorating at an alarming rate. The great whale along with other species detrimental to existing life of marine plants and animals were becoming scarce. Eco systems on the great continents were moving along with most of the animals to higher elevations. It started when the honey bee began migrating to mountainous regions. Soon most ecosystems in lower levels became prone to disease and fermentation. It became a struggle for survival for man and animal. Like most places on earth in the late twentieth century one was dependent on the other for survival.

Quality of life was cheap in most major cities. It wasn't safe to venture anywhere outside as gangs of criminals and lower levels of life would march around neighborhoods stirring up what mischief was available. There was still a crude law system and the general public still had some morals but for the most part life was cheap. Food was hard to come by and was precious so what people couldn't stalk pile they tried to grow, kill or steal to survive. The only things that were practically free were living accommodations although power was scarce and heat in some of the northern cities went back to the stone ages. Water being also precious most fresh water was obtained either through cisterns or primitive means of distillation. Because water was scarce most people drank juices or alcohol, or rain water. Some fresh water still flowed from mountainous regions but most fresh water rivers and lakes in lower elevations were polluted.

What was formally Pittsburg was now a succession of rust and rubble, the streets having been long ago deserted. Many of the old buildings were still inhabited, with much of the parkland being cultivated for food. Most of the food was grown on rooftops or man made gardens built and protected by private individuals or what was left of a law abiding society.

Rowland pulled the cord that sparked the four cylinder generator engine that pumped electricity to the lights that lit the multi acre garden that was protected by him and three others. They had sworn an oath to protect and preserve what was left of humanity and in doing so were given provisions as part of the payment for services rendered. The crops were sown, cultivated and harvested by a group of dedicated people that work as a means to survive. The parkland was formally what was known as botanical gardens in downtown Pittsburg.

It took another pull after checking to see if there was enough gas and the engine fired up with a healthy cough. It was twig light. They didn't always run the generators but tonight was an exception because they were having a special celebration and needed to harvest some of the vegetables for the feast. Most people carried some form of weapon. A knife or club was common, although some people had guns. Ammunition was precious and mostly used for hunting fresh meat.

Rowland and his three partners had guns for protection and to uphold what was left of the law. It was a full time job which was dangerous at times. Casey and his men had gone looking for fresh meat for the feast. This was done outside of town. Sometimes they were gone for days. They were the husbands of some of the woman folk and their families that help cultivate the gardens.

Roland wandered along the outside row of cucumbers surveying the garden's edge for any unusual activity as the local women began distributing themselves with their baskets amongst the vegetables. The women folk were precious and had to be protected in order to carry on the species. Although there were some arguments amongst the men from time to time for the most part women were protective of their men. He was her provider. Not all men wanted the responsibility of a wife and family as there were many mouths to feed.

It was a struggle for survival for man and beast. Each one depended on the other for deliverance from extinction.

Rowland did not keep track of the time. 'The People' had wise men that did that. Casey and his men had been gone for two sunrises and were due back with fresh meat. Rowland was aware of the sunrises and the moon changes but as far as dates or a twenty four hour day he had no awareness. They were celebrating All Saints Day which they did every twelve months. The wise men had explained how they used to keep track of the days months and years but that had stopped long ago. He was aware that 'The People' used to read and write books but that was left for the wise men. They were good at sitting around a roaring fire telling stories.

As he wandered around he noticed one of the power cords

was out so he returned to the power shed and checked the fuse box. He knew enough about electricity to know if a fuse was missing. He found the fuse and replaced it then returned to see if the power cord was working.

"The vegetable crop is good this year eh Rowland?" a curvaceous woman observed who was in her late thirties.

"Yes, the wise say it could have been better had we more insects to pollinate the flowers. They say this crop would have been far better had the honey bee still been around. We should be thankful of the mild winter we had," Rowland explained. Rowland was standing talking to the woman at the end of one of the rows about ten yards from a wire fence. The fence surrounded the entire garden. They always had trouble with thieves but that is what the patrol officers were paid for.

The five women collected enough vegetables in about 45 minutes. It was almost pitch black when Rowland checked the gas in the generator. He went to a shelf that was in the power shed and grabbing a bottle of whisky, took a swig.

"Casey and his men should be back soon," a tall heavy man in his mid forties said standing at the door. "….should be a good feast."

"It's been a while hasn't it, Ben?" Rowland mused.

"I almost forgot what the taste of fresh meat is like," Ben reminisced. "Gary's kid has a slight case of pneumonia and I told his wife I'd look in on her. Are you going to give me a swig of that?"

Ben had a full head of sandy hair and a flat face, with a handsome, gentle complexion. The prominent feature about his head was his overly large ears. His hair was messy. He was one of the four men hired to protect what was known as 'The People'. It was important to keep some sort of law and order in this forgotten society. It was not only necessary for protection but also meant their survival. One of them had to remain on duty while they were feasting.

Ben started to drink and took a couple of extra swigs when Rowland grabbed the bottle. "Easy, I need that for protection," he warned placing the bottle back on the shelf. "It's good to have a feast once in a while isn't it Ben? Make's life worth living doesn't it?"

"If you ask me, there's only two pleasures in life, sex and food," Ben mused.

Rowland laughed and locked the power shed. The moon was full so they made their way in the dull light. Their dwellings were nearby each man having his own place of residence. As they said goodnight Rowland walked towards what used to be a rich neighborhood in Pittsburg, Ben walking in a different direction heading for his bicycle that he used to get to an old abandoned wear house. He was on duty that night not only to protect the gardens but the members of 'the People' as well. The patrol officers lived separate lives each one looking out for their own health and welfare. Some lived alone, others had living arrangements, some with woman and children as in Ben's case, others together as in the case of Ray and Rick the remaining two 'patrol officers,' finding comfort and protection in one another's presence.

Rowland's place was a brick house which was solid protection not only from assassins but from bad weather as well. It had a large fireplace and Rowland had mounted a large cistern out back which was used to collect rain water. It had all the comforts of home but lacked heat and electricity although he had mounted a wood stove in the main bedroom. In the garage which he kept locked but for an air vent that allowed carbon monoxide from the generator, he used for electricity, to escape.

Rowland surveyed his home with caution. He had to be

sure no one had tried to break in. It was located at the end of a dark secluded street not far from a local supermarket which had long ago been pillaged for most food items. He unlocked the gate protecting the front entrance. Opening the milk box he grabbed a flash light and unlocked the small side door leading to the garage. Glancing at the vent he checked to see if the fuel tank on the generator was full. He took a moment to fill the tank and then fired up the generator. Light suddenly illuminated the garage like a candle in the dark as he left through the side door and replaced the flashlight in the milk box. He had flood lights to protect his home but he wouldn't turn them on until someone tried to threaten him. Unlocking the front door he turned on a unique alarm system he used for protection.

After leaving Rowland, Ben walked to a secluded hiding place where he found his bicycle. It was a twenty minute ride to an old abandoned wear house where he and his family lived but he was on duty and tonight he had somewhere else to go. The contents of the wear house were long ago confiscated but in a secluded back room he had a nice little fireplace where he and his family survived. It was not often that they had intruders. Not too many people were interested in an old abandoned wear house. But he had to make a stop tonight to check on Gary's child who had a slight case of pneumonia.

The next morning Rowland knew he and two other fellow patrol officers would be needed for protection at the 'Great Hall' where they held their feasts. The men would be back soon from the hunt and the feast would be held that evening. Rowland locked the front gate. It was about 8 o'clock in the morning. He walked towards what 'The People' called the 'Great Hall' suspicious of any criminal activity going on around him. He noticed an elderly lady with a shopping cart on one of the neighborhood streets. It was full of non perishable items she had obviously been looting out of some of the houses. Most of the homes had already been pillaged but it was only forty, fifty, years ago that they were occupied. Mold and rot, weeds, and insects had already demolished most of them although some were still inhabited. She looked at him scornfully, ashamed of the layers of dirt and her filthy rags.

Ben was already sitting in front of the 'Great Hall' cradling his shotgun as he sat outside looking for any illegal activity.

"Any sign of Ray yet?" Rowland asked curiously as he approached.

"No."

"Are the women inside?"

"Yes" Ben said. "A couple of the women trapped some pigeons and rabbits. So I guess they'll be fresh pigeon and rabbit stew on the menu. And some of the boys caught some silver bass out of the river. But I don't know about you, I'm not too partial to that."

They took shelter under a metal lean to, to protect them from the elements. Later above the quiet sound of only the wind, the roar of an engine could be heard. It was faint at first then continued to a dull roar. A few moments later and Casey and his men could be heard quite loudly. They were sighted, the box van winding down the deserted streets, his men sitting on top, toting shotguns. They began hollering obscenities as they pulled up into the parking lot next to the main entrance.

It began to cloud up and a storm was threatening. The weather was unpredictable at times the elements becoming quite frequent and severe sometimes threatening hail and even funnel clouds. The wind began to pick up and it would be all Casey and his men could do to get the fresh meat inside and prepared for the feast without them getting drenched. They had bagged a couple of doe as well as a small boar, some more rabbits, and some possum. Some of the local farmers had traded some fresh eggs for vegetables so there would be fresh eggs on the menu. They had also traded for some milk and cheese. But in this heat you couldn't always guarantee it was fresh.

The storm picked up and with high winds, lightning and thunder they got the food inside and the women began to prepare the feast. They were quite safe on the inside with the generators pumping electricity to the kitchen, the men and children lounged in the hall drinking spirits, dancing and jesting amongst themselves. Outside the four patrol officers took shelter under the lean to, keeping watch until it was time to be called to the feast.

Rowland sat on an old worn out chair, huddling to keep dry. He knew this misery wouldn't last and that he and his men would be given provisions as reward for their services. Ben's family would be present so he also had his family to think about.

"It's good to have contacts like that farmer," Rowland mused trying to break the boredom by creating conversation. "I wish we'd had more like that."

"Well that, and the water distillery," Ray explained feeling bored as well. "I don't know how long the gasoline will hold out. They say there is an endless supply. It's a pity we have to depend on those generators for power. I wonder what it was like having all those comforts."

Rowland was medium built with a tough masculine demeanor added to his kind and warm disposition. His hair was fair and well kept. He carried a proud air and was quite sure of himself only adding to his good looks and this made him attractive to women. He was usually clean and neat although water was precious and it was not always convenient to shower. He was a man that was useful at most anything he put his hands to.

"Probably like heaven itself," Rowland philosophized. "You can just imagine what's going on in some of the rural areas. At least we're withholding some portion of the law."

Ben argued, "Law, you call this handful of degenerates a society? We're just doing this because we're getting food for ourselves and our families. If it came right down to it, you'd kill to survive."

"It's not a matter of whether you would actually kill is it? It's the difference between right and wrong. Something inside of you tells you when you're doing right or wrong," Rowland stated continuing to disagree.

Ray interrupted, "Hold it a moment. Do you think it's right to kill someone because he steals a few vegetables?"

There was a pause. Then Rowland defensively stated again, "That's not the point. We're not arguing about whether it's right to kill."

There was a sudden flash of lightning and a crack of thunder.

Inside where it was warm and dry, Casey and his men were slowly drying off, as they boasted about their hunt. Casey was an experienced hunter with years of experience at killing wild game. He was a masculine, weathered, woodsy kind of person who spoke his own mind. Most of the other men valued his opinion and this made him a true leader. He was medium height, fair but graying hair with a short well trimmed beard. He was round in the middle but considered a heavy man. He wore a heavy, yellow, checkered cotton shirt and long hunting trousers. He was not neat and tidy and the only reason his beard was trimmed was because his wife trimmed it for him.

A dark haired woman, curvaceous, in her mid thirties wearing a clean, white and red, summer dress came from the kitchen carrying a try of cheese. She placed it on the table and smiled at Casey in a seductive manner.

"Come here, Sandra," Casey demanded holding out his arm enticing her to his knee. She wandered over reluctantly, submitting to her temptations and received his warm embrace. He grabbed her close and kissed her. "Isn't this worth fighting for?" he asked looking at his comrades.

One of Sandra's children asked her when dinner would be ready whining in a polite sort of way playing enticingly with her hands and her feet. "Go and play," she resentfully responded remaining content in her husbands embrace. The child ran away and Sandra waited for a moment and then pushed herself away from the group of men in a seductive wiggle.

Casey began again. "Carry and I were just achieving the crest of the hill when I spotted that possum. We never would have seen him because it was getting dark, but I happened to see his tail move."

Carry recalled the incident and boasted, "It was Casey's shot that bagged him. I didn't see him in time." Carry had an easy going personality, was young and had a light, clean shaven face. He was tall and slim and his clothes looked like they were a size too big.

The kitchen doors swung open and Sandra brought out another platter. Suddenly the outside door opened and they all heard the rain and thunder as Rowland entered. She looked at him and said, "Come on in out of the rain, Rowland?"

Rowland looked at her and answered, "Any reason why we can't join in some of the festivities?"

"You know you and your men are always welcome to be part of our group. That's what you get paid for isn't it?" Sandra warned wiping her hands on her apron. "We're like family."

"That gave me a good excuse to come in and socialize."

"If you don't be careful we'll put you to work in the

kitchen," Sandra concluded with a smile as she walked back towards the kitchen.

Rowland sat on a soft arm chair. There were several soft chairs as well as several couches occupied by men, a few women and children. Ben's wife and children were there as well.

"That cloudburst came up in a hurry. Dangerous to be out in a thunderstorm," Rowland warned being somewhat concerned. Rowland had a 45 caliber handgun strapped over his shoulder but he kept it concealed under his shirt. Things like thunderstorms and food for health concerned Rowland because there were no hospitals and very few doctors.

".......you and your men staying dry?" Casey asked his curiosity taking charge.

"Yeah, there's a shelter out there we can keep watch under. How's your little boy, Gary?" Rowland asked.

"Not well. My wife is home looking after him."

Gary had long brown hair, with tough weathered facial features due to years of Genoese. He was medium height and weighed about 180 pounds.

"It's not too hard to catch cold in this weather," Rowland explained. "It's so unpredictable anymore. If there's anything I can do to help, let me know."

Casey changed the subject. "You and your men are greatly appreciated here Rowland. We try to withhold what is left of a law abiding society, though it's difficult at times. Civilization is coming to an end. Look at what goes on outside 'the People'. You can't survive. We've gone back to the stone ages. Not too many men would risk their lives for what's left of the law."

"I'm sure there are people who know the difference between right and wrong outside in the country. Your men bought fresh eggs, milk and cheese," Rowland mused explaining the reality of their situation.

The wise men sat around and told stories as some of the

children as well as the adults listened with interest. A man in his mid sixties sat in the centre with the children gathered around. He had long white hair and a bushy white beard. His age showed as he folded his arthritic hands on his lap and starred off into nowhere as he talked. His daughter sat nearby keeping watch of his every move.

"First came the electric radio, then the television, they even had microwaves that you could cook a roast of beef in 10 minutes. Before that came the electric light which was known as the best invention of modern times," the old man coughed and Rebecca his daughter got out of her chair and adjusted his collar making sure he was warm enough.

"Cold papa?" she asked.

The old man looked at her and shook his head, then continued, "They had airplanes and rocket ships to take men to the moon. They claimed Albert Einstein was the most brilliant scientist that ever lived."

Rowland looked at the old man and listened. 'It was strange' he thought, 'he was looking at one of the most brilliant minds left. Soon there would be no one left to tell the stories'. He watched as all the children looked and listened with wonder, Rowland liked to listen to the old stories. He thought he detected a twinkle in their eye.

"Unfortunately scientists were more important than what valuable resources nature has to offer. The ground from whence we came has come back to us again." Every body laughed.

Rowland was suddenly distracted when Sandra came out of the kitchen with a platter of vegetables. She glanced in his direction and caught his eyes starring at her.

"Gee the way a girl gets noticed around here you'd think I was a movie star or somethin'," she warned not speaking directly at him but implying it was him she was talking about.

Casey hadn't noticed. He continued talking to his men.

"What man couldn't notice?" Rowland explained trying to be discreet. A moment passed between them and then Sandra exclaimed seductively," We really could use some help in the kitchen, Rowland."

Remaining discreet Rowland waited for Sandra to return to the kitchen then he got up and entered. It was a conventional institutional kitchen. There were five or six stoves along the wall with a long table in the centre for preparing food. Two convection ovens were off to the side. Not all the stoves were in use since it takes quite a bit of hydro and some of the ovens didn't work. Rowland had designed a power shed out back where they had two or three generators pumping electricity. Rowland walked through the kitchen out to the back to check the fuel in the generators. After topping up the fuel he reentered the kitchen.

"If that dinner is half as good as it smells, we're in for a good feast?" Rowland stated walking up behind Sandra, exercising his nostrils, as she checked a pot of potatoes.

"Just about ready," she concluded.

A heavy woman in her late forties dressed in blue jeans and a orange tank top asked Rowland, "Rowland could you help put this roast in the oven? It's heavy and then maybe you could carve it."

After taking the pan out of the oven he washed his hands and then began carving the roast and placing the slices on a plate. As he did this Sandra stood close by and as she helped fill some of the vegetable dishes she admired Rowland's strong hands and his ability to carve meat.

"You have strong hands Rowland," she said. "I wonder if you're touch is as gentle as your ability to carve meat."

"Is that an offer?"

"Tell me why a man like you, who is good at everything, is not with a woman?"

"Guess I never met a woman I really liked," he explained.

"I guess we can carry out the plates and silverware," Joanne the cook explained wiping her hands on her white apron.

The dinner was to be served in smorgous bourge style, each person grabbing his or her own plate and helping themselve's. It was going according to plan. They kept a one man watch in front of the hall just in case something unexpected was to occur. Hours passed as they intermingled between the kitchen and the dinning room, Rowland occasionally checking in with his men. They played, danced and told stories as the time passed keeping warm around a roaring fireplace located in the centre of the hall. Suddenly they heard gunfire.

There were three exits to the building. Rowland exited through the back door to circle the opposite side of the building. Ben took one of the exits. As Ben peered through the exit door he was aware that the opening would create a target because there were three flood lights attached to the side of the building. Outside of the two exit doors was an asphalt driveway and on the right side was the lean to. It was a clear dark, night. There were a few lights in the distance which only made for an easy target. The lean to was dark and there was no sign of Ray.

Ben suddenly heard a shot and the bullet ricocheted above his head. He quickly closed the door as Casey and a few of his men were anxious to hear what all the fuss was about. Ben shouted, "Don't go near that door." There was a shuffle, as some of the people became frightened, some of the men grabbed their guns. Ben then exited the rear door. Casey's men covered the two exits.

After leaving through the back door, Ben circled around to the front of the building being careful to stay out of the light. At the end of the back wall he made a dash to the lean to.

"Where are the shots coming from?" Ben asked after seeing Ray and being careful to stay out of the light.

"Over there towards that house," Ray exclaimed pointing in the direction of the exit to the parking lot.

"Are you hit," he asked.

"Just a scratch."

"How many do you say?"

"Not sure," Ray exclaimed.

They watched in the direction of a vacant house that was next to the hall. It was dark but the reflection of the wet parking lot and the distant lights made visibility possible.

From the back of the house next to the hall they saw the flash of gunfire. Ben and Ray took cover behind a tree and an old telephone pole. Someone began firing from behind the hall. They assumed it would be Rowland. Ben and Ray began shooting toward the rear of the old house. Suddenly everything became still.

"I heard two shots from the rear of the hall, didn't you Ray?" Ben exclaimed.

"Yes"

"Must be Rowland. They must of assumed we didn't have guns," Ben explained. "Then when they realized we did, they fled."

"Looks like this is going to be an all night party," Ray warned. Ben smiled as the rain dampened his face and agreed.

THE END

The Little Stone Statue

Chapter 1

Change In The Valley

It was an overcast morning in the shadowy little hills of Bedfordshire, with the clouds ominously rolling over the meadows embracing the moisture like a saturated sponge and releasing it on the sleepy estate below, with its tiled roof delivering the water to a cistern located underneath the rafters. The trees and flowers of the meadow seemed to cry out in sweet release as if they could talk amongst themselves of how wonderful it was to get rain at last. The animals and insects of the valley took shelter because for them, the rain meant discomfort that would last for twenty four hours. Communication among the animals and insects had also been possible with each new sound, as well as the beauty of the flowers and trees, making even the wind recognize its own name. It became so noisy with the sound that each voice made, that it was detrimental for the wind to carry those sounds from one place to the next. The water lily cried enticingly to the insect to come capture its nectar as the flowers gossiped amongst themselves at how easy it was to lie about all day and do nothing. The tall trees seemed to mock them as they uproariously laughed at what the flowers had said.

The clop of horse's hooves could be heard over the rain as a carriage carrying a lord and his lady came to a stop in front of the sleepy estate. The carriage driver tied the rains as the lord and his lady stepped out into the driving rain. The garden at the lower end of the estate was protected by various artistic stone statues, watching over the garden. One of the more elaborate statues said with a sneer, "Here comes the master again. I wonder what he's going to do this time?"

The statue that was adjacent to it bellowed, "Oh he's probably going to wine and dine the little floozy till he can't get enough of her." The rest of the statues throughout the garden could be heard laughing.

At the entrance to the garden, a small boy, foot stone, was used as a stepping stone to clean one's muddy boots before entering the living quarters and the master proceeded to clean his boots on the statue. Then the lady cleaned her boots on the statue. Then the boy statue complained to all the other statues in the garden, "How I detest being used as a piece of filth. I wish I could be like a real little boy."

As the master walked away with his lady one of the statues envisioned, "Wouldn't it be nice not to be made of stone and to move around as the man and lady do and not be stuck in one spot all the time?"

The garden of the sleepy estate, was such a beautiful sight that everything about seemed to team with life. Even the stone statues had life. There were many animals that lived in the garden as well as many flowers and insects and birds. As they talked among themselves two rabbits murmured, "I wonder if the master is going hunting? It's such a nasty day to be doing anything."

"I don't think we have to worry about him today," the other rabbit answered, relieved.

After this one flower exclaimed to another, "Isn't it nice not to have to do anything, especially on such a dark day?"

Then the second flower answered, "Get used to it because I have a feeling it's going to last all day."

The rest of the day remained uneventful, the lord and his lady spent the day inside keeping warm by the fire. Pouring out a glass of wine and handing it to his lady he boldly exclaimed, "I have some business to take care of in town tomorrow then we have the rest of the day to ourselves."

She responded by saying, "Oh that'll be good. I can cook a nice dinner for you in the meantime."

The morning brought brilliant sunshine. On this day they went for a walk in the garden. As they walked amongst the statues, the flowers, and the shrubs he asked the lady, "Isn't it a nice day to go riding?"

The lady smiled in agreement, "I think I'd like that."

"After I get back from town we'll go." He then kissed her goodbye and left her alone in the garden.

A dominant statue proclaimed loudly, "How can he leave her all alone like that. Who does he think he is?"

Beside, an adjacent statue proclaimed, "That's no way to impress a lady."

Two flowers conversed among themselves, "Sunshine at last, I think I'll stretch as far as I can."

As the lady strolled in the garden, the sounds of her petticoats reselling at her ankles could be heard through the morning breeze, as her sky blue dress silhouetted against the rest of the beauty the garden offered. The lady dreamed of when her master and her would be married and when she would own this dreamy little estate. Her mother would be proud at her having landed such a prestigious husband. She will then supposedly be happy for the remainder of her life.

To the lady, money was not the answer to happiness. But having a roof over one's head and lifelong security wasn't hard for any girl to accept. As she dreamed she strolled down towards the edge of the garden, where the rippling of a small brook brought pleasant thoughts to the young woman's mind.

She knew this. She knew that love and a relationship did not depend on material wealth and on how much people own, but on true commitment and being able to adjust when the chips a down.

Not far away from where the woman was standing, a robust warrior statue proclaimed boldly, "If I were him I never would have left her alone."

A female statue that was standing nearby, softly replied, "I think she's lonely."

The lady noticed the sunlight's reflection on the little brook. It was like a thousand fireflies dancing on the water.

The sun rose high in the sky on this bright spring morning in this sleepy little valley as the hills seemed to absorb nature's rich happiness with each plant and animal that she embraced. Life seemed to thrive on this fresh, new, spring day. Presently a rider approached.

Tying his horse to the hitching post, the lord entered the sleepy estate that seemed to be teaming with life. He was greeted by his lady at the door with a kiss.

She looked at him lovingly and said, "I've fixed your favorite dinner, steak and kidney pie."

"Oh, thank you sweetheart. That was well worth the wait," he proclaimed as he walked to the couch and sat down. She took his arm and went with him as he slowly began taking off his riding boots. There was a fire in the hearth which was causing her to feel quite romantic. He continued taking off his boots and then noticed she was being quiet asked, "What's the matter Elizabeth?"

"It's just that…well, I think that I'd like to get married," she boldly stated looking at him for some romantic support.

The master's eye's rolled away as if he was uncomfortable next to her and answered her saying, "Elizabeth we've been over this dozens of times. I'm not ready financially to make a commitment."

"But I want to have a child, "she continued.

"I know honey I want one too. There's nothing I want more than to get married and have a family but I have to straighten out this matter about my family estate. It'll only take a few more months."

"Oh, Rick."

Suddenly clouds began to roll ominously into the valley as the sunshine was soon blotted out.

After dinner, Elizabeth and Richard went for a ride in the hills not suspecting the weather to interfere. A cloudburst interrupted their ride and in so doing they returned to the estate. After hitching the horses, Richard and Elizabeth proceeded to clean their riding boots on the little boy statue.

"Oh, not again," complained the little statue. "I can't take much more of this. If only I was a real little boy and not made of stone."

Something magical happened in the valley that evening. There's something magical about the love of a family and the love between a man and a woman that changed the entire valley. As the man and woman retired and as the valley went into a deep sleep, a star above shone brightly, brighter than any of the other stars in the sky. It caused a magic that seemed to stand out above the rest of the world. Like the love between a man and woman, like love and hate, like having friends and family, rather than enemies.

Something else caused change in the valley too. The little boy statue miraculously changed into a real little boy. Not only had the valley changed but Elizabeth and Richard's lives would forever change as well.

Chapter 2

First Day At School

The carriage came to a stop in front of the sleepy estate and a young boy got out. Waving goodbye to the carriage driver who passed him his tiny suitcase, he scrambled up the stone staircase and stymied along the walkway. Suddenly stopping he noticed before him, standing erect, a large, stone, warrior statue and studied it for a moment with one eye strategically dipped. Thinking the better of it he continued through the garden to the front door.

Confused as to what to do, he fidgeted for a moment, then hammered on the large, oak, door. Elizabeth answered the door and the little boy looked at her and stated his business.

"Hi, I'm the servant boy they sent you."

"Oh yes," Elizabeth answered, "Do come in."

Richard and Elizabeth had recently been married and they had been trying to have children but had been unsuccessful. In the early nineteenth century couples who couldn't have children were usually not treated and it would be two hundred years before such treatment would be made available. Young boys were also put to work at an early age. It was not unusual for a young boy to work for a living rather than go to school. So Richard and Elizabeth decided to hire a young boy servant from an ad they had seen in the local newspaper. By hiring a boy servant, this could not possibly be the answer they were looking for but at least it was a little closer to it.

Richard, Elizabeth, and the little boy had no idea a change had occurred, but they were going through their daily activities as if nothing strange had happened. For them it was just another day.

Elizabeth took the little boy by the hand and led him into the room. Richard had just come into the room and was wondering what all the fuss was about.

"This is Richard, my husband, and your….what did you say your name is?"

"Jeffrey"

"Richard this is Jeffrey, our new servant," Elizabeth informed him. "Do you come from a large family, Jeffrey?" she asked becoming somewhat inquisitive.

"I don't have a family, I'm an orphan."

"Oh, poor boy," she cooed with an expression of sorrow. "Well this is your family now, so make yourself at home Jeffrey. Here let me take your suitcase. Come I'll show you to your room." She snatched Jeffrey's suitcase and led him to one of the adjacent bedrooms at the side of the house.

"This is where you'll sleep," she gestured, pointing to a double bed in the small, brightly lit, room. "I'll fix you something to eat and then we'll discuss your duties as a servant. In the meantime you can put your clothes in the dresser and wash your face and hands."

She left Jeffrey alone. He did what he was told and unpacked his clothes and placed them in the dresser. Filling the bowl on the table with water, he proceeded to wash himself. Having accomplished this, the smell of bacon cooking, drew him back into the pantry, where he found Elizabeth fixing his breakfast.

Elizabeth was slim, average in height, blue eyes and dirty

blonde hair to add to her pretty complexion. Her pale blue, full length dress was outstanding to her good looks.

Jeffrey casually lingered at the edge of the pantry surrendering into his mouthwatering temptations of crisp, frying, bacon as it cooked in the pan. He had eaten only a stale piece of bread they had given him at the boarding house he had stayed in that morning, and it was all he could do to resist the temptation to ask for a piece., but he knew he must mind his manners on the first day of his new home. He was hungrier than he could ever remember. As a matter of fact he couldn't remember anything that happened to him before living in the boarding house.

"Crack these eggs and then you can set the table," Elizabeth ordered as she handed him a bowl of eggs. "You don't mind, do you?" she asked.

"No, not at all," Jeffrey stammered, his enthusiasm being controlled by his hunger as he snatched the bowl and began cracking eggs.

The dinning room was parallel to the pantry with the huge, oak table filling the majority of the room. There were plates and silver wear in the two hutches at either side of the room. Jeffrey then began setting the plates and silver wear around the table.

After a big, hearty breakfast Richard and Elizabeth sat down with Jeffrey and began discussing duties.

"We don't expect you to work too hard Jeffrey, just a few light duties to help take up some of the load, for example carrying water and firewood. That would be a great help," she advised him with a sincere show of compassion. "Richard can show you how to feed the animals, that shouldn't be too hard, and then you can sweep in here once in a while. Also, Jeffrey we would like you to lead a normal little boy's life and go to school. Would you like that?"

Jeffrey was so moved by the emotions he was experiencing and the duties Elizabeth had mentioned that all he could do was sit with his hands folded as he fumbled with his fingers looking down and remained silent.

The next day they woke Jeffrey up at dawn. To his surprise there were chores to be done before breakfast. He looked forward to a good breakfast, as he knew from the day before that Elizabeth was a good cook. For him this was something to look forward to.

After feeding the animals and carrying firewood and water for Elizabeth, Jeffrey found to his surprise (the second of many that day), that she and Richard wanted him to go to school. So after eating a hearty breakfast, they hitched the horses to the carriage and drove Jeffrey into town.

As the carriage bounced up and down on the dusty road, Richard took the opportunity for some quality time by gesturing to Jeffrey in a friendly way, "Ever been to school before?"

Feeling ashamed Jeffrey answered, "No, can't say as I have."

"It will help us out a lot if you learn to add and subtract, Jeffrey," Richard remarked, glancing at him sideways, "Might turn you into a real gentleman."

He remained silent being uncomfortable with the idea. Jeffrey was average weight and height for a nine year old boy with not too much baby fat. He had messy, brown, hair, and fat prominent lips. His ears were too big but he had a nose that seemed to curve out. He wore loose fitting, dark pants with a blue shirt and had on a small, dusty cap.

Richard had a dark, freckliest complexion, having dark reddish hair and brown eyes. He was tall and lean along with his good looks.

The carriage pulled to a stop in front of the school house. Jeffrey, Elizabeth, and Richard jumped out

The school house was a tiny, white washed building, 20/30 ft., with little wooden steps leading to the front door. Several children were playing in the yard. A young spinster was supervising as they approached. She was plain looking with a grey, colorless ankle length dress. Her hair was tied up in a bun.

"This is Jeffrey," Elizabeth stated. "We'd like him to go to school. And your name is….?" She gestured with a show of affection, by holding out her hand.

"Miss Donnelly," she responded a little hesitantly, shaking her hand. "Hello Jeffrey," holding out her hand to Jeffrey she appeared a little shy. "I think you'll like school."

Elizabeth looked directly at Miss Donnelly and then sternly at Jeffrey and said, "We'll be in touch. See you at lunchtime." She and Richard then turned and walked back to the carriage.

They decided to load up on provisions while in town, so Richard visited the general store, while Elizabeth shopped for a new hat.

"Richard I'd really like to know what they're wearing in Paris," she suggested as they pulled up in front of the general store. "I know I'm being selfish, but please have patience with me sweetheart."

"You're not selfish, Elizabeth, you deserve a new hat. Besides what woman can't resist the desire to shop. I'll meet you back here at eleven," Richard relented, watched as her petticoats swayed to each step she made as she walked away.

Miss Donnelly handed Jeffrey a reader and told him to turn to the first page and read as the lesson began. There were

10 or 12 children of various ages ranging from 6 to 12, sitting in rows facing Miss Donnelly.

After a few minutes of silence, she looked over her spectacles. "Well were waiting," she ordered.

Jeffrey remained silent looking around at the look of expectation everyone was giving and shamefully admitted, "I don't know how to read."

There was a snicker from some of the other classmates. A feeling of shame mixed with fear came over him as he noticed one of the male students,(about the same age as Jeffrey), whispering to a girl seated behind him.

"That's enough children. Jeffrey will just have to learn like the rest of the class. Jeffrey, you follow along while Mary reads. Go ahead Mary," Miss Donnelly advised.

As Mary began to read, Jeffrey remained silent, looking down at his reader with a feeling of embarrassment that was quite foreign to him. He tried catching glances of the boy that snickered at him but was careful not to catch eye contact. 'He'd show him after school' he thought.

At lunch Elizabeth asked Jeffrey how he enjoyed his first morning at school.

"I don't think I like school much," Jeffrey sighed.

"Why don't you like your teacher?" she asked.

"No, it's not that. It's just that, well, the kids laughed at me because I didn't know how to read."

"Oh Jeffrey, you'll get used to it. Once you learn you'll probably show them all up," she said in a soothing way. "Now eat your lunch and let's not talk any more about this nonsense."

Later that afternoon Miss Donnelly asked Jeffrey to brush off the chock board so they could start the next lesson. As Jeffery began to do as he was told, hate began to brew as the same little boy sneered under his breathe and whispered, "Sissy."

It was all Jeffrey could do to control his temper. He resolved again to get even with this little runt.

After school, Mary was standing in front of the schoolhouse and Jeffrey walked over and began talking.

"I don't know what I'da done if you hadn't of read for me, Mary," he began recalling the incident in the classroom.

"Oh that's alright, Miss Donnelly asked me to anyway," Mary recollected.

"I'd really like it if you would take the time to help teach me sometime," Jeffrey asked.

Just then they noticed the boy who called Jeffrey a 'sissy' was pushing around another boy that appeared to be smaller and weaker. Jeffrey left Mary and got in between the two boys and punched the bully in the nose causing blood to flow. Miss Donnelly came out of the schoolhouse. With an appalled look, she approached the three boys and took Jeffrey by the ear, leading him to the side of the schoolhouse. Whispering low so no one else could hear she scolded him.

"Wait till I tell Mr. and Mrs. O'Reilly what happened here today. I'm sure they won't be too pleased, this happening on your first day of school."

She would now have to take disciplinary action, now that Jeffrey had drawn blood. Jeffrey kept silent. He could not comprehend what was happening, when it was the other boy that should have been punished.

"I'd like you to do something for me, Jeffrey," she warned being certain that he would. "I'd like you to go home and tell Mr. and Mrs. O'Reilly what you've done here today." She looked sternly at him.

"OK, Miss Donnelly."

".....and from now on no more horseplay. You behave yourself," she warned letting him go.

Jeffrey was angry that she singled him out as a troublemaker, and he vowed he would get even someway or another. The sun was hot and he knew he needed a bath. He walked home with a bitter attitude, regretting what he'd have to tell his guardian parents when he got home.

The town of Bedford was fixed on a hill that overlooked the valley. The valley was known to the local folk as Bedfordshire simply because there was no other name to call it. He followed the path that led through an adjoining meadow, leading into the valley.

As he walked through the meadow, he decided he would pick some flowers for Elizabeth then maybe she wouldn't punish him so much. The meadow was covered in wildflowers and he had no trouble picking a small bouquet. There were acres and acres of purple violets, yellow magpies, white daisies, and gold colored marigolds. He had a hard time imagining why anyone would want to pick flowers for a girl, but something inside told him this was probably the right thing to do.

Jeffrey scampered into the pantry where he found Elizabeth cooking the evening meal.

"Here these are for you," he gestured handing her the flowers.

"Oh, they look lovely. I better get something to put them in," she proclaimed then asked, "Did you have a good day at school?"

"I'm afraid I got into a little bit of trouble maim," he confessed.

"Oh, what happened?"

"I punched a boy in the nose."

"Jeffrey I told you no more nonsense," Elizabeth warned recalling the incident that he had told her about.

"But he was being a bully," Jeffrey remembered.

"If you think you can just come in here and give me flowers and then everything will be alright your mistaken young man.

That's no excuse to punch him in the nose. Now we're going to discuss this over dinner but I think we'll probably have to punish you," she stammered. "Now go and help Rick feed the horses."

This was quite a blow for young Jeffrey's ego. He became withdrawn and didn't want to talk to Rick as he went about his chores. Richard asked him how his first day at school went, but he just said, "OK", and then remained silent.

Richard knew there was something wrong and later asked Elizabeth, "What's wrong with Jeffrey?"

"Apparently he got into some trouble at school."

"Oh, like what?" Richard asked.

"He punched a boy in the nose," she said.

That night at dinner Elizabeth confronted Jeffrey. "Tell Richard what happened in school Jeffrey."

"A boy was bullying another boy so I tried to stop him by punching him in the nose," Jeffrey said recollecting the incident in the school yard.

"Some of the kids were laughing at Jeffrey in school because he couldn't read," Elizabeth said, recalling the conversation.

"Is that true Jeffrey?"

"Yes sir."

"That's no excuse for bulling, Jeffrey, is that understood?" Richard warned. "That's no way to make friends, young man."

"Are you going to punish me?"

"I think we can let you off with a warning, just so long that it doesn't happen again."

Chapter 3

The Friend

Jeffrey awoke the next morning rested and refreshed. It was a warm, bright, morning as he went about his chores,(as he was supposed to) with a positive attitude, obedient to what he was told. After carrying water and firewood he fed the animals with as much love and compassion as his heart could bear, keeping in mind that animals were inferior to human beings and needed help, something like what he did. Richard had to go to town, so after a big hearty breakfast, he drove Jeffrey to school.

The meadow was alive and fresh as a breeze carried the scent of flowers and insects buzzed around their heads. The carriage made its way through the deep valley and up the steep hill that led to the village.

"To avoid complications with Miss Donnelly I'll drop you off here, now remember no horseplay," Richard warned as he slowed the carriage to a halt about a hundred yards from the little white schoolhouse. "See you tonight."

Jeffrey thought nothing of what he had said as Richard pulled away and he was left standing, because in his heart he knew he had a positive attitude this morning. He was being given another chance and nothing was going to cause him to get into any kind of mischief today. So off he went as he scrambled to school.

As the children were led into the schoolhouse because Mary's seat was in front of his, Jeffrey stopped to talk with her before the children were seated. "Did Miss Donnelly say anything to you?" he asked looking somewhat concerned.

"No," she explained. "I heard you got into a bit of trouble."

"She just scolded me and told me to tell my….."

"Sit down children," Miss Donnelly said, throwing her briefcase on the desk.

"Now Mary, since Jeffrey is unable to read you go ahead and read from your reader."

'Why is she picking on me' he thought. 'She's centering me out in front of the rest of the class again. What did I do to deserve that?' Although Jeffrey was taking a positive attitude, he knew in his heart that somehow he and Miss Donnelly were going to cross wires again one day.

The weather began to turn warm in the valley. The warm air brought the bird's knew life and the flowers new buds as the days grew longer and the sun rose higher in the sky. Animals found new meaning for their young as the grass grew tall and the leaves in the forest turned brown.

Life was normal for Jeffrey for the next three weeks. He came home from school and went about his daily activities as a normal little boy would, making friends with those people who were important to him. He even became friends with the little boy he punched in the nose. An ulterior motive for befriending the little boy was still on the back of his mind but he just wanted to do what was right and not get into any kind of mischief. It was important to him to make Elizabeth and Richard happy after all they were his guardian parents.

Jeffrey was finding out that there was a lot of work to being a servant boy. He was finding he didn't have much time to himself. He was sitting at the dinning room table while

Elizabeth was cooking dinner, one Friday night. Richard was busy outside somewhere.

"Billy wants to take me fishing tomorrow, is it OK if I go?" he asked.

"I don't see why not. You'll be home in time for dinner, I gather."

"Yes," he stated.

"Well go and wash up, then set the table, Jeffrey."

During dinner, the conversation became informative when it came to Elizabeth and Richard's attention that Jeffrey was going fishing with Billy.

"Where did you meet Billy, Jeffrey?" Richard asked.

"He's the kid I punched in the nose."

"Oh you've forgiven him have you?" he asked with the slight hint of a frown.

"Yeah, we're great friends," but deep down he still carried some bitterness. He really didn't understand these feelings he was having. To forget that someone did a cruel act against you did not make sense.

The next morning, while he was doing his morning chores, Elizabeth told him Billy had come and was ready to go fishing.

"You'll be home for dinner right, Jeffrey? Now remember behave yourself you two," she warned looking directly at Jeffrey as the two boys left.

"She can be so strict," Jeffrey stated as they defeated the first hill and proceeded to enter the valley.

It was a bright, clear, morning. The air was cool and it was a perfect day to go fishing. It hadn't occurred to Jeffrey that they needed bait although he noticed Billy was carrying a fishing pole. For that matter it hadn't occurred to him that you had to use a fishing pole.

Billy accessed the matter and said abruptly, "We need to find some worms."

"What for?" Jeffrey asked.

"We need to find some bait."

"Oh yah right."

Billy was thin. His sandy colored hair was messy and his ears stuck out which made his head a little too big for his body. His cotton trousers and long sleeve shirt was two sizes too big. But he had a clean complexion and was generally a good looking child.

On the way to the 'fishing hole', Billy began turning over large rocks and picking worms from underneath, putting them in an old can he had brought.

The small brook that wound through the valley provided drinking water for the tiny community and it made an excellent place to go fishing.

"This looks as good as place as any," Billy proclaimed as they made their way to a clearing beneath two large, oak, trees beside the babbling brook.

Billy took a worm from the can and began baiting a hook.

"What are you doing that for?" Jeffrey asked.

"Don't you know anything about fishing?" Billy remarked.

"No"

"How come? You're father never took you fishing?" he asked again.

Not only did Jeffrey feel degraded by this last remark but deep inside Jeffrey still held some bitterness towards the little boy about the incident in the schoolyard.

"He's not my real father," he confessed to him a little reluctantly. "They're my guardian parents."

"What's a guardian parent? You mean their not your real parents?" Billy asked.

"No, I was hired as a servant boy and they're sort of like taking care of me."

"How do you like that?" Billy again asked.

"What do you mean, 'do I like it,' of course I like it," Jeffrey protested. "Why shouldn't I like it."

This really hit a sour note with Jeffrey. Something inside made him feel angry.

Billy then said, "I don't know. Maybe it's not fun not having any parents." Then he asked, "Have you always been an orphan?"

Fury raged in Jeffrey, especially after the last question.

"How'd you like a punch in the nose?" he threatened with a look that was full of hate.

Billy stood up with his fists clenched and proclaimed boldly, "Yah, and who's going to give it to me?"

Jeffrey then stood up and laid into him with a vengeance. The boys ended up wrestling each other, Jeffrey being the bigger of the two, punched Bill in the nose and again drew blood. They rolled in the dust, both boys getting dirty with torn clothing. Billy took the worst of the beating.

Jeffrey had every intention of explaining why he was home so early and why his clothes were dirty and torn. But as he walked into the lodge he realized he couldn't say anything without telling a lie. He also realized he was faced with an even bigger problem, because when he got there he found Elizabeth talking with one of the workers from the orphanage.

"What happened to you?" Elizabeth asked as the two women gazed on Jeffrey's appearance with astonishment.

"I was wrestling with Billy," he explained.

"Oh, Jeffrey you weren't fighting again?"

"Yes, maim," he related the incident with shame.

She looked at the social worker with a puzzled look.

"Jeffrey I thought I told you no more fighting," scolding him a little reluctantly. There was a moment's silence where all three remained speechless and then a little uncomfortably Elizabeth opened up, "Jeffrey this is Mrs. Rothchild from the orphanage. She is here to draw up your papers for adoption."

Jeffrey was stunned. All that he had accomplished in the last three weeks was slipping away.

"You mean you were going to adopt me?" he asked.

"You should be ashamed of yourself young man," the social worker related. "What do you think we should do Mrs. O' Reilly?"

Elizabeth was at a loss for words. "I don't know," she hesitated.

"I'll tell you what I'll do," she implied. "I know a poor widow who needs help. Why don't we put him to work for her and in the meantime that will give you and Richard time to reconsider?"

The social worker was an older lady that carried an air of sophistication. She had jet black hair that was streaked with grey, and rolled up in a bun. Her plain grey suite was modest by present day standards.

Elizabeth could see that Mrs. Rothchild was a mean spirited lady. In all probability she didn't like children either. Elizabeth sensed this and noticed Jeffrey sensed it too. Her conscience was telling her to do the right thing but she also wanted to help Jeffrey. A sense of responsibility overtook her.

"Yes, I think we can arrange that," Elizabeth agreed glancing sideways at Jeffrey.

As Mrs. Rothchild was leaving she said goodbye and then turned to Jeffrey and warned him, "If I were you I'd pull up my socks young man. Otherwise you might find yourself back at the orphanage."

She then turned to Elizabeth and stated, "We'll be in touch."

After she had left, Elizabeth scolded Jeffrey. Making herself useful but also ignoring Jeffrey, she warned, "If I were you I'd make myself scarce, young man."

He scurried out to the stable where he found solace with some of the animals. He was alone for the afternoon with his thoughts. To him animals were useful. 'At least they don't talk,' he thought, 'They can't hurt anyone that way.'

A young colt was drinking water at one of the troughs and patting it on the head he said, "You don't want to hurt no one do you boy?" The colt lifted his head and looked at Jeffrey as if it could talk.

Later that afternoon Richard walked his horse into the stable and finding Jeffrey in a daydream exclaimed, "Something must be bothering you Jeffrey you're very quiet."

"It's just that sometimes things don't turn out like you expect them to," he confessed.

Richard became somewhat concerned, lifting the saddle from the horse, as he listened to Jeffrey. "Explain son."

"Well I just found out that you and Elizabeth were planning to adopt me."

"So what's wrong with that?" Richard asked looking puzzled.

"It's just that, I just got in a fight with Billy and now she and the lady from the orphanage are thinking twice."

Chapter 4

A Mortal Blow

For the next three weeks Jeffrey was obligated to do,(in his spare time), work for a poor widow that lived just outside of Bedfordshire. He wished he had never set eyes on Billy, who unfortunately for him had suffered a broken wrist as a result of the fight they had had. Mary on the other hand had thought Jeffrey quite the troubadour for having stuck up for the little boy who got bullied in the schoolyard. But there were rumors going around that it was Jeffrey who was the bully and most of the village thought he was the instigator. For Jeffrey life became quite difficult for the summer.

Jeffrey worked on Saturday and Sunday for Mrs. Carmichael which took up the time he had off from school and doing chores. He cleaned up the yard and painted the fence, ran errands for her and chopped and carried firewood and water. He planted vegetables and flowers in the yard and inside he cleaned and mopped floors.

He walked into the general store one Saturday. He was on an errand to pick up some flowers for Mrs. Carmichael as well as a few odds and ends. As he walked down one of the aisles he noticed two women gazing at him and whispering under their breathe, "There's that bad little boy who broke Billy's arm. I wouldn't want him playing with my Leroy. Who knows what he'd do." Then they grabbed whatever they carried and left the store.

This was a mortal blow for young Jeffrey's ego. As hard as it was he was trying to do the right thing but he kept getting into mischief. He knew Richard and Elizabeth were deciding whether or not to adopt him but he didn't know how to change. What did he care if some bully got hurt? He was just giving him what he deserved. After all Mary thought he was doing the right thing. He might have prevented some other kid from getting hurt by punching Billy in the nose.

He lazily dreamed at a herd of cows that were grazing in the meadow as he stymied along towards Mrs. Carmichael's. As he wandered he thought, 'At least those cows can't talk. They can't get me into trouble that way anyway.'

There was a wonderfully pleasant aroma as he entered her cottage. She was baking cookies. Upon entering Mrs. Carmichael stood in the kitchen with a tray of fresh baked cookies. "Like a cookie, Jeffrey?"

He set the bag down giving into his temptation he snatched a couple of cookies showing the old lady his appreciation. As he was about to go about another chore he noticed some money she had left on a nearby table. After seeing the money something inside told him to take it. At first he ignored the temptation. He went about his chores and when he finished he told Mrs. Carmichael he was about to leave when she offered him another cookie.

He snatched the cookie blurting a weak goodbye and upon leaving he made sure she wasn't looking and quickly stuffed the money in his pocket.

"So things have been going well lately have they Jeffrey?" Richard asked Jeffrey at dinner that night.

Things had been going too well. Jeffrey was making

everyone around him think that this silly rumor was really only a rumor after all. It hadn't occurred to him that he had been doing something good. As a matter of fact his work was going so well he didn't even think about what had happened to him.

"Is Mrs. Carmichael pleased with your work?"

"Yes she is, actually," Jeffrey stammered not realizing he was lying.

"People seem to be taking a more positive attitude towards you lately," remarked Richard, "Have you made any more friends?"

"Well there is this girl at school."

"Oh there is eh," Richard said acknowledging what Jeffrey had said.

"Yah I think she kind of likes me."

Elizabeth suddenly interrupted, "That's great Jeffrey, that's the kind of young man I want to see. Would you pass the beets please Rick. If this keeps up we may have to reconsider our decision."

"How would you like that Jeffrey?" Richard asked, "Would you like to be a part of a real family?"

The thought that he had stole the money had not registered in his mind although he became excited at the thought of having new parents. He didn't realize that they could change their decision again. His thoughts became tangled and confused. He hesitated before answering.

"You know it's a responsibility being the member of a family," he warned. "Do you realize that son?"

"Yes"

Elizabeth opened up, "You know we have to stick together as a team. But just remember one thing. We'll always be there for you."

Suddenly something terrifying flashed through Jeffrey's

mind. Guilt seemed to take possession of him as these new feelings seemed to pour through him. He became so overwhelmed by guilt that fear became a passion that entangled and confused his thinking. He put these feelings out of his mind and thought only of at last being a normal little boy.

"We've decided we can lighten the work you've been doing as well, Jeffrey," Richard stated. "You'll still have your chores to do but until we contact Mrs. Rothchild you'll still have to work for Mrs. Carmichael. Is that OK?"

"Sure," he mumbled.

Later as he looked at the money he had stolen, he didn't know what to do with it. He looked for a place to hide it and decided to hide it in the barn in some remote corner. He thought 'If I forget about it and pretend it didn't happen then maybe no one will ever know.'

It was midweek, Elizabeth was just finishing up the evening dishes and Richard was out shooing the horses. Jeffrey was drying dishes for Elizabeth, when a stranger approached.

The sun was low in the sky because the days were getting shorter. It was late summer and the evenings were getting cool. The sun was almost totally blotted out by some evening cloud cover that was threatening rain. As the rider approached his image started off as a tiny speck and as it grew larger it became more visible. Richard couldn't make out who it was as he stood in the opening of the barn door until the rider got closer because the shadows from the nearby trees seemed to play tricks on his vision.

The stranger dismounted and as he held the horse's bridle he walked his horse closer to the barn door. Richard then noticed it was the town sheriff.

'Evenin', sheriff," he said "What can I do for you?"

"Evenin' Mr. O'Reilly. Looks like we might get some rain," the sheriff mused looking up at the clouds.

"Now I'm sure you didn't come all the way down here to talk about the weather, did you sheriff?"

"Well now that you mention it. Mrs. Carmichael has a complaint against a boy called Jeffrey that seems to be living here," the sheriff relented with some hesitation.

"Oh, what about?" Richard asked.

"'Appears he may have stolen some money from her."

Elizabeth and Jeffrey suddenly appeared out of the house. Jeffrey caught the tail end of the conversation.

"Evenin' maim," the sheriff shouted tipping his hat.

"What's all this about?" Elizabeth asked wiping her hands on her apron.

"Apparently we have a complaint against Jeffrey from a Mrs. Carmichael, maim'" informed the sheriff. "I guess he stole some money."

"I think I get the picture," she confessed. Turning to Jeffrey she starred and said angrily, "So now we've turned to stealing things, have we Jeffrey?"

Jeffrey became silent and withdrawn, not knowing whether to react or not.

"What did you do with the money?" she asked.

Ashamed he looked at them and confessed, "I can get it for you."

He then turned and scurried into the barn. Snatching the cash he hurried back to where the three were standing.

Elizabeth and Richard were quite embarrassed by the ordeal and stumbled with words to say to the sheriff.

"We're sorry we didn't know the boy would do such a thing," Richard apologized a little ashamed for the way he was feeling.

"Well you know these orphans, they don't have much of an upbringing," the sheriff explained.

"I promise you we'll take the necessary disciplinary action, sheriff," Elizabeth promised.

"Well now that Mrs. Carmichael has her money back I can't see as there should be a problem, maim'," he said taking the money out of Jeffrey's hand. "I'm sure he won't give you any more trouble."

He then tipped his hat, mounted his horse and began riding away.

For Jeffrey, adoption was now out of the question. He not only had the reputation as a mischief maker, but would forever make Elizabeth and Richard's lives a misery as well. They kept him on as a servant possibly because they had grown attached to him and since they didn't have a child of their own, he was just nice company to have around. He would also help keep them from causing a scandal. If word got out that they couldn't have children their lives would be forever ruined as well. They were secure enough financially with Richard's inheritance that they could hire another servant boy but unfortunately for them it would not be the same.

Rain became the norm for the next few months. The clouds moved ominously into the little valley and the days grew dark and dismal. The flowers in the meadow and the leaves on the trees withered and died and the birds and animals disappeared. The winter months became monotonous as the days dragged by.

Jeffrey continued to do chores for Elizabeth and Richard and continued to go to school. For Jeffrey, he had a family now. They were his parents. As long as he lived under their roof he was part of a real family. But for Elizabeth and Richard, their lives were just an existence. They had each other but their dreams of having children dissolved.

"Mrs. Rothchild knocked at the huge oak, front door as she stood waiting for a response. Elizabeth answered the door.

"Hello, Mrs. Rothchild. Can I help you?"

She responded by stating if they were interested in their decision about Jeffrey's adoption.

"Won't you come in?" Elizabeth offered being the good hostess that she was.

Richard was in town on business and Jeffrey was in school. Mrs. Rothchild shook the rain off her umbrella and absorbed the warmth of the roaring fire from the hearth inside the room.

She offered her a cup of tea and she accepted willingly.

Chapter 5

A Huge Disappointment

"As you know children tomorrow is Valentines day and this year we plan to do something special," Miss Donnelly related to he class on a cold, cloudy day in February. "Each student must write an essay….." Suddenly there was an outburst from one of the children. Jeffrey whispered loudly, "Yah, how about a holiday."

Miss Donnelly took off her spectacles and shouted at Jeffrey in turn startling the whole class. "How dare you interrupt my class. Another outburst like that and I'll have you stand in the corner for the rest of the day." She had a mean expression on her face but realizing where she was her appearance changed and she continued sharing with the class.

Jeffrey was experiencing new feelings and sensations that were foreign to him and was unsure of what was happening. He had never led a normal little boy's life and did not understand these new feelings. To him people were strange and not very understanding. He knew he should do what was right and not get into so much trouble so he decided it was time for a change. He didn't know how to go about changing but decided he should not expect as much from people as he thought he should. Maybe by doing this his attitude would change and then maybe he wouldn't get into so much trouble. His attitude towards Miss Donnelly changed as well.

He stayed after the other boys and girls left and confronted her. "I apologize Miss Donnelly for anything I might have done to offend you," Jeffrey explained.

She suddenly became compassionate. "All right that's very honorable of you. I see you've finally seen the error of your ways. Have you decided to make a change as well?" she asked.

"It'll never happen again" he boldly stated.

"Well now we both know what your going to write your essay about don't we Jeffrey?"

Jeffrey looked away from her and down to the floor. "Yes, Miss Donnelly," he exclaimed rather embarrassed in a bashful sort of way.

Unfortunately for Jeffrey people weren't that forgiving and life wasn't necessarily that simple. As he left the schoolhouse he was confronted by Billy who was just recovering from a broken arm.

"Hi, Billy, want to go hang out," he asked half expecting he would.

"No, I learned my lesson the first time. I don't need another broken arm. Go beat someone else up," he scowled.

Jeffrey didn't expect this anyway but it was still difficult for him so he decided to go home.

He had to stop at the general store on his way home because Elizabeth had asked him to pick up a few things. The screen door swung with a loud bang as he walked in. He recognized Mrs. Carmichael and noticed her talking in the corner to a few of the popular lady's of the town. They looked at him with astonishment and whispered amongst themselves as they scowled.

Jeffrey gathered what he came for and was checking out when Mrs. Carmichael took the grocer aside and whispered something to him. The grocer gave Jeffrey an odd look as he checked out the articled he had bought. "You best behave yourself when you come in here young man," he added looking right at Jeffrey.

As Jeffrey left the store a light rain began to fall and he flipped up his collar and began crossing the street when he noticed the sheriff standing against a post on the corner. He at first didn't notice but suddenly recognized him. "Did you pay for those items Jeffrey?" he asked being somewhat respective of the law.

"Yes sir."

All at once there was a flash of light and a roar of thunder.

"Best you be getting on home now, you here," the sheriff muttered.

Jeffrey scampered into the lodge and scurried towards the pantry where he knew he'd find Elizabeth. "Here's the stuff I got from the general store," he blurted, the rain dripping from his drenched body.

"Thank you," she replied "Did you get caught in the storm?"

"Yes"

"Well go change your clothes and set the table for dinner."

"Yes, maim."

As he placed the plates around the table he decided he would try something different. She was peeling potatoes when he approached.

"I know I've been a bad boy, but can't you and Rick try and like me just a little. I've decided to change my attitude towards people," Jeffrey stammered.

Elizabeth was surprised, "Jeffrey we like you. What ever gave you that idea? Everybody makes mistakes, nobody's perfect."

Suddenly there was a flash of light and a crash of thunder.

"I have to write an essay for Valentines day and I think I know what I'm going to write it about," he confessed.

"Oh what?"

"Love."

Jeffrey knew little about the true meaning but had taken a positive attitude towards people and he was willing to learn all he could.

Elizabeth stopped what she was doing and looked at him, "Oh, that'll be nice," she replied with little emotion, "So you can write now can you?"

One day a few weeks later he came home from school. The weather was beginning to make a change. The buds were sprouting and the trees and flowers were beginning to stick their heads up from the earth. The sun was shinning and bringing new life to everything in the valley.

He slammed his reader down on the table and entered the kitchen. Elizabeth was peeling vegetables. "I have a surprise for you," she whispered. "Come here with me." She led him into the master bedroom. In the corner was a small child's crib.

"What's this for?" Jeffrey asked looking somewhat puzzled.

"Where going to add another member to the family," she confessed.

This was a bit of a blow for Jeffrey. He looked confused, "What do you mean?"

"Oh, come on Jeffrey. You know what I mean? I'm going to have a baby."

Jeffrey's world was slipping away. Things would no longer be the same in the sleepy estate, and he knew it.

"Richard doesn't know about this yet so let me tell him," she warned.

Jeffrey became gloomy and withdrawn. Elizabeth began to fold some of the baby clothes and Jeffrey, dazed and confused, slowly walked out of the room into the garden. He felt a real sense of loneliness.

There was a gentle breeze amongst the flowers and trees as he sat on one of the stone benches that were in the garden. A fly buzzed around him as the sun shone, making the day warm in the fresh spring air.

Later that evening as they were finishing dinner, Richard took the news rather surprisingly as he starred in wonder for a moment, before suddenly snapping back to reality. As he began glancing around, Elizabeth was saying something, when he noticed Jeffrey. As if something was blinding his senses he became lost in another world. A world full of empty hopes and dreams, of broken relationships, full of sadness and death. Jeffrey became uncomfortable when he noticed he was starring at him.

"You haven't heard a word I said have you?" Elizabeth asked.

"Oh excuse me Elizabeth," he muttered not looking at Jeffrey.

"I said I have to go into town tomorrow to pick a few things up for the baby."

He looked at her forcing himself to say, "That's fine."

The next day, after dropping Elizabeth off in the middle of town, he pulled the carriage up in front of the saloon. Jeffrey was in school because it was a working day. Forcing the shutters open with one hand, he wandered into the saloon.

Chapter 6

Tragedy

As the months passed Elizabeth got farther into her pregnancy. Jeffrey didn't know the first thing about childbirth but to him everything appeared normal other than the fact that Elizabeth talked quite a bit about the coming child.

Richard began to drink more; more on his own rather than around people. He could usually be found down at the local saloon. He was making quite a habit out of having a few drinks and getting a little drunk. He usually carried a bottle with him and it began to have an effect on Elizabeth and Richard as well. One day just before dark, Jeffrey halted his horse by the barn as Richard fell off in a state of drunkenness.

"Here Rick let me help you," Jeffrey said as he lifted him out of the dirt.

Richard suddenly came to himself, pushing Jeffrey he mumbled, "Get out of my way."

He pulled the screen door open and closed it with a slam.

Elizabeth was just finishing the evening dishes. She was about seven months pregnant and it shocked her to see him this way. "Richard how could you?" she blurted as Richard mumbled something lifting his hand towards her and fell beside the table dragging the table clothe and its contents to the floor. When Elizabeth tried to run to help him she screamed then fell to the floor as well.

Jeffrey ran into the kitchen to try to help Elizabeth. As he revived her, she weakly moaned to Jeffrey, "Get a doctor."

Jeffrey didn't know what to do so he jumped onto Richard's horse and rode to get a doctor.

Doctor Rice the town Physician was an elderly man about sixty. He had a long handlebar mustache to go with his weathered clean shaven face. His sideburns were longer as well. He wore a old, dark, pin stripped suite. As he strolled out of the master bedroom wiping his hands, Jeffrey was waiting for him.

"Well she'll live but she lost the baby," he stymied. "Richard is going to have quite the hangover when he wakes up. I'll contact the undertaker when I get to town." Then he left Jeffrey alone.

Jeffrey was on his own for the next couple of days and Richard took to the bottle. Once he found out the child was dead he began drinking heavily. Guilt began to gnaw at him as he remained in a state of drunkenness. It was dark and blustery on the third night as it rained in torrents. Thunder roared and lightning flashed as Jeffrey sat and watched Rick became drunker and drunker. As a flash of lightning struck it lit up Richard's face making him look demonic in his state of madness.

He starred at Jeffrey as if in a trance. He mumbled something like, "If it wasn't for you this wouldn't have happened."

"Why blame me?" Jeffrey asked watching him slosh down another drink.

"Because if it wasn't for you this whole thing wouldn't have started," he shouted slurring his words as he spoke.

Jeffrey became frightened, "I'm sorry Rick for causing you and Elizabeth all this grief," he confessed.

"You better be," Richard warned as he stood up grabbing a

bottle. He walked towards Jeffrey with a threatening attitude. Suddenly he raised the bottle and threw it at him barely missing him. Thunder roared and lightning flashed as Jeffrey ran.

Elizabeth and Richard rode up and dismounted their mares just before their entrance to the estate. It was a brilliant, bright spring day and everything in the valley seemed to be teaming with life. Taking hold of the mare's rains, Richard proceeded to clean his boots on the small foot stone next to the hitching post, as Elizabeth straightened her skirts in a somewhat lady like manner. She then cleaned her boots looking down at the little boy statue in a trance like daze, she looked at Richard and said, "I think if we have children I'd like to have a girl."

Richard took a moment to think, then added, "Yes I agree. I think I'd like one too."

"Can we get married soon?" she asked.

"Yes"

He pulled her close, leaving the two horses at the hitching post and courted her into the main entrance.

Life came back to the valley for them but for Jeffrey things went back to the way they were before the change had occurred. For him being a real little boy wasn't the answer. For Elizabeth and Richard maybe the good things in life are worth waiting for. Even though life becomes difficult at times good things should be cherished patiently. You should appreciate what you have and not be covetous of what you don't have.

Kateland

Kateland's mom found it difficult overlooking the fact that she being a small town girl planned to spend quality time with her father in Pickering which is the suburb of Toronto. The two of them wanted to spend time at the African Lion Safari and Mike her former husband had proven himself irresponsible, lacking good common sense. They had been good years, in ten years of marriage she had learned a lot about family relations.

Mike's older brother had been a stumbling block in their relationship, his promiscuous wife always throwing herself at good looking men in her path. His sister was so naive that she was practically impossible to communicate with and Annette's mother-in-law lacked good common sense like her son. So for Annette it was a no win situation. But they were good years with a lot of good memories. After all she had sired a daughter. Now it was up to her to pull together the remainder of their lives.

Annette's side of the family was a little more laid back although they had personal problems as well. Like the time her younger sister lost her car in a residential neighborhood in the middle of the night. She had to call her father who lived 25 miles away to come and pick her up. The police found the car within 48 hours. Or like the time her parents got their luggage lost while switching planes in Chicago.

Annette was unloading dishes from the dishwasher when Kateland entered the kitchen. A friend that had a car had dropped her off at the corner of their rural neighborhood after school. She had walked from there.

Not much happened in a rural country neighborhood other than normal everyday activities. You had to make your own entertainment.

"Hi sweetie. I've got chicken in the oven and made an apple pie for desert. It should be ready in about an hour," Annette explained closing the door of the dishwasher.

"Can't I skip dinner, Mom. I want to go and visit Janet," Kateland asked. Janet lived three miles away and Kateland was hoping her Mom would drive her.

"Oh come on honey. I made this especially for you, "Annette demanded. "Eat something, then I'll drive you."

Kateland sat down. She wasn't hungry but forced herself anyway. Her mother sat down and also began to eat. Helping herself to the vegetables she decided to talk about Mike. She knew this was a touchy subject with Kateland and she was at a loss as to what to say. Suddenly she began.

"I want you to do me a favor Kateland. When you and your father go to the 'safari', I want you to promise me you'll use common sense," she again demanded.

"Like what, Mom?"

"Like leaving the windows rolled up."

"Oh, Mom. Don't you think Dad's smart enough not to do that?" she explained.

"No", Annette warned.

There was a moment of silence between the two of them.

"Well I disagree," Kateland stated. "You don't know him like I do."

"I know him better than you think."

Kateland's relationship with Mike was a good father daughter relationship. As Kateland grew up they created a bond that was rare considering most parental relationships. Due to the fact that it would be better for Kateland's health, Annette did not discourage the influence Mike had over Kateland. The rest of their family had their share of problems and Annette was prepared to avoid them if at all possible.

She ate some of the chicken, but picked at the rest of her food until finally her mother said "Well at least have a piece of the apple pie I made you."

There was silence as her mom drove her to Janet's then she told her she would pick her up in a couple hours. As she opened the door of her mom's '97 Volvo she grabbed her schoolbooks and climbed out.

The rest of the night remained uneventful; Annette watching television until it was time to pick up Kateland.

Kateland was tall for her age. She had straight, brown shoulder length hair, with a straight, noticeably attractive, face. Her figure was slim but curvaceous with an average bust size. She had her mother's hair color, but Annette was a little more filled out in the hips but was also attractive.

Kateland was in her 4th year in high school. Academically she was in the top half of her class. She was due to graduate in June and she had 9 months to go. Annette and Mike were proud parents that were willing to encourage her in any way possible.

Kateland's cell phone rang Friday as she was coming home from school. She had an hour to get ready for her job which she had at one of the local food chains in a small town not far from where they lived. Her mother would drive her there too. Annette didn't mind driving her around. She was paying for her own cell phone as well as earning extra spending money.

"Hi, daddy," she shouted in excitement.

"How was your week, honey?" Mike asked capturing her attention as she strained to listen above the rest of the noise on the school bus.

"Uneventful," she exclaimed at a loss of something better to tell him. She didn't want to tell her father of all the unsuccessful relationships she had had with her friends and acquaintances during the week.

"You busy tomorrow?" Mike asked.

"Well I have to work till 3."

"How'd you like to go for a bite to eat after work?" he asked.

"Sure," she conceded.

"I'll pick you up after work."

"Mom, I only have to work till 3 Sunday, so Janet and I are getting together to do homework at her house," Kateland explained to Annette that night at dinner. "And Saturday night we're going to hang out at Jerry's." Jerry's was a coffee shop which was a local hangout for some of the younger crowd. Annette liked to know where her daughter was. She was still young and in today's world it is important to know what your children are doing. Part of the reason was that Annette saw herself in Kateland and she didn't want her making the same mistakes.

After dinner that night Kateland was helping with the cleanup. Annette asked, "What's your plans for the weekend, honey?"

"Dad's picking me up after work tomorrow and we are going out for a bite to eat. So don't make dinner tomorrow," Kateland warned.

"Sure sweetie."

Kateland punched the clock at three the following day and ran outside. Her father was waiting.

Kateland climbed into his three year old Nissan when she remembered she forgot the new sweater her mother had bought her for Christmas.

"Hang on Dad I forgot something," she explained as she climbed back out and ran into the Harvey's restaurant.

The sweater was on a chair in the change room when she grabbed it and headed for the exit. She met Roy her boss who stopped her.

"Can you work on Tuesday night for a couple of hours, Kateland?" he asked.

"I'll have to ask my Mom. I'll call you and let you know," she explained. Then she turned and left.

She and Mike went to a fancy, plush, Asian restaurant that was about ¾ of an hour's drive. They had window seats where they had a beautiful view of the Aurora River which due to the hot summer was the color of tea.

"Remember all those camping trips we took up north when I was young in the summer Daddy?" Kateland reminisced while they waited for the waitress to bring their menus.

"And the day you caught your first fish," he reminded her.

Kateland was silent as she thought for a moment. She looked at the manly, handsome, expression her Dad had on his face. He had blue eyes on either side of a bulbaceous, weather affected, but prominent nose. He was short and stocky, slightly overweight, with sandy brown hair.

"I still don't like fishing," she explained.

"Were they happy times for you, Kateland?"

"Yes"

"Are you still happy?" Mike asked.

"I just wish it could have been different between you and Mom," she explained.

Her mother was folding clothes when Kateland entered their moderately, spacious, living room. Annette was renting a small house in a rural neighbor hood in the outskirts of Brampton. It was an hour's ride to Mikes place in Pickering which was accessed by jumping on the 401 highway. She was receiving child support, the remnants of an unsuccessful marriage and their two bedroom home was considerably cheap for its size.

"I have to work Tuesday night for a couple hours. Should I call and tell him it's ok?" Kateland explained upon entering.

"Sure, honey" Annette conceded.

Jerry's Coffee House was busy that night as Kateland and Janet entered and began looking for a seat. They had a hard time finding one so they joined some friends. They ordered drinks that Kateland paid for. They usually sat and chatted for a few hours on Saturday night. Annette had no problem with them hanging out as long as she was home at a reasonable hour.

"Yah well my dad works for the Board of Education," Carrie an attractive red head exclaimed in the middle of a heated discussion on whose Dad brought in more bread and butter.

"Yah well my Dad makes more money than your Dad because he works on the oil rigs," Janet argued determined to make a point.

"I don't think anyone's Dad should be judged by how much money he makes. I think he should be judged by what he believes in," Kateland demanded causing the argument to change to a different light.

"What's your Dad do, Kateland?" a not so attractive girl in her late teens asked sipping on her shake.

"He works for the post office," Kateland was proud to respond.

"Oooh, government employee. Must have a lot of benefits."

"He does alright. But that doesn't make him a better Dad," Kateland argued.

"Does he spend time with you?"

"Him and my Mom are divorced," she explained.

"It's nice to get a second opinion on a subject besides its easier to get away with something when you have a Dad," the good looking girl named Carrie relented sending their conversation to new levels.

"I know what you mean," the not so attractive girl who was known as Linda said, "I look up to my Dad. He's my mentor."

This caused some discouragement with Kateland but she didn't let it get her down. She was thankful to have a Dad and was able to spend time with him.

Later when Kateland got home her Mom asked, "Meet any good looking guys?" It is every mother's wish that her daughter meets the male of her dreams. Just like everyone else she was young once too. But for Kateland growing up with no father made things a little difficult.

"No. Guys these days only want one thing. Besides I'm too young to get married and start a family," Kateland explained grabbing a fresh piece of apple pie. She liked her Mom's apple pie. She makes good apple pie.

"Honey, keep yourself pure. Don't let them take advantage of you," Annette warned. "Don't make the same mistake I did."

"What, so now you're telling me I'm a bastard," she exclaimed keeping herself from losing control. She was becoming quite emotional and Annette became defensive.

"Kateland, the beginning of becoming a responsible adult

is to be able to take advice. I don't want you to make the same mistakes, that's all."

Like most Harvey hamburger joints, the one Kateland worked at had a drive through. Kateland had a few admirers in high school but she was yet to have a real date. So when John a secret admirer pulled up at the receiving window the following Tuesday Kateland was not surprised when he began addressing her as a friend.

"What are you doing Friday night Kateland?" John asked sitting next to his buddy in a supped up 1994 orange Dodge Charger, as he grabbed their food and reached for his wallet to pay her, Kateland became a little nervous. She was attracted to John but was a little reluctant to step out of her comfort zone. Boys were only after one thing but just maybe John was different. She knew that someday she would have to take a chance.

"Actually I didn't have anything planned other than hanging out with my girlfriend," Kateland responded after a few tense moments.

"You want to go to a party?"

"I'd probably need an escort," she warned.

"That's cool. I'll be your escort," John explained being careful not to be too pushy.

There were other people waiting in line so Kateland had to move along. "Why don't we discuss this at school tomorrow? I've got people waiting," she said as John reluctantly agreed and pulled away.

The next day in school he asked Kateland again if she would go to the party and she said yes. The next few days were exciting for her as she told her parents and closest friends, she became nervous thinking about what to say or how to act on her date. She was suddenly becoming very self conscious.

When she told her mother that night, her mother was ecstatic. "That's great honey. Have you thought about what you're going to wear?"

"Actually, I hadn't thought about it," Kateland responded in confusion.

"I guess all you have to decide is slacks or a dress," her mother mused. "I can help you with that."

"It's really something to think about isn't it."

"Dressing is always important on a date," her mother warned. "You can keep his interest or scare him away just by what you wear."

She decided she had the rest of the week to think about it. She and Janet got together that night to do homework and began discussing Kateland's date.

"I heard John works for his wealthy father on the side," Janet her best friend explained, "and he and his brothers plan on taking over the family business."

The fact that John had a future wasn't on Kateland's mind she was more enchanted by the fact that it was her first date. It is every woman's fancy to be swept away by prince charming gallantly riding a white horse so it being Kateland's first date also put a twinkle in her eye.

When her father called her Thursday and found out she had a date his advice also came at a precise moment. "Don't let him take advantage of you," he warned capturing her surprise and catching her off guard.

"Oh, Daddy, maybe he's different?"

"Sure sweetie, just be careful," he agreed showing her a little fatherly affection and the maturity of his age.

Friday night finally came. John came to pick her up at 6.30PM. Knocking on the white vinyl front door he was dressed in faded blue jeans and a dark red, white and black flowery sports shirt with matching white sneakers. John was tall, athletic and good looking with brown eyes and dark brown hair combed thick to the right side. He was Canadian by birth but had a Scottish background.

"Now behave yourself and don't be home too late," her mother warned watching her climb into the orange charger dressed in a light blue skirt with matching blue and brown vest. She wore a pair of white pumps. It was a warm, starry, September night.

It left her mother wondering as he left a rubber slick showing off to Kateland as he sped down the road. 'My they do grow up, don't they' she thought.

John and Kateland became bored after a few hours at the party, their friends drinking and flirting amongst one another. Lucky for John he was smart enough not to drink too much so he and Kateland decided to go and have a bite to eat.

"So what's the teacher's pet got planned after her senior year?' John asked creating conversation as they waited for their food at a Chinese restaurant in one of the local strip malls.

"I think I'd like to go to teacher's college," Kateland explained letting the cat out of the bag about her new ambition.

"What age preference?' he asked. John was a tech student but his future was pretty secure with his father's business. But he was no dummy.

"Primary," she boasted.

"You think you could handle twenty, thirty screaming kids?"

"If their ever going to change and be disciplined, it's in their primary," Kateland explained. It was a brilliant revelation that gave Kateland a much needed advantage over the average individual.

"You're not planning to be rich?' he philosophized. This didn't discourage Kateland.

"I think you should be happy with what you do. Money shouldn't be an issue. How about you? What's your plans for the future?"

"Probably take over the family business. There's a future in the clothe industry, especially with all the denim being used know days," he explained. Denim was a raw product that was manufactured at a lucrative price which added needed capital. Kateland was reluctant to talk about marriage on their first date. The fact that John might be interested didn't spark her fancy besides she wasn't interested in thinking about the subject for the time being.

About midnight John walked Kateland to her front door to say goodnight. He held her hand and kissed her gently on the lips sending butterflies down Kateland's curvaceous spine.

"Can we see each other again?" he whispered so that her mother, who was standing watching in the dark, could not hear.

"Of course."

Thanksgiving came and Kateland was spending it with her father in Pickering. He picked her up Friday night and Saturday they went to the African Lion Safari. Excitement for her was so overwhelming because she had never actually seen animals that big up close. She now understood why her mother was so concerned about rolling the windows down. She had never been to a zoo and seeing lions and giraffes up close was a new experience.

"So is this guy John getting serious?' her father asked on the 1 1/2 hour drive home.

"No, we just hang out together," she explained.

"But you're seeing him quite a bit aren't you?"

"I guess we're going steady," she explained.

"You know about the birds and the bees I hope?"

"Oh Daddy."

Mikes mother had the two of them over for a thanksgiving dinner the next day which was in a small community in the north end of Toronto. Mike's sister Anne and her boyfriend Danny were also invited.

"Now that you're interested in boys, you'll probably see less of your father eh, Kateland," her grandmother stated embarrassing Kateland as they began passing around the food.

Her grandfather warned his wife that she was stepping out of line. "Don't embarrass the poor girl, Emma," he said handing Kateland the turkey. He was short and over weight and his wife was muscular from many years of hard work. It was normal for their family to get together on thanksgiving. Annette would have been there as well had her and Mike still been together.

"Guys are OK. They just need to be kept in line," Anne said looking at Danny to see his reaction.

Kateland continued to see John for the remainder of her senior year. They were parked on a hill overlooking the Aurora River one spring night in June, as the sun began to set behind them, they sipped on a couple of milk shakes.

"So you're taking out a loan to go to university in the fall?" John asked.

"Yes"

"Which university have you applied?"

"University of Waterloo"

"Do you think you'll be accepted?" he again asked.

"There's no reason why I shouldn't," she explained.

"Kateland, it's time we started thinking about the future."

"What do you mean?" she asked.

"I want to settle down and start a family," John warned, "And I don't want to wait."

For Kateland it was a new beginning. A new career, probably a new home, maybe even a new boyfriend. It was this challenge that began to mold her into a mature, responsible, intelligent, young woman. Her future was bright. The fact that she now faced another disappointment didn't discourage her motives. It only made her stronger.

Nude M.D.

Chapter 1

Audrey is a normal suburban housewife, living in any ordinary residential neighborhood in America. Her life is far from boring. She has three hungry mouths to feed and her socialite husband (who is to her, anything but boring), is as successful an entrepreneur as she could ever hope for. Who would have thought at approaching forty she would have her own SUV, let alone a two car garage in a ritzy neighborhood in local suburbia.

She does what any normal housewife will do each day, gets up and makes the family breakfast, then kisses her husband goodbye and sends him off to work and the children off to school. If the weather is uncertain, she will make preparations for their journey, taking precautions in their dress as well as driving the children to school. Part of the daily routine is to make sure there is food in the house and plan all the meals. It is her duty not only to make provisions for her family but to make sure they are eating healthy. This requires some planning as a well balanced diet is important to every housewife and is a necessary requirement when entertaining. She does not have a housekeeper but a woman comes in and cleans and helps with the laundry as well as cooks the main meals of the day, so it's up to Audrey to make preparations in advance. By doing the shopping, all she has to do is get a shopping list from the cook. The rest of the time she has to herself.

Audrey is 5 feet 6 inches tall, with an attractive figure,

brown hair, shoulder length and green eyes. People tend to say she is a 'ten'; although she is not drop dead gorgeous she is accepted in most circles to be moderately attractive. She is a self made women, although not too liberated, she likes to make minor achievements out of each new goal that she tends to allow herself. She is well on her way to manipulating her husband into making his dreams a reality. This she does with each personality that she engrosses to allow them into her world.

Fredrick who is known as 'Freddy', has trouble with his vision and as frightening as it seems to his mother Audrey, he will probably need optical equipment. Freddy is ten, two years older than his brother and five years older than his sister. He has brown hair that is cut too short, because his ears stick out and seems to be too large for his head. He is average in height with a lean build, mostly from the fact that kids his age have a lean build and as they grow older will acquire added weight. He has a prominent nose on his face which only adds to his good looks. Freddy is an aggressive child getting into mischief as most boys do, occasionally having anxiety attacks, but maintaining none the less. He enjoys the great outdoors where he finds solitude which makes him a bit of a loner. Audrey finds he has help seeing clearer if he receives aid from some other source. She finds he spends too much time watching television, but has the interest to learn. Audrey will have to set aside time to take him to see an optometrist, which means cutting into her daily activity as well as Freddy missing time from school

Annie, who is Audrey's five year old daughter, has just started school, and her teacher made it clear she wants to talk to Audrey. Audrey is aware of her children's learning capabilities; Annie being able to type a message on the computer at three. David who is Audrey's second son is a great thinker as well, sharing his engineering skills with the children by building huge buildings with his logo set. He claims he wants to be an engineer when he grows older. She encourages her children, by manipulating them as creatively as she is capable in everything they pursue. Annie is a normal sized little girl with blond hair and blue eyes. She is average in height and not overweight for her age. David has brown hair and green eyes.

Audrey's success is not something that happened out of the blue. Her mother Anne Billingsby who had married a prominent lawyer, had encouraged Audrey at an early age to marry someone with money. Audrey always thought her mother practical, so when she met her husband Barry, who had made his success in business,(establishing himself with Pennington & Associates), thought she had married for love and not money, regardless of the fact that he was a successful entrepreneur. Her mother, for all practical purposes, was an overachiever leading her daughters and sons down the road to success, being somewhat temperamental, and not too domineering. She would need some quality time with her as she was coming to visit for the weekend. Anne's better half, her life long partner and loving husband, William Billingsby, had retired from practice seven years ago. In the last ten years of practice he was asked to join the bar, but refused mostly due to lack of ambition. The pathway to success for Bill wasn't easy. Getting to the top of one's field meant true dedication and determination. This was not achieved overnight and because of this, Bill was tired. He just wanted to spend the rest of his days sitting quietly in some remote corner reading or spending time with his grand children.

The Billingsbys had two other boys both older than Audrey,(one was a success in law and the other was trying to succeed in business), and the last child being Jenny. Audrey was a role model for Jennifer, Jenny being the younger of the two always trying to be like her older sister. Jennifer was still single and had a successful career in interior decorating. Over the three years she was in business, Audrey gave her many of her own ideas, as Audrey had such good taste in everything. Although Jenny went to college to learn, it was not unusual to use someone else's ideas, Audrey being the most likely candidate. Jenny lived a few blocks away from Audrey and living in a large bungalow, it was easy for Jenny to come and visit on occasion. Jenny had no trouble finding potential dating partners. She was attractively beautiful like Audrey, not overweight,(as she exercised and watched her diet), with firmly developed breasts, thick thighs and an average waistline with a cute figure. Her hair was cut short and reddish brown. Jenny had a close, nit, group of friends, whom she used when her boyfriend or family members were not available. Her repertoire was not too overbearing.

Barry and Audrey have friends they entertain on a regular basis. Barry has a wine cellar with a collection of wines, exotic and tastefully rare. He also collects rare brandies and cognac. It helps when selecting wines for dinner. Barry is not artistic in nature but tries to be very liberal and open minded when it comes to things like entertaining, maintaining a business like attitude, even with his closest friends. That leaves Audrey to plan the meals and arrange the hors d oeuvres. Barry and Audrey are a team, each one perceptive of the other's need, sharing each day with family and friends, and making one another's life tolerable, as a single marriage unit. Barry is an inch taller than Audrey and has a good build, is slightly overweight, and has fair hair and brown eyes. He is considerably good looking with a handsome, manly, but not too tough, complexion.

Barry met Audrey through her father Bill Billingsby when he needed legal advice on some shady business deal that he had come across while climbing the ladder to success with

Pennington &Associates. He graduated at the top of his class in business from Yale, making him a high commodity in a business he took an interest in. The cosmetic industry covers a wide range of territory, so receiving a tip about a facial cream, it introduced him into the industry, which gave him the added incentive he needed for success. 'Laurier' the patent name he named his business, was created as a result of this tip. The capital investment required to launch the business his father-in-law forfeited on condition of a 45percent investment in the company, making Barry sole owner.

So for Audrey, landing an entrepreneur husband like Barry was a real challenge, especially with the ripe competition that would be available to Barry. Although being Bill's daughter had added advantages,(Audrey's father owning 45 percent of the business,) being the socialite Barry is has its added advantages for the two of them as well. It gives Audrey the opportunity to improve her social skills which she needs in order to be a success not only as Barry's wife, but as a young socialite herself, and for Barry it gives him the opportunity to learn more about his business. The team the two of them make together makes their socializing all the more entertaining when they get together with friends and acquaintances. For Audrey, it creates a new challenge.

They usually set aside Saturdays, and spend them with family, friends, and business associates. It is a way to rest and relax from life's inconveniences. This Saturday the Petersons are coming. He is a business associate who is introducing Barry to some colleagues related to a minor business deal. The evening would have to be perfect and it is up to Audrey to make it that way. The cleaning will be done a day or two ahead and then Audrey will just have to straighten a few things up during the day Saturday. Their wives will be there as well, so Audrey has to make a good impression. She thought it appropriate to serve prime rib as it was a formal occasion and to make sure everything is done to perfection. She also will have to prepare and serve the drinks and hors d oeuvres as well.

The Pennington's live a fast paced lifestyle, in no way above their means, making prosperity a tool that they manipulate to their advantage. They live clean, honest, hard working lives, being the best they can be with success being the ultimate outcome.

Chapter 2

Audrey noticed the half eaten sandwich on a plate, on the end table, as she walked through the main living room on Saturday afternoon. As she looked around she saw everything was neat and in order, then looking at the half eaten sandwich she starred at it for a moment as if she saw a reflection in a mirror. Contemplating what would be the night's outcome she remembered she needed to make sure there were enough hors d oeuvres. Turning her pelvis, she swung herself around and continued towards the violet colored dining area where she crossed and entered two adjoining kitchen doors. As she did she looked towards the white, stucco ceiling and shouted, "Annie, come and take your sandwich plate out to the kitchen." Discipline was a necessary commodity when maintaining a household and Audrey felt it necessary to keep strict discipline with her children. To Audrey discipline was a way of life. Kingdoms were created by discipline. If discipline was essential to an army, it would be essential to her family too.

"Shelly, how's that avocado dip coming?" she stammered as she entered the kitchen and approached the counter in the middle of the floor. Shelly was a heavy set woman of about forty. She wore a white dress and apron reaching just below her knees. Her hair was pinned together in a bun covered with a hair net. She was a muscular woman with a facial complexion that revealed her many years of hard work. With a look of shock she conceded, "Its' ready maim'"

121

"Now make sure the children are all fed," Audrey demanded. "I'm taking the two youngest to their aunt Jenny's and Freddy is staying with a friend. I should think dinner should be ready by seven, that'll give me two hours to break some ice with the guests"

She looked down at her purple top and blue jeans and thought, 'I have to drive the children to their sitters, that won't give me much time to get ready.' Taking a more positive attitude, she turned and walked through the two swinging doors pushing them open with both hands.

Annie was lingering along in the living room when Audrey entered. She quickly took two skips and landed in her mothers arms. Audrey gave her a stern look and asked her again, "Would you be a good girl and do as you're told or I'll tell Aunt Jenny not to give you any treats tonight?" Annie smiled and went to fetch the plate.

Audrey took another look around making sure everything was neat and in order and proceeded towards the stairs.

She entered David's bedroom and the first impression she got was shock. "David, would you please clean up your room? We have visitors coming tonight and I don't want a dirty room. And then wash your hands and go see Shelly in the kitchen," she again demanded.

Shelly had a good relationship with Audrey's children. The children liked Shelly because she gives them treats, much against the orders and knowledge of Audrey. Shelly was just making her job a little more pleasant and the children's lives a little less strict against the better recommendations of Audrey and Barry's busy schedule.

Winding down the street of their suburban neighborhood in her 2 year old SUV, Audrey checked the time, 'Three thirty,' she thought. 'Just enough time to drop Freddy off at his friend's and prepare herself for dinner. What would she wear? I think something bright and cheerful to put her guests in the right mood. Barry was out playing golf and would probably be home when she got there.'

As she pulled into their driveway she shoved the transmission into park next to her husband's blue Mazda, and gave herself a pat on the back for being right.

Audrey opened the shower door to their private bathroom, and stepped in next to her husband. He slid his arms around her and gave her a wet kiss, as the two took a moment to share each others nakedness. The aroused nipples of Audrey's pink breasts gave her goose bumps as Barry's hands,(along with the warm shower water), slowly rolled down to her firm, warm, buttocks. Passion began to possess the two of them as they made love, stealing each moment as if there was no tomorrow.

Audrey and Barry had a healthy sex life. When they could find time they snatched a few moments here or there when the kids weren't around or once in a while in their bedroom. Their bedroom was in a secluded part of the house making it possible to muffle their screams of neglected passion. Lately, their passion had been rekindled, which improved their marriage life considerably.

Audrey was just finishing putting her makeup on when the Petersons arrived. They were accompanied by a business associate and his wife. Including Audrey and Barry, there would be three couples dining. Barry answered the door.

Amusingly the host expressed himself, "Welcome to my castle. My 'valet' has the night off. I trust you found your way alright?"

"Pennington & Associates must be doing better than we thought if you can afford to hire your own valet," laughed a good looking client of about 50. He was about 5'8" tall with a dark complexion, mainly because of his dark, clean, shaven beard. He had a full head of black hair that was combed straight back. His wife had black hair as well and wore a cream, colored, full length, evening gown. She was exceedingly pretty.

"You can't condemn a man for having a sense of humor, now can you, Eugene?" Barry who was quick with a comeback asked, somewhat surprised.

Amusedly, Eugene remarked, "An advantage in this business right?"

Pennington & Associates was a fast growing company and with the economy fluctuating up and down the way it was, it made business a game of Russian roulette. Eugene had the need to acquire some services from Pennington & Associates to improve revenue for his company which was a fast growing chemical business.

Barry led the two couples into the living area. "Help yourselves to the hors d oeuvres. Dinner won't be for another hour or two. My wife has done an excellent job, don't you think?" Barry proudly asked, directing them to the dinning area that was located openly next to the living room. "What can I get you people to drink: cognac, wine, bourbon?"

"Cognac for me," Mr. Peterson suggested. Henry Peterson was a tall, medium built man, with a blue, pin stripped suit that seemed to be tailored fit. He had a full head of hair that was graying, combed to the right side to cover his growing baldness. He had the appearance of sophistication with the distinct look of a deep thinker. His weathered face was clean shaven with sideburns medium length.

"Red or white for you, Emily?" Barry offered. She was a visionary compliment to her husband, Henry. She looked as if she and he were meant to be together. They were both an aging couple that along with their intellectual looks, complimented one another. She was not too attractive, but had a distinguished appearance with her red hair cut shoulder length. An obvious feature which curtailed her appearance was an unattractive mole on her left cheek. She wore a brownish, red, skirt suit with a matching wide black belt.

"Red, please," she proclaimed with a smile.

"The same for me thanks," Eugene's wife added.

With as much worldly wisdom as only an astute connoisseur could muster, Henry reassured them, "It may interest you to know that Barry has a wonderful collection of rare wines and brandies."

"A meager collection according to some standards," Barry reassured them.

"Don't be so modest," Eugene contradicted. "I know Henry has a good knowledge of wine and I'm sure we can learn something from it."

"I recall you saying that, 'to have wine at dinner was a rare treat', am I correct Barry?" Henry recalled recollecting the conversation they had had many years ago.

"Now Henry you know there's no point in stirring up old memories unless they have some truth to them," Barry stated regretfully. He warned them, "Besides my better half should be down shortly. I'm sure she can tell you more about that than I can, and she won't be so modest."

"Are you saying that women are just as capable as men?" Eugene asked with a frown. He got a shocked look from his wife who wasn't shy to show that she was somewhat perturbed at the last remark.

"Well I'll say one thing about women," Barry informed them changing the subject, "They sure know how to keep you waiting."

There was silence as Barry poured the drinks. As he handed out the last cognac, Audrey came strolling into the room wearing a shimmering, burgundy, full length, evening gown. It was sleeveless, leaving little cleavage and was slit up to the top of her hip which gave her added sex appeal.

Putting a hand gently on her shoulder, Barry showed her off proudly, "Everybody, this is my wife Audrey. Audrey you know Henry and Emily Peterson?"

"Yes." Audrey shook Emily's hand smiling and acknowledging the Petersons warmly.

With an inquisitive glance Barry said, "And this is Eugene and...."

"Carol"

Carol took Audrey's hand and they both greeted one another.

"Barry tells us he's an astute connoisseur of wine, is this correct, Audrey?" Eugene asked. For him this was a bit of a challenge seeing how he had put his foot in his mouth earlier.

"Barry taught me everything I know," Audrey reminisced. "He can be such a good help now and then," she smiled glancing sideways at Barry for support.

"Ah, ha, then he is being modest. Is it safe to say that he enjoys a little wine for dinner?" he asked trying to reopen the conversation they had had.

"Privileges have their rewards don't they Eugene?" she stated looking at her husband. Barry being modest ignored the glances his two business associates gave him because where business was concerned Barry knew when to keep his mouth shut. A shrewd business man always knows when to play his cards.

Now it was Barry's turn to play the cards. "I assure you, Eugene that my wife is as organized if not more so than any man I know. It would be an advantage having her in the business, isn't that correct Henry."

Henry was a chief supervisor with the company having more authority than anyone but Barry. He was also a valued friend. He became intrigued by the conversation that had started and reacted at once to the opportunity, "Better late than never."

"Touche'," Barry frowned.

Confused with what was being said no one but Barry and Henry reacted.

Being somewhat curious, and being the shrewd business man that he was, Eugene again reacted, "Speaking about business, am I correct in understanding the Pennington's shares have gone up 25%."

"The stock market has soared in the last week with one of the benefactors being cosmetics. I am informing everybody I know to invest," Barry explained not letting the cat out of the bag too soon. Eugene was owner of a reasonable size manufacturing company and for him to invest in Pennington & Associates would add increased revenue to the company.

"So am I to understand that by investing in this company I would in turn save at the cost of my retail investments," he asked suddenly becoming interested. For Eugene that would mean doing business with Barry at a cheaper cost. Barry would have more stocks which would add increased revenue to his business. That was the price of doing business.

Out of a need to socialize, Audrey interrupted, "I don't know but whenever they start talking about business I seem to draw a big blank, Shall we go and talk over here ladies," Audrey stated directing the ladies to the opposite side of the room.

"Absolutely," Barry declared continuing his conversation. Then he took a brief pause, "Excuse us ladies, business before pleasure."

"I understand completely," Emily added as they maneuvered to the other side of the room.

The evening continued smoothly as Barry convinced Eugene to buy 10000 shares in his business and Audrey psychoanalyzed the other two ladies personal lives rather fluently.

Once again the conversation evolved over wine as the guests made their way towards the dinning area. Shelly was serving the meal when Eugene opened up the conversation again about spirits, "Where did you learn so much about wine, if you don't mind me asking, Barry?" his curiosity getting the best of him.

"I became interested when I happened to sample a rare 300 year old bottle of Madeira a wealthy friend of mine tasted. So after a few courses I took I learned. You also learn through experience," Barry concluded.

"Do you think that Bordeaux' is a good wine?" Eugene persisted.

"Yes, obviously but by today's standards, it's one of many good wines. Good wines are not necessarily made in France anymore. There are good vineyards all over the world now. It depends on the age of the vineyard as well as the type of soil and the weather," he said reassuring them.

"Have you been to France?" Carol asked.

"Oh, yes," Audrey interrupted, "We love it there. One of our dreams is to own a chalet on the French countryside."

"Do you speak French, Audrey?" Carol again asked.

"No but it does open up new opportunities, doesn't it?" Audrey stated.

There was silence as the six of them tasted their food.

Persisting with the conversation, Carol broke the silence, "I understand the French never drink water, nothing but wine."

"Yes as you know you have to be careful drinking the water anywhere in Europe," Barry philosophized, "Which probably is one of the reasons why there are so many good wines coming from there."

"That reminds me Barry, Freddy has an appointment with

the optometrist on Thursday, so I'll probably take time to talk with Annie's teacher while I'm at it," Audrey reminded him.

Barry frowned. "Audrey you know I never question your activities. Why bring it up now?"

"Well it's just that Annie needs a little bit of discipline and I'm a bit concerned about her," Audrey warned

"I'm sure she'll be just fine," Barry reassured them smiling at his guests. "She takes after her mother so there's no reason to worry."

"Speaking about mother," she warned him again, coaxingly, "Mom's coming for the weekend, so I'll expect you to be on your best behavior."

"Do I suspect a lack of trust here, Barry?" Emily mused. She was obviously amused with what was going on between them. So were the others. Emily was using psychology to coax one of them into a misunderstanding.

"I assure you, we have a close relationship Emily," Barry relented remaining on the same level of thinking as the others, "We trust each other completely."

Audrey remained in the dark as they sparred back and forth. She wasn't ready to put her foot in her mouth too soon. Suddenly every body starred at Audrey expecting her to say something. As if in a trance she suddenly snapped out of it.

"Absolutely," she smiled as politely as possible. She paused for a moment then continued.

"Emily, I hear Liz Walker is having an affair with her therapist," Audrey reminded her stirring up the local gossip that registered with their social activity. This dissolved any ideas Emily was entertaining.

"Well their marriage was on the rocks anyway. You remember Liz Walker don't you hone?" Emily asked turning to Henry being as compassionate as possible.

"Yes of course the country club, I remember," Henry

recollected. "You don't say? It must be a boring business being a therapist. Makes house calls too I imagine."

"Free of charge, no doubt," Barry added. "I'm sure her husband is going to appreciate that."

"They say that adultery has become legal in Kentucky," Eugene added amusingly. The others laughed.

"I guess it pays to become a therapist," Henry added.

"Speaking about country club," Barry exclaimed, "Are you and Henry going to the barbecue?"

"That's a week from Saturday isn't it?" Henry reminded them.

Their country club was an elaborate estate, located on the edge of Louisville, with plush meadows and rolling fields offering fresh air and solitude to its 300 members scattered throughout the state. Membership had its privileges, with each of the members having sworn secrecy about their membership. It was taken for granted that their wives were included although outside members were discouraged. Once a year in the summer they held a barbecue where all the members and their families were invited. It was an annual event so attendance was essential.

"Yes we'll be going," said Emily reassuringly. "You two going?"

"We're going to try but we may be a little late," Audrey confessed. It wasn't difficult to be on time but by the time they rounded up the rest of the family and got them ready it would probably take the early part of the afternoon.

Tuesday afternoon Audrey looked for Freddy who was told to wait for her in front of the public school. On this warm, clear day she noticed there was no one in the rearview mirror as Freddy opened the passenger door and climbed into the white SUV. He remained silent as Audrey reexamined the rearview mirror and pulled away. The optometrist was about a

15 minute drive due to the increasing traffic which was getting dangerously close to rush hour.

"Billy wants me to go hang out after dinner. Says his Mom is making something special. Is it OK if I go?" Freddy pleaded as Audrey caught the next traffic light.

"You'll have to wait until after I talk to Annie's teacher," Audrey demanded. Freddy felt the heat of the sun as he enjoyed the breeze from the open car window starring out in contentment.

The optometrist looked at Freddy's eye through the scope as Audrey sat looking on. He then set the scope aside and asked him to put a card in front of his right eye. "Now what letters do you see?" the doctor asked.

"UVBY" Freddy read off the letters from the largest to the smallest, stumbling and making mistakes. The doctor then told him to place the card over his left eye and read the letters. He read most of them correctly.

"It appears as if there is a problem with the right eye," The doctor said completing his observation.

"Will he need eyeglasses?" Audrey asked.

"Most assuredly."

Freddy waited in the car as Audrey talked with Annie's teacher. To Audrey's surprise, Annie didn't need discipline after all. The teacher just wanted to encourage Annie's unique learning ability.

"She seems to have an enormous capacity to learn," the teacher commented.

"I knew she was smart," Audrey remarked to the teacher obviously aware of her children's talents.

She dropped Freddy off at Billy's and pulled into the double driveway of her three quarter of a million dollar home. It was late spring as she noticed the fresh buds on the rose bushes, the heat of the day already beginning to cool. Barry's blue Mazda was in the driveway.

"You're going to get a reward for this young lady," Audrey leading Annie through the wide front entrance to their home. "Grandma is coming for the weekend and we have a surprise in store for you. Now it's a surprise so you won't know till then."

Barry overheard the conversation while lounging on the sofa reading the evening paper.

"What's this about a surprise? Now what did my little princess do to deserve that?"

"Her teacher said she was an outstanding achiever. I don't know about you but I think she deserves a reward," Audrey bragged being careful not to let the cat out of the bag too soon.

`David came running into the room. "What's the surprise? Can I have one?"

"I'm not telling till Grandma comes. So you'll just have to wait till Saturday," Audrey warned, frowning "Buy the way. Freddy is going to need glasses."

Saturday was cloudy and dark. The forecast was calling for rain but there was only a slight drizzle as Barry carried Anne Billingsby's suitcase through the wide door at the front entrance of their home. As Anne entered the twin oak doors the children were sprawled around the living area each preoccupied with their own business. Annie was reading a book, David was playing with a few pieces of his logo, and Freddy was trying to create mischief for the other two, lost in his own little world. All three snapped to attention upon hearing their grandmother's voice.

"This damp weather is really affecting my arthritis, oh hello children," she murmured at once acknowledging their presence.

"Hi grandma," they shouted.

"I know one little girl that's going to get a special treat if she behaves herself," she confessed. Anne Billingsby had a weakness as most Grand parents do, of spoiling the children and Annie was no exception. She had learned of Annie's outstanding achievement through Audrey's conversations.

"Mother says she has a surprise for me Grandma."

"I heard you've been a good girl, is this true?"

Annie nodded her head.

"And what about you guys?" she asked.

"Not Freddy. He's been bugging us," David argued.

"Let me take your jacket," Barry demanded.

Anne, suddenly realizing where she was, began taking off her jacket as Audrey walked into the room.

Anne Billingsby was 5 feet 6 inches tall with black hair streaked grey. She was in her autumn years being self conscious of the wrinkles that seemed to be affecting her pretty complexion. The fact that she is an overachiever gives her sophisticated, intellectual facial features. Old age and disease seemed to be slowing her down. Anne visited Audrey some weekends not only to get a chance to spend time with her grand children but so she and Audrey could take time to shop. She wore a casual blue and beige pant suite with matching wide brim hat.

Chapter 3

Saturday came the following week. The country club had its members wandering in with intentions of enjoying each of the day's festivities. It was 30 degrees centigrade, and bright sunshine, with clouds ominously rolling by giving shades of grey in patches. There was no chance of rain as Barry pulled his white SUV out of the driveway and continued through the suburbs towards the freeway. The country club was a twenty minute drive through an endless intertwining of freeway which wound like ribbon till it reached the gentle rolling countryside outside of the city. The radio announced the freeway would be free of traffic delays as a chopper hovered past, Barry doing an easy 80 kilometers as he eased into traffic.

They reached the club in record breaking time.

"Now remember kids behave your selves and don't forget to get along with the other children," Audrey warned showing off her authority as Barry finished parking the white SUV.

Barry and Audrey left the car and wandered towards the garden as the rest of the family disappeared.

The gardens covered a large part of land that entailed a small lake, two baseball fields, two putting greens, a golf course, a driving range, swimming pool, and a place for lawn bowling as well as a large picnic area.

There were lawn chairs spread all over the patio, (a number of them filled), when they made themselves comfortable amongst a multitude of friendly faces many of them well known to Audrey and Barry.

"I'm surprised you dragged yourself away from the stock market," one distinguished, average, slightly above middle aged gentleman expressed boldly as they descended into their seats.

"Denying oneself can be so much fun, don't you think?" Barry reassured him as he began his road to self discovery. Barry wore a sun visor to shade his eyes. His expensive shorts and multi-colored south sea shirt was accompanied by sock less sandals. There was a grey cloud passing over as he twirled his sunglasses in his hand.

Audrey wore a light blue blouse with white short shorts. Her hair was tied back with a wide dark blue hair band.

"How's the dog grooming business, Dan?" Barry asked in the same exertion of energy and breath.

Dan was medium built, had graying hair, with tired lifeless eyes. He wore khaki pants and a short sleeved pin stripped checkered shirt accompanied by white sneakers. He was sipping an orange daiquiri. Accompanying him was a gentleman of about the same age, slightly thinner, a weathered clean shaven face that for all appearances was pleasantly happy. He wore slightly faded beige colored shorts with a short sleeve yellow flowery shirt

The waiter came and asked them what they were drinking, wore black suite pants and a white short sleeve shirt. He had black hair as Audrey noticed his good looks she also noticed he was wearing white sneakers as well.

"I'll have a Singapore sling," Audrey stated ignoring the others.

"Make mine a margarita," Barry added.

The waiter looked at the old gentleman and asked, "What can I get you Walt?"

"A Caesar please," Walt said.

The drinks along with the food were paid for as part of the membership. It came at a high price with the country club, getting as high as $10000 per person. Of course there were special privileges as well such as a free golf membership along with the use of any of the facilities, as well as parties and special occasions,; although there was a fee for them.

"Walt I have a business client who is interested in doing business," Barry asked somewhat inquisitive of Walt's thorough knowledge of business matters. "He's an important client so I want to make sure I make all the necessary arrangements in advance. Are there investment forms I don't know about that I think I'm overlooking?"

Walt was a business consultant for a popular business management company and had done some business managing for Pennington & Associates in the past. They knew each other fairly well.

"I'll contact your secretary on Monday and inquire as to what investment forms you have Barry. When did this transaction occur?" Walt's explained his curiosity getting the best of him.

"Two weeks ago."

"I'm surprised you haven't done something about it yet," Walt mused. "Let's not mix business with pleasure. Talk about something else."

Suddenly Henry Peterson spotted them as he was talking amongst friends. "Hey, there you are," he shouted as he swiftly wandered over to where they were sitting.

"Where's Emily," Barry insisted.

"Oh, she's around somewhere," Henry stated.

Later Audrey was surrounded by a group of lady friends conveniently discussing the latest local gossip. Among them were Liz Walker, Emily Peterson, and a few ladies whose husbands were preoccupied.

Liz was discussing her relationship with her therapist accompanied with the snickers and frowns of her so called friends standing close by. She was 5 feet 4 inches tall along with an attractive slim figure. Her modest, firmly developed (32 inch D cup), breasts were covered with a bikini bra and a matching blouse-shorts outfit with her dirty blonde hair, shoulder length and tied back. Liz had a tanned, appealingly attractive complexion, her blue eyes making everything she said attract those around her.

Audrey was a strong Presbyterian, being introduced to the faith at an early age. She firmly believed that the legal bond between husband and wife was ordained through a higher power. Liz's husband new there was something going on between her and her therapist. It didn't seem to matter to Liz. It was against everything Audrey believed pure and wholesome. Christian values and a clean healthy lifestyle were important to Audrey. She could never consider cheating on Barry and expected him to return the favor. Audrey was raised believing that it was important to have a healthy marriage. Although Barry kept a pistol locked in his dresser drawer and although she didn't go to church regularly, she went enough to believe she had a sound relationship with her maker. She was glad that Liz Walker was only an acquaintance and not a close friend.

"Want to get a breathe of fresh air?" she whispered to Emily who was standing close by.

"I thought you'd never ask," Emily gasped.

They grabbed a table and the two of them ordered drinks.

"How can anyone do that?" Emily frowned, half caring, trying to spark life back into Audrey.

"Believe me Emily, life has a way of catching up on

someone like that," Audrey hissed. She was shocked at what she had heard. To Emily it was just another one of life's little inconveniences being the older and wiser of the two.

Audrey and Emily were just getting back their bearings when Mary Harpwood wandered over to their table. She was about 35, with sandy brown hair and a prominent nose on her pretty face. Mary was tall and slim. A yellow, full length, pant suite was more or less draped over her slender form. She had known Audrey for a few years from various functions of local women's groups. Emily didn't know her until being formally introduced.

"Seeing that you're here Audrey, you'll never guess who I saw in the bookstore flirting with one of the clerks?" Mary announced ignoring Emily's inquisitive glances.

"I can't imagine," Audrey blurted, preparing herself for what was about to take place. She knew who it was she just didn't want to admit it.

Suddenly out of nowhere Annie approached their table.

"Mom, Freddy was supposed to pick a team for baseball and there were only two kids left and he wouldn't pick me," Annie reminisced explaining the afternoon's activities in a few short exertions of energy.

"Oh, excuse me Mary. This is my daughter Annie. Annie won't you say hi to my friend Mary?" Audrey frowned looking directly at Annie and catching her attention, "And say hi to Emily too," Audrey said looking at Emily apologetically.

Annie looked at the two women shyly in a fit of silence guiltily looking at Audrey for support.

"Children, you never know what they're thinking," Audrey philosophized looking apologetically at her friends. "Run along and play Annie. We'll talk about it when we get home."

The waiter arrived with their drinks. Audrey tipped him

and looked at Mary and said, "Now what did my cheating husband do that I might catch him and get an annulment in my marriage?"

"Oh Audrey don't you think your overreacting?" Emily began explaining.

"Not at all. The gossip that goes on around here is enough to damage anyone's eardrums let alone ruin someone's life," Audrey scowled.

Emily touched her arm in a comforting gesture and warned Mary, staring at her but ignoring Audrey, "She's just overreacting. She overheard one of our acquaintances was fooling around on her husband." Emily thought it a good time to change the subject. "Are you interested in jewelry by any chance, Mary?" Emily asked.

Audrey swallowed her pride and remained silent as the other two ladies discussed jewelry.

Barry walked to the bar with Henry and approached the bartender, "Give me a shot of your best Kentucky Bourbon."

The bar was located inside the club house which was centered in the middle of the club's facilities. It had a high ceiling as well as a moderate sized dining hall which was closed to the weather. A fire place was in the middle of the room.

"I'll have the same."

He looked at Henry and began discussing the annual derby that was only a week away while the bartender poured their drinks.

"They say Greased Lightning is a sure bet in this weekend's race," Barry expressed himself informingly taking a sip.

"What does he pay?" Henry asked.

"10 to 1. I don't regularly drink bourbon but it's such a pleasure when I do," Barry reminisced looking at the drink.

"I heard Freedom is a late starter but being so green has been given 2 to 1 odds in winning."

"If I'm going to place a bet I think I'd go with better odds," Barry warned him.

"It's kind of like doing business isn't it?" Henry mused.

"Yeah, business is a bit of a gamble isn't it."

"A bit like Russian roulette."

They approached Audrey and Emily's table after leaving the club house and remained standing holding their drinks. A blue grass band was playing, the music becoming louder as they raised their voices above the sound. There was a stage to the left where all the lawn chairs and outdoor dining area were located.

"Barry, where are the kids. Don't you think we should make sure they have something to eat?" Audrey demanded catching Barry's attention. Barry was lost in his own little world and the question suddenly caused him to snap back to reality. It was difficult due to the rhythm of the music and the number of drinks that had passed Barry's lips. Another of Audrey's demands took a sobering affect on Barry's mind bringing his attention.

"Honey round up the kids I think we should have something to eat."

Barry wandered around the bandstand breathing in the richness of the country air. He wasn't feeling the affects of the alcohol that much that he couldn't make sure his family was safe. He thought he saw Freddy when he was overtaken with surprise to see someone he hadn't seen in years.

"Why, Ben, good to see you, "he said shaking his hand.

"Barry, you're doing well for yourself I hear. Took her old man for some money and created your own empire," Ben said with a cynical smile.

Barry ignored the accusation but was determined to be

friendly. He knew Ben as an old acquaintance he met in his university days at Phi Beta, the fraternity he belonged to. Barry's memory was sharp and from what he could remember Ben was a prankster going so far as to cause disruption in relationships.

Ben wore a sharp looking dark, navy suite which because of his muscular physique looked a size too small. His shoes were black and brightly polished. He had a dark Caucasian complexion.

"And what scheme did you come up with since the last time I saw you?" Barry asked his curiosity getting the best of him.

"Well I have this great plan to rob Fort Knox. Let me tell you about it," Ben boasted and then he began to tell the story.

"Haven't changed a bit have you?" Barry said half interested. "Listen Ben I have to find my kids. Nice seeing you. Are you a member here now?"

"Yes, just recently."

"See you, "Barry said excusing himself politely"

The Pennington's ate their meal along side of another family that had young children. Sarah Woodward and her husband Ron had known them for some time.

"David have another hamburger," Audrey commanded as she continued devouring her chicken stopping to comment on her children's eating habits. "If you don't remind them they won't eat."

"Oh, isn't it the truth," Sarah returning the comment. "I have the hardest time trying to get Ron to eat. He's always doing something."

"Well you know what it's like raising a family, always on the go," Audrey mused passing Sarah the salad. She took a napkin and wiped Annie's face.

"It's hard to find time to spend alone with your husband don't you think?" Sarah asked taking the salad.

"Well I'm so busy taking care of the rest of the family and then entertaining, you know."

"They're nice to have around though," Ron said slyly, "What would you do without us? We make excellent bread winners don't you think? How's your steak?" he asked looking at Barry.

"Mine's good," Barry reflected.

Ron Woodward was part owner of a prominent manufacturing company. They made mold casings for plastic parts and he was chief supervisor, a responsibility that he relished with enthusiasm. He didn't take his position lightly which was one of the reasons why he bought his membership at the country club. Ron was lean and muscular. His wife was a petite natural blonde.

Later that evening Audrey and Barry were getting ready for bed.

"I met an old friend that I hadn't seen in years this afternoon," Barry recalled the meeting he had had with Ben as he buttoned his baby blue, pajamas.

Audrey was brushing her hair in front of her vanity. She had on a long, burgundy, sleeping gown. She looked at him and said, "Oh, who?"

"Oh, just some prankster I had met at college," Barry reminisced. He quickly recalled the conversation and then added climbing into bed, "He commented on my road to success."

"What did he say?"

"He went on to say that I took your father for some money and created an empire."

"I'm surprised you're so concerned what other people

think," Audrey commented half interested putting the brush down.

"Now darling you know I'm only trying to create conversation so I can seduce you," he said changing the subject. "By the way can you make an appointment for me to see Doctor Harris?"

"Why is something wrong?" Audrey looked startled.

"No I just want to make sure everything is working properly."

Barry didn't know it but their lives were about to change forever.

Chapter 4

The following week Audrey needed to arrange to have Jenny baby-sit Annie and David because Saturday was the annual celebration of the Kentucky Derby. Gambling was one thing but horse racing was another. Barry just liked to go and place a small bet on a horse. It was tradition. Besides celebrating was part of the occasion and Audrey and Barry,(being the socialites that they were), just wanted to follow tradition.

Jenny arrived at the Pennington's at 4 o'clock as she pulled up behind their white SUV in her own reddish brown Honda Civic. She knocked and then entered where she found all three children sprawled as usual around the living room. Barry came wandering in dressed in a blue and white sports shirt with a comfortable pair of dark, loose fitting, expensive pants.

"….Rodger's mother going to be alright?" Barry asked looking directly at Jenny with an inquisitive glance as he threw on a pair of shoes.

"Yes she's home now," Jenny calmly stated. "I think she'll be alright." She was not surprised to be asked that. Rodger was her steady boyfriend and it was not unusual, Barry having known him quite some time.

"Gee mom you look great," Annie shouted as Audrey strolled into the living room wearing a pair of black slacks, white and black diamond checkered top, with a traditional white and black, wide brim hat. She looked like she just walked out of Paris. It had a black ribbon and bow wrapped around a black centre. The brim was white with one side curled up.

"Are we ready, hone?" Barry asked.

"Ready," Audrey mused, then turning to Jenny she stated, "We shouldn't be too late. Thanks again Jenny for helping out like this. How's Rodgers Mom?" she asked. Jenny's boyfriend's mother had been in a car accident.

"She'll be just fine," Jenny explained. She kissed Jenny warmly on the cheek.

Jenny took Audrey with both hands and looked at her in the face. "If there's a prize for the best dressed female, you're going to win." She looked at Barry and warned him, "And don't you drink too much bourbon."

The local radio station was playing blue grass music as Barry's sky blue Mazda wound around the curves in their urban neighborhood. Churchill Downs was in downtown Louisville and the traffic was usually congested prior to the race so Barry and Audrey left in plenty of time. They traveled south until they came to exit 132 and then veered right to Crittenden Drive. From there it was right onto Central Avenue and continued straight. Churchill Downs was about 1.6 miles from the expressway.

The weather was promising sunshine for the rest of the day as there had been a light morning drizzle followed by higher humidity. The crowds were gathering as the admirers placed their bets on a lucky winner, some horses holding more promising odds. Barry had instructed Audrey in advance that Greased Lightning was a sure winner so as they found their seats in the stands, Barry proceeded to the ticket booth to place a bet.

Audrey held her head high as she noticed the other ladies with their wide brim hats it being partly prestige and partly tradition. She frowned as she noticed Liz Walker and her husband in some of the lower seats.

Barry returned handing her the racing program. It was 45 minutes to the race and already the excitement was beginning to build. The racing program had a list of all the different horses telling a little bit about each horse and its owner. The Kentucky Derby was the first of the Triple Crown races and if the horse won here it would go on to compete for the Triple Crown. There was big money here and if a horse wins the Triple Crown it would become very valuable. Their offspring alone would be worth millions.

Barry looked at Audrey. "Hon do you want a drink?" he asked.

Audrey was looking over the crowd, but as she heard Barry's voice she lifted the program above her face to shade her eyes and looking at Barry shook her head.

"I might'a known I'd find you here." At the top of the crowd, Barry heard a familiar voice and turning to see who it was he saw a tall muscular figure as the sun distorted his vision. As Barry moved his head to the shade his vision suddenly became clearer.

"Ben,… nice to see you again. How's the wagering going. Got any lucky tips?" he asked. Barry was a little reluctant to ask him for anything knowing who he was and what he was capable of. People do grow up and move on so Barry thought it best to keep old prejudices aside for the time being.

"Is this your better half that I heard so much about?" Ben smartly remarked turning his attention to Audrey.

He took Audrey by surprise. 'She was not only impressed with his appearance but he was bright too' she thought.

"What did my charming husband say about me that is so impressive?" Audrey mused.

"Nothing short of telling me that you helped him build an empire," he boasted.

The sunlight was bothering Audrey's eyes as she tried to get a good look at this so and so who called himself Barry's friend. She was fairly certain that this was the guy Barry was talking about from the country club. She reached into her purse and grabbed a pair of sun glasses. Getting a better look at him gave her a strange impression. This guy was a clean cut, exceedingly good looking guy. To Audrey men had to have more going for them than just good looks.

"Barry, where's your manors, aren't you going to introduce me to your friend?

Barry politely introduced Audrey to Ben.

"Now then Ben, don't you wish you had a better half?" she bluntly stated trying to catch him off guard.

Ben was quick with a come back. "Yes I do. She's over there," he said turning and pointing to a female in the crowd. "Say we're going to a party afterward, why don't you two join us?"

Barry looked from Audrey to Ben like a lost puppy. Audrey noticed Barry's frustration and was quick to bail him out. "Sorry Ben to be so antisocial but we already have plans."

"Well then maybe some other time, by the way Barry. I got a tip on a horse called Mayfair just in case you don't have any thing to wager on. Nice meeting you Audrey"

As Ben walked away Barry expressed his discouragement to Audrey. "That guy is charming but the Ben I used to know was a cad," he warned.

"Let me guess, the guy at the country club?"

"Yes," Barry confessed.

"Their off….."

As the excitement of the crowd intensified, the announcer

described the race in detail as the horses made their way around the track. The crowd got to its feet each ticket holder, holding their tickets in expectation of a sure win.

As they approached the finish line Greased Lightning was a head above the rest with Mayfair a length behind. Suddenly out of nowhere Freedom was gaining strength fast. He passed all the other horses and became neck and neck with the leader. Both horses crossed the finish line. It was a photo finish.

There was confusion everywhere. There was a long pause and then, "Folks there seems to be some confusion as to who the winner is. It's a photo finish and we won't know until the judges make their decision."

Audrey was excited. "I hope Greased Lightning wins. How much did you wager on him Barry?" she asked as they settled down into their seats again. Barry handed her the ticket. She looked at it and noticed it was worth 250 dollars. "...Last of the big time spenders, huh."

"It's ten to one odds. If he wins it'll give us 25 hundred dollars," he boasted.

"Well at least you won't lose your shirt," she warned.

"Come on," Barry demanded, "Follow me."

Audrey and Barry made their way to the winners circle.

There was a crowd gathered around a horse and its jockey, with wreaths and bouquets of roses everywhere. It was tradition to have roses at the winners circle.

Barry handed Audrey a rose and said, "Here's a two hundred and fifty dollar rose."

Just then the winner was announced.

"The winner of the 2011 Kentucky Derby is Freedom."

Henry and Emily Peterson found them in the crowd. The crowd was thick as many horse lovers made their way to congratulate the winners.

"So I should go with the better wager eh," Henry reminded

Barry about the conversation they had had at the country club as he patted him on the back.

At first it was unclear to Barry what he was talking about. Then suddenly it clicked in.

"Well I only lost 250," Barry confessed.

"Not bad for a green horse huh," Henry boasted.

"Just a lucky guess, Henry," he warned. "That's what gambling is all about isn't it? How much did you wager?"

"200 dollars"

"You guys squeak," Emily protested.

"I'm sorry I met too many guys that lost their life savings betting on horses," Barry philosophized.

"Shall we head over to the party for some refreshments folks," Henry suggested changing the subject.

"I think that's a great idea," Audrey agreed.

Tuesday the following week, Audrey made an appointment for Barry to see Doctor Harris. It was a warm evening as the lights went out Barry snuggled up to Audrey in bed wrapping his arms around her in a warm embrace. They didn't notice the heat because they had a central air conditioner.

Barry had some family members that were coming on Saturday so Audrey reminded him of the busy weekend.

"I was planning to barbecue some ribs on Saturday," she fantasized. "The weather's supposed to be nice and I thought it would be good to spend it outdoors."

"You do whatever your little heart desires," he stated smothering her right ear with a succession of warm kisses. His hand wandered over her hip.

"By the way, you have an appointment to see Doctor Harris on Tuesday of next week."

Audrey suddenly became excited and wanted Barry to make passionate love to her. As she felt the heat and intensity increasing he suddenly turned over and left her unsatisfied. This was unusual for Audrey. They had a healthy marriage life and for her to be left hanging was not part of the arrangement. Marriage worked with two people, each one working as part of a single unit.

As Saturday approached, Audrey arranged the tables on the pool deck where the meal would be served in smorge-us-bourge style. Barry's parents were there, as well as his sister and her husband. Mr. and Mrs. Pennington had three grand children from Julia and Ron Harrington, Barry's sister and brother in law. Barry's three children made six grandchildren altogether. Barry's children were preoccupied having cousins they could play with for the afternoon. Jenny and Rodger, were there as well as Audrey's mother and father. It was up to Audrey to make sure there were side dishes to go with the ribs.

It was a sunny Saturday with a few cumulous clouds patching the warm landscape as they gently rolled past. Summer was usually hot in Kentucky with cold fronts squeezing out warm air which in turn created violent thunder storms. Tornadoes were not uncommon in this part of the country but for the most part it was pleasant.

The children were playing in the pool when Shelly brought a round of drinks for the guests. Jenny took a drink and told Annie that there would be no treats for the children while they played in the pool.

"I understand that Freedom, the winner of the Kentucky Derby, had won twice before," Mrs. Pennington explained to Audrey taking a soda from Shelly who was passing out the drinks. "I heard the owner's got him up for sale."

"That doesn't surprise me. Living in Louisville you learn quite a lot from people. I was born but I wasn't born yesterday," Audrey reminded her making her laugh.

"Well don't forget I was born a few years before you," Mrs. Pennington warned politely.

Barry and Rodger were sitting close by.

"Your mother's made a full recovery I take it," Barry asked his curiosity making it all the more necessary to hear.

"Absolutely," Rodger confessed sipping his drink.

Rodger was tall and slim, but somewhat muscular. His beard was dark and clean shaven supporting long sideburns. His hair was somewhat dark but uncombed. He had blue eyes that portrayed his image but behind these eyes one could detect fear. He was wearing grey designer shorts and a casual green shirt.

"Are you on holidays Rodge?" Barry asked.

"Yes"

Rodger worked as a shoe salesman. He was nursing his drink when he added, "I've got two weeks which doesn't really give me a lot of time off."

"Oh, you and Jenny got something planned?"

"No it's just I've got a lot of work to do on the side."

"Honey would you start the barbecue," Audrey interrupted.

"Yah Barry, you going to show us your expertise?'" Anne Billingsby was quick to make a remark who was sitting on a lawn chair next to her husband. Julia and Ron were sitting next to them.

"I'll show you all that I learned in my cooking course," Barry said.

"I didn't know you took a cooking course Barry?" Bill added. Bill was a fair sized gentleman with a full set of graying hair that was cut short. The weathered grains on his face not only showed his remarkable intelligence but his many years of hard work. He wore a full length pair of grey pants and a pin stripped white shirt.

"Yes, it was a gourmet cooking course given as part of

a promotion for a wine that I was sampling. Carignan ever heard of it?"

"That's a Californian wine isn't it?" Anne interrupted.

"Yes"

"Yes I've tried it," Anne reminded him.

"Mary and Don you're from California. Have you ever tried Cari…..what did you call it Barry?" Audrey asked giving Mary and Don Pennington an opportunity to join the conversation. She felt some good conversation was needed to replace the small talk.

"I think I've tried it," Mary Pennington added.

"Do you drink a lot of wine Mary?" Audrey's curiosity continuing the conversation. It was about this time that Annie came running over,(dripping wet,) and spoke to her grand mother.

"Grandma watch me jump in the pool."

"Ok, sweaty," Mary said and watched as Annie ran back to the pool and jumped in. Mary was slightly overweight, petite, with straight white and brown hair cut short. She had a pleasant disposition to add to her chubby facial features. She was wearing a white flowery dress and was slightly overweight.

Julia Harrington walked over to the table displaying hors d oeuvres, grabbed a cracker and bit into it carefully making sure not to get any of the seafood sauce on her chin. "What is this smoked salmon, Audrey?"

"Yes," Audrey answered still waiting to get an answer from Mary.

"Well my doctor says I should watch it on the alcohol but occasionally I do have the odd glass of wine," Mary replied ignoring Julia's intrusion.

Bill with the lack of something better to say exclaimed, "Anne would you get me one of those crackers?"

Anne looked at him perturbed, "What did you're last servant die of?"

"Over exhaustion," Bill explained.

"Ron and Julia, how was you're trip from Ohio?" Barry asked, "The weather wasn't too bad."

"We got in last night," Julia exclaimed. "The weather was wonderful. Of course Ron did all the driving. There's a lot of pretty country through Ohio."

"What's life like in Cleveland?" Barry asked continuing the conversation.

"Probably the same as anywhere else," Audrey reminded him.

Ron was a school teacher and Julia worked part time on the side just to make ends meet. Being a school teacher does not pay all that much. Ron was 5'6" tall with a light brown, Caucasian complexion. He had Asian descent. He had an average build with straight black hair. Julia was a tall,(5'6"), curvaceous 28 year old lady with dirty blond hair.

Barry parked his sky blue Mazda in the parking lot of Doctor Harris's office at 2 pm on Tuesday afternoon.

"Barry Pennington", he said as the secretary checked his name on the list of appointments.

"Just have a seat," she stated.

Barry sat in the waiting room with another group of people for 45 minutes. Then he entered the examination room

"What brings you here, Barry?" Doctor Harris requisitioned looking over Barry's file with interest.

"Just thought I'd better have a checkup

"Audrey not taking care of you?" she asked.

"Oh she is, I just want to make sure everything working properly."

Barry found it odd that Doctor Harris had taken an

interest in how Audrey had been taking care of him but thought nothing of it. The examination went well, she claimed his blood pressure was a little high and told him to drink more water.

'Drinking alcohol isn't affecting this is it doctor?" The possibility that alcohol could be causing high blood pressure had occurred to Barry but he wanted to avoid it if at all possible.

"It shouldn't," she warned.

Barry found Doctor Harris an attractive lady, curvaceous with a pretty face that was on the verge of being beautiful. She had jet black hair cut shoulder length. He was not sexually attracted to her; he loved his wife. He knew he had responsibilities as a family man and he took it seriously.

"We have to take care of ourselves as we grow older," Barry reminisced to the doctor on the way out of the examination room.

"Yes don't I know it, "she exclaimed."

"…Any messages?" Barry demanded, passing his secretary on his way to his office the next day.

"No sire."

Barry entered and then closed his office door. He had a list of reports on his desk that he had to look over and sign so he had his morning work cut out for him. He noticed a naked photograph because he was always getting pop ups on his computer screen of naked women. But this particular female caught his eye. As he looked closer he could not help but notice that this particular female looked exactly like Dr. Harris. 'But that was impossible' he thought.

"Here's your coffee sir," Carol said entering the room and placing it on the desk.

"Thank you, Carol."

The more he looked at the photograph the more he thought

it looked like Doctor Harris. It kept eating and eating on his conscience. He was sure it was Doctor Harris. But how could it be? He decided to find another photograph. As he clicked onto the web sights he discovered nine more. He decided to make prints of them.

He examined the photographs for a moment. Dr. Harris had been their family doctor for the past five years. The possibility of her being a ludicrous lady was absurd but it was possible she did it for the money. As he examined the photos he had to admit, Doctor Harris did have an attractive figure. Barry placed the photographs in an envelope and filed them in a drawer.

Chapter 5

Dr. Janice Harris dropped her keys and purse on the hall table upon entering her luxurious townhouse in Louisville's Park Avenue, which was a part of an elite district in a newly developed urban neighborhood on the outskirts of Louisville.

"Mama's home," she shouted upon entering their plush living room and collapsing in a refinished early 19th century sofa. She put her feet up on her ottoman for a few moments before her four and six year old children came running and tumbled into her lap.

"Oh, not so ruff," she gasped reshuffling the two of them in a furry. "How was your day at school, "she asked her six year old whose name was Gary.

"Oh, fine," Gary was reluctant to say. "Frank got in trouble with the teacher again."

As innocent as Gary appeared, he was a normal little boy getting into mischief as most boys do. Janice took her son with both hands and looked him in the eye, "Why don't you go and wash your hands and face before supper and we'll talk about that later."

The two children scurried off towards the bathroom as Janice took a few more moments to relax before dinner. The front door clicked open and Mike Harris walked in. Dropping his briefcase by the door he acknowledged her presents.

"Hi honey. If your day was half as bad as mine I think we should both have a good stiff drink?" he warned.

Mike Harris had dark hair, was tall and well built. Aside from the fact that he procrastinated occasionally (he didn't have the ambition to exercise).his muscles were loose and sagging in places. He exercised his brain more than he did his body although he was exceedingly handsome. He was wearing dark suite pants and his short sleeve shirt that was missing a tie and was unbuttoned

"You know honey I've been thinking," she mused changing the subject, "Maybe we should go to Lexington for the weekend. I think the change will do us both some good."

Mike exclaimed, "Might be nice to get away, I know the kids would like it." He walked over to the lazy waiter by the bar and poured himself an Evan Williams Bourbon. "What's your pleasure?"

"Oh nothing for me, I've got a head ache. I just want to take a nice long, hot, bath and go to bed early."

During dinner Mike began talking about his day. He had recently been promoted to a senior accountant for a huge banking firm which was for him a huge responsibility. There were meetings and business trips not to mention the dinner engagements and lonely nights at the office working overtime. They would be lucky to get away to Lexington for the weekend.

"Jack could not accept the fact that there was a joint account for his company that had one foot in the poor house to start with," Mike insisted as he cut Gary's meat into tiny pieces.

Virginia their housekeeper placed a bowl of fresh vegetables on the table then scurried back to the kitchen to fetch the cheese sauce.

"Thank you Virginia. Well what seems to be the problem then?" Janice asked.

"The problem is he didn't trust his partner who was cheating him behind his back."

"Well why didn't he close the account?" she asked.

"It's not that easy. You can't just dissolve an account. There is a lot of legal mumbo jumbo involved," Mike stated.

"Yes, I know honey, but that's got nothing to do with you," Janice explained, taking an interest in the conversation, as Virginia returned with the sauce. "The next time you think you've got it tough just think what it would be like to walk in my shoes."

Mike hesitated and then sighed. "Your right honey." Picking up his glass of wine he looked at her and offered a toast. "Shall we toast to the weekend?"

"Of course."

At once Dr. Harris gave in.

Later that evening, after having her bath she began wrapping her kimono around her in her adjoining bedroom. Mike came in, took her shoulders with both hands and passionately kissed her.

"Interested in a little hanky panky?" he asked quietly, desperate to change the mood.

She wiggled out from under him and resisted his seduction, "Not tonight honey."

She then walked out of the bedroom and into the children's room.

Janice Harris was slightly tall, had shoulder length, jet, black, hair and her curvaceous figure made her an attractive woman with her slender, long, legs coming together at her oval hips. She had a cute 34-26-36 figure together with a winning personality that was attractive to any man. Her husband she met accidentally through an acquaintance of hers just before graduating from medical school. Along with their busy schedules they dated enough to get married in a few short months.

Dr. Harris was not your average, ordinary, everyday, run of the mill, doctor. She had acquired her career through some very ludicrous activities by keeping a low profile for a number of years. To Doctor Harris nudity was extremely natural. She had worked her way through medical college with some of the funds raised by exposing herself on the internet. All that she and Mike had achieved was as a result of perseverance and hard work. To her nudity was natural and all apart of her job. Mike had no idea Janice had such a dark past and she wanted to keep it that way. It would only create a scandal if people found out.

"All ready to see the sand man you two?" Janice asked as she entered the children's room. It was an average sized single bedroom with navy blue wall paper covered with small panda bears, each of the single beds placed side by side. On either side were two adjoining night tables. In the middle was a light blue love seat. She sat on Gary's bed and tucked him in.

Gary was a healthy little six year old with fair hair and blue eyes. He was average in height for his age and carried light body weight. John her four year old had the same color hair, had green eyes and was 2 inches shorter.

"What did Frank do to get you in trouble, Gary?" she asked folding and straightening out the covers.

"He lied," Gary explained in a furry of excitement.

Janice's eye's glowed with astonishment. "He lied to the teacher?" she asked.

"He lied because he said he would bring a picture to show and tell and he never brought it and now he's in trouble," he explained bluntly.

"Really, don't you think the teacher will understand? Maybe Frank just forgot?" she asked.

"Mom, don't you think if I forgot to bring something to

show and tell she would punish me?" Gary said his curiosity getting the best of him.

"Of course not sweetie," Janice found she needed to change the subject." How would you two like to go to Lexington for the weekend?"

Both children jumped up in excitement.

"Now it's not for sure yet, so don't get your hopes up too high," she warned.

"Is there stuff for kids to do?" John her four year old responded excitedly.

"There's a small lake with paddle boats and a park you can play in," she concluded. "Now go to sleep." She then walked towards the door and turned the light out. "Sweet dreams my pets."

Dr. Janice Harris walked into her office on Remington Street the following morning checking in with her secretary.

"Is there any mail Molly?" she asked.

Molly responded by handing her the morning mail.

"Any messages?"

"No maim'"

There were people in the waiting room waiting to be treated. "Mr. Colby has an appointment this morning at 10.30. Let me know when he's here and remind Dell Pharmacy about Mrs. Desmond's prescription," Janice demanded. She then looked at the first patient and nodded encouragingly, "Cheryl."

Her day continued as any normal day. It was a bright, sunny Thursday, not a cloud in the sky. About three o'clock she got a phone call from Mike who called from his office. Janice dropped what she was doing to take it.

"Honey, I'm sorry but we won't be able to go away this weekend. I've got too much paperwork."

"Oh all right. If you simply must", she responded with discouragement.

"I'll make it up to you Janice, I promise."

Frustrated she walked back into the examination room and looked at the patient. "Shall we continue?"

The patient sat in the chair as Janice looked over his file with interest. "Everything working fine?" she asked.

"Yes"

"Are you sleeping regularly, Alfred?"

"Yes"

The gentleman was about middle age with dirty blond hair and short sideburns. Dr. Harris was just doing a regular checkup on him so she didn't really expect to find anything wrong. She checked his vital signs while continuing the examination.

"Your blood pressure seems to be a little too high, are you eating properly?" she asked.

"Yes, doctor."

"Well try cutting down on the caffeine. I'm going to request a blood test for you. If there is anything wrong we'll call you." She filled out a referral and handed it to him.

She then led him back to the waiting area where there were other patients. She thought maybe her eyes were playing tricks on her when she saw Barry Pennington.

"Did you have an appointment today Barry?" she asked.

"No, but I was hoping to have a word with you."

"Certainly please step this way," she stated. She led him into one of the examination rooms. "Wait here a moment while I get your file."

The thought of him having a file made Barry a little squeamish. His thoughts were jumbled and confused as he was about to make the decision of his life. Not only his personnel health was at risk but his family's as well. He began thinking that he still had a chance to turn back as the seconds turned into hours a force inside him had been eating at him for days. Was he really trying to protect her or did he have greed in mind because he was becoming a changed person not through any choice of his own? Only Barry knew about the photographs and he was a little reluctant to have them exposed. What he was thinking would take a little bit of determination on his part but he began having second thoughts.

Three days ago Barry had been working under a lot of stress. His business was being lucrative but Barry was finding it difficult to find grease to make the wheels turn. He seemed to have an endless amount of paper work and too little help making minor decisions. Henry Peterson was a chief assistant but it was still up to Barry to make decisions about the company.

Henry walked into his office on Monday afternoon.

"Express transport has been after us for the past month with a transaction that we have no record of. They're threatening to liquidate their services if we don't comply," Henry warned being uncertain but firm as to what to do.

"Henry, what do I pay you $18. an hour for. Can't you just find out who was responsible for the shipment?" Barry stammered feeling somewhat perturbed with the conversation.

It was not just Henry Peterson that was having trouble making minor decisions but people down the ladder as well.

Money had not been Barry's only ambition although it was a large part of it. His lust for fine dinning as well as his influence over people drove him with the determination to succeed as well as meet the cost of his luxurious lifestyle.

Janice Harris was not proud of her dark past. She had received success at a huge price and the fact that she was happily married and had two growing boys made it all the more difficult for her to forget. She would give anything to do it over the right way, but she knew she could not change the past. She had found a way of making things right in her life and she was determined to prove it.

Dr. Harris walked into the examination room with Barry's file in her hand and began looking through it. Barry saw this and stopped her immediately.

"No, doctor I'm not here for an examination, I wanted to talk to you about something."

Doctor Harris paused looking surprised. "Is there something the matter?" she asked curiosity overwhelming her.

Barry appeared healthy at first glance but the fact that she had examined him only a few weeks ago sparked her curiosity. 'Something could be the matter with his family', she thought, 'or maybe something wrong in his personal life.'

He paused. He was still having second thoughts. "Yes doctor. I was wondering if you knew anything about some images that were being exposed?" Barry blurted. His voice seemed to sound far away. Deep down he knew he was about to do something wrong. He contained himself. But Janis Harris could not believe what she had just heard. She was not sure what he was implying. She decided that ignorance was the best policy.

"What is it you're trying to imply Barry?" she asked.

"It's about some explicit photographs I've come across merely by accident."

"Of who?"

"Of you Dr. Harris."

Dr. Harris could not believe this was happening. The examination room suddenly began to close in around her as she came to rationalize the ultimate consequences of this accusation. Suddenly she became very frustrated and looked at this 'subhuman creature' thinking of himself as a man and paused as if time had suddenly stood still. But then it occurred to her that Barry was after all a family man. Maybe his intentions were good and he just wanted to protect her. After all she was a doctor. But what if these photos became exposed. It could ruin her life and others as well. What was he doing looking at pornography. His intentions could be dishonorable.

Looking away from him she managed to say, "Look I have other patients waiting. Can we talk about this another time?"

He had to think fast. "Why don't we have dinner together?" he paused, "We can talk about it?" He was impressed by the response.

"Certainly," she replied, "When?"

"How about tomorrow?"

"The Keg-8 o'clock." She walked out of the examination room and continued her practice. Barry found his way out.

The following evening Dr. Harris waited patiently for Barry in the restaurant. She had told the mat radix that Barry would be coming. Her thoughts were anxious but confused as she played with the swivel stick and twirled the ice in her soda water. She wasn't drinking alcohol because she needed to keep her wits about her. She had had a long tiring day and she wasn't sure what to expect. Reaching into her purse she clicked on a mini-tape recorder.

The mat radix led Barry to her table. Barry tipped the waiter then sat down. "Scotch, single malt," he said acknowledging the waiter. The waiter bowed and then backed away.

Barry was more confident in the restaurant than he had been in her office the day before. He had taken the night to think about what he was doing. He had examined the photos again and was being driven by his lust. This was strange because after all Barry was a family man. But it would have been a temptation for any man.

He kept his two hands folded on the table in front of him as he bluntly stated, "Are you hungry I'm starving?" Dr. Harris just sat and stared at him.

The waiter brought his drink and handed them a menu. Janis left hers on the table and Barry opened the menu, glanced at it and then closed it and handed it back to the waiter. "Are you ready to order?" the waiter asked looking at Dr. Harris.

"Nothing for me thanks," she said.

"I'll have the number three, medium rare, no onions, and baked potato," Barry stated. The waiter left.

She took a look around to make sure no one was listening and whispered`, "Barry, what do you think you're going to gain by these accusations?"

Barry's boldness was overtaking him. "Well the fact that you're a happily married woman with a family kind of explains it doesn't it?"

"But why are you accusing me of this? Is it because you want to protect me or something?" she asked. She became frustrated. "First of all the accusations are false. I don't know where you got the photos from."

Barry was wearing a casual grey, tweed, sports jacket and from inside he produced a yellow envelope. "Look at these," he stated handing her the envelope.

Dr. Harris opened the envelope and gazed in horror. She suppressed her emotions as she went through the pictures burning with anger not only at him but at herself for being a part of such a fiasco in the first place. Was it lust that was driving this man on or was he really trying to protect her.

"Yes they look like me but whether they are is out of the question," she warned. "What are you proposing?"

Barry was beside himself as to whether to go through with this plot or throw in the towel. He paused as the thoughts kept crossing his mind. Suddenly he just came out with it. "If we don't agree to arrange for a settlement, I'm going to show the pictures to you're husband."

"That's blackmail," she warned suddenly in a state of shock.

"Call it what you like."

Dr. Harris tried to reason with him. "Look Barry you're a family man why would you want to pull a stunt like this?" She tried desperately to keep her voice down. She was hoping maybe he'd grow up and see the error of his ways.

"Let's just say some people are willing to take the risk," he relented.

Dr. Harris reached into her purse and casually switched the recorder off and then took out a bill and left it on the table. She got up and walked out.

Barry closed the huge oak door after entering his three quarter-a-million dollar home. Hanging up his sports jacket in the front closet he discarded his shoes by the door. Audrey was straightening a few things up and acknowledged his presents, "…late night at the office, Hon'?"

"Sorry I missed diner. I ate out," he mumbled and tried continuing to a secluded part of the house. He wanted to be alone. Annie and David were playing in their rooms and Freddy was visiting a friend.

"I think I'll go to bed early," Barry proclaimed.

"Donald and Lee should be here about three tomorrow," Audrey warned. Donald was Audrey's older brother. He and his wife were coming for the weekend. Barry gave her a smug look that caught her attention. "Everything alright, Barry?"

"Yah, sure."

Barry had to pick Audrey's brother and his wife up at the airport the following day. Their plane was half an hour late. Barry recognized his wife's dark shoulder length hair and Donald's slim physic in the crowd, not mistaking the unenthusiastic, phony, smile he always had on his face. His wife looked like she could care less with that 'leave me alone attitude' she carried. Barry knew he was in for a lousy weekend.

After leaving 'The Keg' Janice Harris climbed into her car and drove to Waterfront Park near downtown Louisville. She parked her car and began to stroll. She needed to clear her head and think this thing out. With the conversation that she had had with Barry recorded, her marriage or her career was not in any real danger, although her reputation might be. She knew she had the evidence to convict him. But with her reputation at stake she wasn't sure whether she should. It might be a good idea to keep it quiet for the time being. After all, what would her family think if they found these explicit photos. She was not sure her husband could trust her knowing the truth. She needed that trust. She decided she would keep it a secret between her and Barry. She knew he was a reasonable family man. What would it gain if he were to expose her? He also had his reputation to think about. Janice had learned through hard experience that guys like Barry came a dime a dozen. But then what would it accomplish by having Barry convicted. She would still have her and her family's reputations ruined. Then she realized Barry really had her in a dilemma. If he demanded something from her she just might have to comply. She thought these things out in her mind as she strolled along the Ohio River. It was a clear, warm, summer night. There was a full moon. Her world was secure for the time being but what dangers were lurking out there. She missed her family and decided to go home.

She walked into her Park Avenue townhouse and kicked off her shoes by the door. The air was cool in her suite because the air was regulated in her condominium. She felt something different upon entering as the unusual silence was noticeable. She wandered around looking for her family whom she found in the children's room. Mike was sitting on the sky blue love seat reading the children a bedtime story. The boys were in their pajamas in bed. Suddenly they shouted as Janice approached the door, "Is a mother allowed entrance into her child's room?" she asked.

"Well what do you boys think, shall we let her in?" Mike exclaimed.

In unison the boys shouted, "Yes."

"Two against one, I guess I'm allowed."

"How did your dinner meeting go?" Mike asked.

"It was over sooner than I thought. Did you two guys behave yourself with daddy tonight?" she asked completely interested in her family's quality time.

"Yes. We watched Lady and the Tramp," Gary exclaimed, explaining the night's activities in a few short breathes.

"Well you two, time to get some sleep." Mike demanded. "Mommy and I want to spend some time alone together. We'll finish the story tomorrow night."

"Night my pets," she said as they turned out the light. "Sorry you had to baby-sit, Hon, but it was an important meeting" she explained as they descended the landing. 'Yes, I definitely need that trust,' she thought to herself.

Chapter 6

The following Wednesday Dr. Harris was just finishing with a patient when she got a phone call from her husband Mike.

"I think I can manage to get away this weekend. Are you still willing to go to Lexington?" he asked, "I can call and make the arrangements?"

"That would be nice Hon, can we talk about it tonight?"

"Over dinner?"

"Alright."

That gave her the incentive to continue. It had been a struggle for a few days after what had happened on Friday night with Barry but she had managed. Knowing that she could get away from the rat race gave her the incentive she needed. She was not willing to have her reputation blackened after all she and Mike had achieved. There was too much at stake. She would not press charges as long as Barry would not interfere with her life.

It was cloudy the following day and Dr. Harris was just finishing her daily practice. Molly had gone home and she was answering a few e-mails before she could lock up. She heard the office door swing open so she went to see who it was.

"Good afternoon Dr. Harris," mused Barry Pennington. "I thought maybe we could have a little talk."

"We've got nothing to talk about."

"Oh, but I think we do," Barry demanded.

"Look if it's about Friday night, I've got enough evidence to protect myself and I'm sure you don't want to jeopardize your reputation," she warned him.

"What do you mean?" nievely he asked.

"I recorded the whole conversation," she explained. "You don't think I was stupid enough to let you get away with it do you?"

Barry was suddenly shocked back to reality. There was a moment's silence as he got a hold of himself. 'How could he be so stupid' he thought Then reluctantly he asked, "So what now doctor?"

"I want you to leave me and my family alone," she warned, "I'll continue to treat you and your family but only on a business like basis…..and I want you to keep this between me and you."

Frustratingly Barry turned and walked out.

"Expect six people not including Barry and I," Audrey insisted as she accepted the grocery list from Shelly on Thursday night. Shelly was finishing cleaning up from the evening meal. "And plenty of hors d oeuvres on the \pool deck, I 'm expecting good weather on Saturday."

"Yes, maim'", Shelly explained, "Don't worry about me, I'll find my own way home."

Audrey was in the super market that night going about her regular routine. She picked up a box of crackers. Looking at them she suddenly heard a familiar voice.

"Nice to see you're still behind the eight-ball Audrey," Ben said in a polite softening tone of voice. He was alone picking up a few groceries and for Audrey a turn in the wrong direction. It was one of the last persons she wanted to see. The smug remark didn't impress her a bit.

"Oh, hi, Ben, fancy meeting you here," Audrey stated. "Run out of horses to bet on?"

"Actually, I'm tired of horses but I've got this great plan to rob Fort Knox," he fantasized. "Care to join me in a drink to discuss it?"

"No I think I'll pass Ben," she said protecting herself. She knew where this was leading. "We've got some company this weekend and I've got to finish this list. Maybe some other time," she acknowledged as politely as she could.

"Well the offer's always open," Ben reminded her.

'You never know who you're going to meet in a supermarket' Audrey thought as she continued shopping.

Gene Mayberry and his wife Catharine were good friends with Audrey and Barry Pennington. They had known them for years. The peculiar circumstances that occurred at their meeting made their introductions all the more peculiar. David and Freddy were barely infants when Audrey and Barry were attending a function for their children. Catharine and Gene's child Mary and David found each other and the introductions turned to embarrassment. Soon the parents made the introductions and fortunately for Mary and David (due to the fact that Mary threw him a kiss) it became the beginning of a beautiful friendship.

Audrey planned a dinner with Kate and Gene which would be a special gourmet treat, (Shelly being experienced at such things) and it would be a treat for her and Barry as well. The Mayberry's brought Mary so her and Annie could play together, and David and Freddy could stay with friends. Presenting a special bottle of wine for the occasion, it would be a good opportunity for the two men to talk business and the ladies to catch up on the latest gossip.

It was mid August, a warm, sunny day, the temperature was in the low nineties. The forecast was calling for rain but that wouldn't be for 24 hours. The sun was getting low on the horizon and the cool of the evening was settling on the city. The Mayberry's arrived in their four door sedan, parking it in the front of the Pennington's luxurious home, in their urban neighborhood.

Gene was dressed casually in a blue sports jacket, with matching dark slacks and Kate wore a grey and red dress that was taper-cut just below the knees. Mary was dressed in red shorts with a white and red flowery blouse. They walked slowly; Kate in her red matching high heels up the driveway to the huge twin oak doors.

Audrey answered the door. "Hiiii, come on in," she shouted as they exchanged greetings. "I don't know where my other half is but he'll be out shortly."

The Mayberry's took their shoes off and made their selves comfortable.

"I'll go see how dinner is going and see what's keeping Barry," Audrey explained politely. "Mary, why don't you go and see if Annie is in her room?"

Audrey left Catharine and Gene alone in the front room. There was silence as the two of them passed the time.

"You might be interested to know that Audrey runs a military like operation here, Gene, seeing how you're a military man?" Kate boasted trying to break the boredom.

Gene's expression changed to surprise. "Really, what do you mean?"

"She claims if it's good enough for the army, its good enough for her family too."

"She would have made a good commanding officer," Gene mused.

"I'm sure Barry wouldn't like to here that," Kate warned him.

"Well now we know who where's the pants in the family," Gene said amusingly.

The twin kitchen doors squeaked open and Audrey walked out of the kitchen and into the dinning and living room.

"We're planning a special gourmet treat tonight. Dinner should be ready in about an hour to an hour and a half," Audrey said to the couple, then looked around confused and said, "I don't know where Barry could have gotten to?"

"Having trouble keeping Barry disciplined, Audrey?" Gene asked.

Audrey looked frustrated and confessed her anger to her friends. "Barry hasn't been himself lately. I think something is bothering him.".

"You re sure your not imagining it Audrey?" Gene frowned.

Audrey looked directly at Gene. "Gene you know as well as I do that I'm not imagining it."

"He's not seeing another woman is he?" Kate asked.

"I don't know." There was a pause and then pleadingly she confronted Gene. "Would you talk to him, Gene? You're his best friend."

"I'll see what I can do."

They made small talk for about a half hour, mostly about their children, family and friends when Barry came strolling in from the back door unaware that he and Audrey were entertaining.

"Hi Gene, hi Kate…. I completely forgot we were having company. It must have slipped my mind," Barry half heartedly said when in reality he was just being antisocial. He was really avoiding people as much as possible. Not that Barry was an introvert because he was a good public relations person especially being in a business involving women's products. But since his confrontation with Doctor Harris he was hiding deep inside himself.

Conversation continued steadily for a while. Before dinner was served Gene took Barry aside in the den and asked him, "Barry is there anything wrong?"

"Why should there be?" Barry was quick to say. 'Why would he think there's something wrong,' he thought.

"Audrey seems to think there's something wrong."

"She must be imagining it Gene."

"Come on you can tell me, I'm your friend. Are you seeing someone on the side?" Gene kept pressing him.

"No," Barry insisted.

"Look if anyone would know it would be Audrey."

Gene was an average built clean cut guy like Barry. Not overweight, he had a fair, full, set of hair and stood 2 inches taller. He had a handsome intellectual appearance, his jaw completed by two identical creases. His forehead had distinct lines of intelligence.

"I'm just under a little stress at work that's all. I probably need a vacation," Barry was reluctant to say.

Dinner was a combination of rice with tiger shrimp in a Thai green curie, coconut, sauce. Kate was a lover of shrimp, which naturally Audrey was partial to as well. The two of them used to visit seafood restaurants together.

Catharine had reddish brown hair which was loose, having a natural curl, but uncombed. Her eyes were green and she had a slim figure being of medium height, she wore brand name clothing. Her bust size was 34D but she wore her tops a size too small. She was pleasantly attractive and she liked to show it.

Conversation during dinner turned from cognac to bourbon but soon turned to real estate as the Mayberry's were upgrading their property. Gene was a bit of a handy man, doing a lot of the work himself. Kate loved decorating and was quick to get Audrey's advice. Barry included himself in some of the conversation which everyone noticed.

A few days later Audrey had a doctor's appointment for a check up. She slammed the office door,(not intentionally) and walked into the office and up to the receptionist checking the time of her appointment.

"Just have a seat, Audrey," Molly said.

Audrey waited about 45 minutes before entering the examination room. After looking over her file, carefully sticking to business, Dr. Harris began checking her vital signs, as Audrey sat up straight on the examination table.

Audrey looked tired and distraught. Little wonder with what was going on between her and Barry. The doctor noticed this and confronted her.

"Anything wrong, Audrey?"

"I think Barry's been cheating on me."

"Do you have proof," Janice asked.

"No"

"That makes it hard doesn't it," Janice concluded.

"Is your minstrel period regular, Audrey?" the doctor asked.

"Yes"

Dr. Harris gave her a thorough examination and found Audrey healthy and fit. She dismissed her but the examination left Janice Harris angry and frustrated. She had known the Pennington's for six years. She had not thought Barry capable of such things and it disturbed her. 'Why should this little runt get away with blackmail?' The thought kept eating at the back of her mind. 'Here was a happily married woman with a family and this criminal was not only screwing it up for the Pennington family but for the Harris family as well.' Janice could not contain her anger. She continued to work on a short fuse but suppressed her anger being careful not to be sharp with her patients.

Audrey was home alone as she walked into her den on a Tuesday in early October. The room was well lit with the autumn light casting shadows across the room's polished mahogany floor and centered, multicolored, area rug. She wandered around watering the numerous plants that were strategically placed to catch the room's sunlight. She could have spent her time reading. Instead out of boredom she wandered over to the ebony desk and began checking the family computer for any mischief her children might be into. Finding nothing she then began scrum aging through the desk drawers. She found a DVD that was labeled 'confidential' and found it odd that Barry would leave this available for anyone.

She slipped the disc in the computer's drive and opened up the program. What she found shocked her. It was pictures of Doctor Harris as naked as the day she was born. Audrey was surprised to see her in such provocative positions. 'So that's it', she gasped. 'Barry's having an affair with the doctor.' She slipped the disc back into the sleeve and shut the computer off.

Audrey packed a suitcase with the necessary toiletries for a few days and piled it into her white SUV. She made sure that the DVD labeled 'confidential', was packed.

"Shelly I'm leaving for a few days. I can't explain where I'm going or why but I will make contact in a few days. Would you make sure the children are fed?" Audrey warned finding it difficult to explain herself to Shelly. She did an even thirty kilometers an hour as she wound around the curves of her suburban neighborhood to go where…. she didn't know.

Audrey and Kate were sharing a cup of coffee the next

day. They were sitting in an elite restaurant that was popular with the dinner crowd in a busy business district of Louisville.

"It's too bad Gene doesn't have a membership at the country club," Audrey reminisced, "You two missed a good barbecue." She felt a need to talk this out. That's the reason she asked Kate to go to the restaurant in the first place.

"Well you should consider yourself blessed," Kate warned, "Gene and I could never afford it on his income."

"Well I think your too late Kate."

"What do you mean?" she asked

"Those days are over."

"Audrey unless my ears are playing tricks on me, you'd better explain yourself," Kate warned.

Audrey took a look around the restaurant to see if anyone was listening and then began.

"Barry's having an affair."

"You seem awfully sure of yourself. Do you have proof?"

"Absolutely," Audrey boasted.

"Did you catch him at it?" she asked.

"No, it's a little more complicated than that. I have the proof on a disc."

"Well what's so complicated about that?" Kate again asked.

"Well I didn't actually 'catch him at it' but I found some explicit photos of 'her' in the desk drawer."

"Don't keep me in suspense. Who is it? Do I know her?" Kate was coxing Audrey on.

"The family doctor," Audrey confessed.

"Nooo. Audrey, I'm so sorry. Have you thought about what you're going to do?" She was making herself responsible for Audrey's affairs, her curiosity getting the best of her.

"No, I haven't had time. I just found out yesterday."

Kate was at a loss for words. She had a good Christian upbringing like Audrey. She believed in an honest marriage and had the same beliefs about her maker. She stumbled with the next question.

"Wa what are you going to do?"

"I've already left him with the kids, but I'm going to get them in a few days," Audrey explained. "I'll get a job I guess."

"But it will be weeks before you find one, what will you do till then?" Kate contemplated.

"I'm sure my parents can help me out," Audrey mused.

"Listen if there's anything I can do to help," Kate concluded.

"Thanks Kate."

Anne picked up the phone after hearing it ring for two or three times. "Oh, hi Audrey," enthusiastically she said.

"Mom I've got some bad news." Audrey warned.

"What"

"I'm leaving Barry," Audrey contemplated. She was talking from a phone booth in a secluded shopping mall.

There was silence as Anne listened to Audrey breathe.

"Well I guess you've got your mind made up," Anne concluded. "Do you have any proof that he's cheating on you," she asked.

"Yes"

"Well I hope it'll stand up in court." Anne being married to a lawyer and promising judge was used to the idea of a fair trial.

"It will," Audrey warned. She looked around her to see if anyone was listening.

"What are you going to do in the meantime?" Anne asked.

"I was hoping you and Dad could help me out till I get a job."

"Well I I don't know, Audrey I'm sure we can help you out,

I'll have to talk with Bill," Anne recommended. "What are you going to do in the meantime?"

"Look for a place," Audrey concluded.

After Audrey hung up the phone anger began to broil in her. It was not all cut and dry like it was when she was discussing it with Kate. All she could think about was how to tear a peace out of Barry. To think that he could cheat on her after twelve years of marriage. It was not just Audrey that was involved here. She had the rest of her family to think about.

She left the shopping mall, got into her SUV, drove to Remington Street, parked down the street from Doctor Harris's office, and sat and waited. She had to think this thing out and this was as good a place as any. What was she going to say to Dr. Harris when she saw her? Would she give her a peace of her mind? Under the circumstances she felt she had to say something if it was only to get it off her chest. Was she doing the right thing?

She checked the time, 5 o'clock. She would be leaving her office soon and she would have to talk to her on the street. Better she go into her office and talk in private. She got out of the SUV and locked it. Walking into her office, Molly was sitting at her desk. There were no patients in the office. Doctor Harris walked from her office up to the front desk, and seeing Audrey acknowledged her with a warm smile.

"Hello Audrey what can I do for you?" Dr. Harris asked.

Audrey seemed to be losing control and tried with all her will to suppress her anger and said, "Dr. Harris can I talk to you alone?"

"Certainly, come this way," Janice directed. Audrey followed her into one of the examination rooms. The doctor closed the door. With all the determination and self control that Audrey could muster, she began.

"Dr. Harris I come from a good Christian linage and if

I were in your profession I would never dream of ruining a good family man's life let alone the rest of the members of his family."

"What do you mean, Audrey?" the doctor asked. "I'm not fooling around with anyone's husband."

"I thought you might have a little more class than that," Audrey hissed.

Suddenly it occurred to the doctor that Audrey knew a little more about what was going on between them than she realized. Audrey must have seen the photographs. Compassion seemed to overtake Dr. Harris as she took control of the moment.

"Hold it, Audrey, I wasn't the one that was out of control. Hold it Audrey, just calm down," as she could see Audrey was clenching her fists, "It seems your husband was capable of a little more than just adultery."

"What do you mean?" Audrey scowled.

The doctor took Audrey in her arms and directed her to a chair. "I think you should sit down before you hear this Audrey." Audrey sat in a chair. "It seems that Barry is not the good family man that he appears. Barry tried to Blackmail me."

Audrey screwed up her face in an expression of distaste and blurted out, "For what sex or money?" Her world was falling in around her and she was reluctant to hear what would be more of a tragedy. But she was forced to hear the inevitable.\

"Apparently he found some explicit photos of me on the internet and threatened to show them to my husband if I didn't agree to a settlement. I have the conversation on tape."

There was a moment of silence as Audrey got a grip on what was happening to her. She had faced the inevitable and now that she knew she didn't know if she could face it. It hit her like a slap in the face. She was stunned. Dr. Harris continued.

"I think for your family's sake and mine, we shouldn't press charges. We have our reputations to think about," the doctor stated.

Audrey was numb. She managed to make her way out of the office but was confused and disorientated. She would go to her parents for a few days. They would understand.

Chapter 7

Janis Harris held her arms out with intent to capture her four year old John who jumped up into his mothers arms. Gary crowded around to greet her also. "Hello my pets. John were you a good boy in daycare today?"

"Yes mom and guess what? One little boy wet his pants," John exclaimed.

"Nooo," Janice shouted, "And what about you Gary? What did the teacher say about your homework?"

"What no greeting for me?" Mike asked taking hold of her and kissing her in desperation. "You'd better hope mommy remembered to order dinner. Honey the housekeeper has the night off, remember."

"How could I forget my family? Dinner should be here in about a half an hour," Janice warned causing much enthusiasm amongst her family.

They were gathered around the dinning room table after dinner arrived. "Are you two hungry? I'm starving.," the doctor asked both of her children looking at them greedily. "I think for your sake Mike you'd better not eat it all."

She had ordered pork ribs from a popular restaurant and it was one of Mike's favorites. As she fed John it occurred to her that family values were important and that all the money in the world could not replace what her and Mike had achieved. It gave her determination to carry on and she wasn't going to let anyone take it at any price.

After dinner Janice and Mike put the kids to bed. They were lounging in their living room relaxing from an exasperating day when Janice started the conversation.

"If I were to tell you something about myself, do you think you could handle it?"

Mike looked puzzled. "You're going to tell me you found someone else?"

Janice waved her hand in denial avoiding that question, "No, nothing like that. Just answer my question. Do you think you could handle it if I told you that I haven't been honest to you about something?"

"Yes of course Honey what is it?" Mike explained surprised that he was hearing this.

"You're not going to like it Mike."

"Try me."

"I've been threatened with Blackmail," she explained letting the cat out of the bag.

Mike looked hurt and confused, "How....where....when?"

"Honey I've led a double life."

Mike interrupted and shouted, "Not prostitution?"

"No, I've been exposing myself illicitly for profit when I was going through university," Janice warned and began to tell Mike of her encounter with Barry.

Barry was disturbed after finding out that Audrey had left him. Twelve years of marriage was not easy to give up. How could he be so stupid to think that the doctor would agree to his demands and yet how did he feel he could get away with it. When he checked the desk drawer in the den his expectations were confirmed. She had found the disc. Barry knew he should have kept that disc in a locked drawer. She was probably thinking he and the doctor were having an affair. That's why she had left him. This was a humiliating blow for

Barry. He was supposedly a good family man. What was he doing looking at naked women?

He found solace in a bottle of liquor. Each drink brought relief as he watched the bottle slowly slip away it brought little comfort to know that soon his sins would be exposed. What would it gain for a family to have a doctor that was an alias porn star? This disturbed him and the drink helped to relieve these thoughts. But what disturbed him more was that he would be exposed as a criminal.

Audrey walked through the threshold of her parents elaborate turn of the century, Spanish style, home which was built on 20 acres of valuable property on the outskirts of Louisville. Her parents had been encouraged to sell for years but it was Anne's dream home where her family had grown up. They had roots here and wouldn't give it up at any price.

Bill was reading the newspaper in the main living room when Audrey entered without knocking. Her nerves were wound up tight. Bill could tell something was wrong.

"What's wrong honey, you look like you lost your best friend?" he asked.

"I did," Audrey confessed with her fists clenched.

"Come over here and sit by me." Audrey collapsed next to her Father in a blue and white wing chair. "Now tell me what's wrong?" he said taking hold of her left hand and comforting her. She began crying as she put her right hand over her face. Audrey was losing control and she knew it. She waited a minute or two till she got a hold of herself.

"Barry just ruined our marriage," Audrey bluntly cried.

"How," Bill asked.

"He blackmailed the family doctor."

"Come on Audrey, your not being realistic," Bill exclaimed, "What do you mean, Blackmail?"

Between tears and sobs Audrey finely got it out. "He found some naked pictures of the doctor on the internet and threatened to tell her husband."

"Are you sure?" Bill exclaimed, "It will have to stand up in court."

"Yes Dad I'm sure. I have a copy of the pictures and had a conversation with the doctor. Listen is it OK if I bring the kids and stay here a couple of days, just till I find a place?"

"Certainly, you can stay as long as you like," Bill stated. "Audrey you sure he's not just cheating on you? I mean blackmail, that's a hell of an accusation."

"I got all the information from Dr. Harris. She thinks I should keep it quiet for the sake of our reputations."

Bill was silent for a few moments as he stared off into the distance. Suddenly something registered in his mind. "Why, that little weasel," he concluded.

"I'm going to find a job, Dad," she confessed. "I just need a couple of days to think this thing out."

"Of course you are, sweetie. We'll help you out the best we can," Bill warned.

Three days later Barry was relaxing after a tiring day in his luxurious living room. He was frustrated and lonely. The children were absorbed in their own activities in other parts of the house. Barry was about to find something to do with himself when the front door opened. Audrey came barging in looking around for the children.

Barry thought that ignorance was the best policy. "Hi, honey, where have you been, the kids were wondering?"

"I'm taking the children to my parents seeing how you're not responsible enough to take care of them," Audrey warned giving Barry very little warning.

"What do you mean, honey?" nievely he asked.

"Dr. Harris told me everything." Audrey wandered around looking for her children. She found Annie in her room and told her to pack her things. Freddy and David were in the family room watching television when they were also told to pack.

An hour later Barry was alone. His wife and family had left him. He was feeling destitute and insecure as his whole world was falling apart something inside him began to snap. The humiliation of being caught with his pants down suddenly changed his attitude towards the opposite sex. He began losing respect towards women. As he poured himself a second cognac, his inhibitions began to loosen.

He envisioned the family doctor as she had been in the pictures and something inside him began to stir. He finished the bottle and collapsed in a drunken stupor.

Barry continued to drink heavily, alone for some time later. Those who knew him knew something was wrong but were reluctant for sake of the family, to say. His friends suffered and little known to Barry his business as well.

Audrey picked up a job at a gift shop and was soon looking for a place of her own about a month later when she and Kate shared a cup of coffee while looking through the 'Courier Journal', Louisville's local newspaper.

She had a couple of apartments circled and looked at Kate. "This one's got three bedrooms and is close to a park. It's reasonably priced too."

"What neighborhood?" Kate asked.

"Here I've got the address written down," Audrey stated holding the paper so Kate could see.

"Charles Avenue, that's a pretty good neighborhood too. When did they say you could look at it?" Kate asked, making Audrey's business hers as well.

"This afternoon," Audrey blurted.

"Let me come along then."

"OK"

"Why don't we have lunch at Murphy's?" Kate proclaimed, "I'm dying for some shrimp."

Kate and Audrey passed a large Coores floor sign as they followed the host to a booth near a window with a view of the Ohio River which was one of the nicest seats in the restaurant. He left two menus and came back with two ice waters.

"So when are you going to file for a divorce?" Kate asked after the waiter had left.

"To tell you the truth I hadn't even thought about it," Audrey confessed, "I have to get my life in order first." She was making excuses because she wanted to avoid a conversation about the doctor. She had her reputation to think about and she didn't want Kate to know it wasn't just adultery.

"Well you'd better not wait too long," Kate explained.

"Why"

"Audrey you're talking about your love life."

"Yes, and I have the rest of my life to think about it," Audrey explained. Audrey decided to change the subject. "You know Kate. Jenny is pretty good at decorating and I mentioned the fact that you two are renovating. She's willing to help."

The two of them began discussing this for the next hour until they had finished lunch and it was time to go for their appointment.

Kate left her car parked at the restaurant and Audrey drove. The number was 23 so after finding the address they parked in front on the street. The street was not busy as they walked to the front door and rang the bell.

"May I help you?" a woman of average height that was slightly over weight answered the door. She had wiry curly hair that was tied back, neat and was wearing a clean cream colored dress.

Audrey paused and then answered, "Yes we're here to look at the apartment."

At once the woman blurted, "Well it's not actually an apartment....it's a duplex, but you can have a look at it. Wait here. I'll get the key." She disappeared back into the building then reappeared moments later.

There were a number of duplexes next door as they walked two units down following the side walk. They stepped up to the front door and unlocked it. Everything was clean and freshly painted.

"The good thing about a duplex is that you only have one neighbor and no one above or below you," she said, it obviously being a sales pitch. "Are you working?"

"Yes," Audrey confessed. "You don't mind children?"

"No, or animals"

Audrey breathed a sigh of relief. "What do you think?" she asked looking at Kate. She began looking around.

Kate wanted Audrey to make up her own mind so she blurted, "Nice neighborhood. You know you're the one that has to live here, Audrey."

Sarcastically Audrey said, "Oh, thanks Kate. Remind me next time I need your advice. We'll let you know," Audrey exclaimed looking at the woman with sympathy and after checking the bedrooms, prepared to leave.

Audrey entered the popular drinking establishment and found it was not too busy on a cool Tuesday in November. She was not in the habit of entering bars alone but she needed to get away from the rat race even if it was only for a few minutes. She had taken the duplex and with Kate and Gene's help had moved most of her things in. She and the children were now living on their own she being sole breadwinner, although she would be receiving child support from Barry. She considered withdrawing visiting privileges.

The waitress brought a glass of house wine and then left her alone. Audrey was seated at a corner table near a window which had a clear view of the street where she could watch the busy, rush hour traffic.

"To think we've waited this long to meet again," a familiar voice broke the silence from behind her. She turned around and to her surprise was sympathetic to where the voice was coming from.

"Oh, hi Ben," she answered.

"Care to share that drink now?" he asked imposing on her time alone but she suddenly had a change of heart. She needed to be around people. Because one person screwed up doesn't make everybody bad.

"Sure"

The waitress came and Ben ordered another drink. "How's your drink?" he asked looking at Audrey.

"All right," she exclaimed. The waitress left.

"I won't bore you with my plan to rob Fort Knox. I'm afraid that's not very original," Ben explained in a moment of embarrassment.

"That's all right. I probably need human companionship," Audrey was quick to say.

"That bad eh?"

"Barry and I are no longer living together. As a matter a fact my father is preparing a law suite," Audrey explained. "I don't know why I'm telling you all this?"

"How unfortunate….," Ben was reluctant to say and after a pause exclaimed, "For you I mean."

"Well I'm afraid life goes on," Audrey philosophized.

"No matter how hard it seems," Ben warned, "Some good

will eventually over come all the suffering and eventually it will be all worth while."

Audrey paused for a moment to think about this and it brought her some satisfaction. Playing with her drink she thought, 'If only he knew the truth'.

Ben and Audrey talked for quite a while and she came to realize that he wasn't the type of person she had thought. As a matter of fact he was a sincere, compassionate individual. It was the beginning of a beautiful relationship.

Barry parked his sky blue Mazda in the driveway of his three quarter of a million dollar home. The wind was blowing the leaves around. It was an overcast day as he unlocked the twin oak doors and entered the deserted house. He wandered into the main bedroom and unlocked the drawer next to the large king sized bed. The revolver that was in the drawer was not loaded so after fetching it out he entered the huge walk in closet and grabbed the ammunition off of the top shelf.

Chapter 8

Barry climbed back into his sky blue Mazda and placed the loaded gun on the seat next to him then put the car in reverse. Unless someone had pinched him he would have thought he was living a nightmare as he left the suburban neighborhood thrusting on the accelerator. How could she humiliate him like that, taking the kids and leaving him alone? Dr. Harris wasn't charging him. Now his whole life was falling in around him. He drove to Remington Street and parked just down the street from Janice's office and then shut the car off. Barry had had two drinks after work at a local bar.

Dr. Harris was just locking up as Molly left the office and walked to her 2007 Taurus. Barry recognized her and watched her as she fidgeted for her keys unlocking the car and climbing in. 'It would be easy at gunpoint' he thought. 'It was getting dark and there were very few people around. It should go smoothly.' He waited for another five or ten minutes till the lights in the office began to go out then quickly started the car and parked it in the parking lot at the side of the office building with the engine running and waited.

The doctor didn't disappoint him not seeing him she walked past on her way to her car. 'Well it was now or never he thought.' He quickly grabbed the gun, opened the door as she fidgeted for her keys, he walked up behind her with the gun pointed.

Janice was wearing a light beige swade jacket over a casual

dark blue skirt and white blouse. She had on a low pair of matching shoes and her hair was tied back in a pony tail. Janice wasn't quick enough to get the car unlocked as Barry held the gun to her head.

"If you value your life you'll do as I say," Barry warned as he grabbed her right arm and twisted it behind her. Janice was not about to argue with a loaded gun. He made sure she could see the gun as he motioned her towards the car opening the right door and forcing her inside. She tried to struggle but he was stronger than her. He took a quick look around to make sure no one was watching then opening the driver door climbed inside next to the doctor and locked the door from the driver's side.

"What is your problem buddy?" Janice warned not thinking about her abductor with the loaded gun. Barry tucked the gun in his belt started the car and drove out of the parking lot.

Janice had to think fast. She thought it was better to use psychology in a situation like this so she stayed calm and began to sweet talk him.

"Come on Barry, you don't want to get into any more trouble. What would your family think?"

'I don't have a family' Barry thought but remained silent. Barry's lust was driving him on. Something inside him had snapped and his lust was out of control.

"You're going to be in big trouble mister." Janice panicked. "Where are we going?"

"Shut up."

Fear began to grip her. She looked out the window trying to figure out where he was taking her. She suddenly realized that unless murder was on his mind that he must be sexually motivated. The fact that he ordered her to keep quiet was like a slap in the face but she continued to think of a way to talk him out of this.

"Look Barry, if you turn this car around and let me go, I'll forget this ever happened," Janice shouted.

He pulled into the driveway of his suburban home and shut off the engine.

"Now do exactly as I say and you won't get hurt," he suggested as he opened the car door and went around to the passenger side. He opened the door and told her to get out. It was dark. It started to rain. Janice Harris considered it a life or death situation being held at gun point. 'One slip and this guy could be crazy enough to pull the trigger' she thought. 'Not only that. What would people say if she was found out, it would create a scandal.'

Barry led her through the dark house that was being lit by flashes of lightning to the master bedroom. He turned on the light. Thunder could be heard outside.

Janis was frightened as she sat on the king sized bed watching Barry's every move. She could see the gun as he pointed it in her direction.

"Do you mind not pointing that thing at me?" she demanded taking her jacket off, folding it and laying it on a chair that was beside the bed. "I'll do anything you say just don't point that thing at me."

Barry hesitated then said, "You better do as I say," and then laid the gun down on the chest of drawers. Barry was not stupid. He knew the doctor could just grab the gun and turn it against him.

"Just what is it you're going to do to me Barry?" she asked point blankly letting down her guard. It confused him slightly and again he hesitated. There was a pause then she blurted, "You have me in your power now. You can do anything you like." Another pause. Dying was not an issue now to Janice. It was all a game of wits. "You are a coward."

He suddenly clenched his fists and quickly covered his face. He began crying like a baby in an uncontrollable breakdown.

"What's the matter tough guy?" the doctor asked trying to be sympathetic.

The circumstances that made the photographs available to Barry were something that could not be predicted or controlled. The fact that he was having a nervous breakdown was the result of all this.

"Look Barry why don't we forget this little incident? You drive me home and we'll forget this ever happened." There was a pause and then "Look Barry I can help you."

He continued to sob then suddenly started coming to his senses. Janice's sympathy with Barry's situation started to take effect and then, "Your wife and family have left you haven't they?" The doctor was trying hard to save her own life but at the same time she felt it her duty to help him. She had known the Pennington's for six years and she made it her duty.

"Audrey found the photographs," Barry cried and then remained silent waiting for the doctor's response.

"I know"

"She told you?"

"Yes"

"I think this whole thing can be straightened out. We can forget about the past and get on with our lives," Janice warned him. "Think about your family, Barry."

"Audrey's sure to divorce me now," Barry exclaimed.

The doctor rubbed her hands and remained silent.

"Then she said, "I think you should think about your children. Why did you want to blackmail me? You certainly don't need the money."

Barry began to sob again. His whole body shook.

"Look Barry I think you should get therapy. I can help."

Barry walked over to the chair with the doctor's coat and grabbed it and offered her a sleeve. She accepted politely and he led her out of the bedroom and out to the car. They were silent as he drove her back to her office. Before he let her out she said, "Think about what I said Barry, and call me next week."

Audrey walked into her parents early 1900 century Spanish style home early on a Monday morning in November of 2011. The weather was overcast as a light drizzle fell, Audrey shucked her umbrella shaking off the precipitation before entering. Her father was expecting her. He was making necessary arrangements for a law suite and he needed some information from Audrey about the case.

"I'm in here sweetie," he shouted as he stirred the cream in his coffee and carried it into the front room. Audrey began taking off her coat and hanging it in the large closet at the front entrance.

"Hi Dad," she said acknowledging him as she entered the room.

She sat next to him on the sofa and looked at him.

"Aren't you going to offer me a cup?"

"Yes of course. Help your self Audrey."

Audrey got up and went into the kitchen. Carrying her coffee she re-entered the living room and sat next to Bill.

Bill began shuffling papers and explained himself, "I just want to go over a few questions before we make the final preparations."

"Ok"

Being presumptuous and taking control of his own destiny, Bill informed Audrey of the legal action he was taking. "When did you first realize Barry was unstable?"

"I suppose when I first realized there was something wrong," Audrey explained.

"Are you aware of the exact date?" he asked.

"It was around the beginning of last summer."

"Ok, July 5" Bill stated writing the date on a piece of paper. "When did you become certain there was another woman?"

"It was in October," Audrey explained.

"And when did you file for divorce?"

"November."

"Just so that you know what I'm doing I'm filing a suite for 55% ownership of the share of Pennington and Associates, on condition that Barry continues to see a psychiatrist," Bill warned with much enthusiasm and parental compassion. "I want you to manage the business. I'm sure it won't be too difficult. You'll catch on after awhile. What do you think?"

"It's a bit of a challenge. Do you plan on getting rid of Barry altogether?" Audrey's asked her curiosity taking charge.

"He'll still own 45% of the business, all he'll be doing is drawing a pay check No your job will be easy. You'll have to make sure the business is making money. You don't even have to be there." Bill explained with much enthusiasm, "Some day you'll take over ownership. Isn't that exciting sweetie?"

"Dad I think you should know that I'm not giving Barry visiting privileges of his children unless he gets psychiatric therapy," Audrey warned.

"Good."

"I think we should celebrate. How about I take you and Mom out to dinner?" Audrey managed to express herself.

"On your income, not on your life? I'll take us out," Bill warned putting his money where his mouth was.

Barry checked with Molly to see if Dr. Harris would have time to see him the following week. He didn't have an appointment but she had asked him to come. She made him wait for close to an hour before she had him come to one of the examination rooms.

"Nice to see you followed up on my advice, Barry," the doctor exclaimed.

"Yes, well I think I'll get some help," he explained somewhat disorientated.

"That's what doctors are for, right?"

It had taken all Barry's effort to bring himself there. He was reluctant to talk considering he really shouldn't be talking to anyone but his attorney. The past few days he had had a lot to think about and with the chasers he drank he was a little confused. But he had no one to turn to. Surely Audrey would want a divorce. There was a lot of legal mumble jumble going on so he was prepared to accept a soft shoulder to cry on.

"Have you been drinking since the last time I saw you?" the doctor asked.

"Yes"

She took out her prescription pad and scratched on it ripping it off and handing it to Barry. "I'm giving you something to help you sleep. Take my advice Barry and stay away from the liquor. In the mean time I'm going to refer you to see a psychiatrist. If you value your job and the visiting privileges of your children you'll get therapy," the doctor concluded.

Kate Mayberry knocked on the door of Audrey's duplex, opened the door and walked in. She knew Audrey would be home seeing her white SUV in the parking lot at the side of the building.

"It's me," she shouted, looking around for companionship upon entering. She found Annie on the floor in front of the television. "Where's your mother?" Kate asked.

A loud voice came screeching across the air waves, "I'm in here." simultaneously with the soft voice of Annie saying, "She's in the bathroom."

Kate followed the hallway down past the kitchen to the three bedrooms and bathroom. The door was open as Audrey walked out past her into the bedroom.

"Hi Kate," she exclaimed pinning her hair back with a grey beret.

"I was in the neighbor hood and thought I'd drop in and see if you were free but I guess you're not," she explained looking disappointed. "Does Annie have the day off.?"

"No she's not feeling well," Audrey explained.

"Anything I can do to help?" Kate asked.

"Well you can help me get lunch for David and Freddy," Audrey stated "They'll be home soon. Like a cup of coffee?"

"Ok"

Audrey made coffee and prepared the boy's lunch as Kate sat at the modest cedar kitchen table. Audrey had picked it up at a second hand store with Kate and Gene's help.

"When do you go in again?" Kate asked referring to her job at the gift shop.

"Not till Freddy gets home from school. He has to watch the two younger ones while I'm working. He's the man in the family now. I'm starting late today. Usually I start around three."

Kate sipped her coffee contemplating Audrey's situation. Audrey remained silent. She wanted to avoid conversation about Barry understandably Kate being in the dark about the Blackmail. Kate and Gene still thought Barry was having an affair.

"Are you going to be free from the kids soon?" Kate asked.

"What do you mean?"

"Well Barry must have visiting privileges of his kids?"

Audrey tried to avoid eye contact. She didn't want to tell her she was considering withholding visiting privileges. In her situation the less people knew of the case the better. She was not trying to protect Barry for his sake but for the sake of the children.

"I'm fighting it," was all she said.

"I hear there's a new love in your life?" Kate stated putting a different light on the situation.

"Who told you?" Audrey asked.

"You did more or less in your conversations. Don't you think it's a little soon?"

"I didn't really expect it to happen. Besides he's just a friend," Audrey explained.

"Where did you meet him?' Kate asked.

Audrey wanted to keep the conversation short so she just said, "Through Barry."

Freddy and David slammed the front door. "We're home." They came stammering into the kitchen.

"Well hello my two little munchkins," Kate exclaimed a little excited. "How have you two been? Getting used to your new home?"

They both mumbled a shy "yah". As young boys usually think they tried to avoid conversation with the opposite sex. Of course this didn't include their mother. After a short pause Kate out of boredom asked what they had learned in school.

"Geography and history," Freddy proclaimed unconscientiously protecting David's shyness.

"Really, what do you know about geography?" Kate asked the situation appealing to her curiosity.

"Well," said David, "There are 52 states in America."

"And where are we?" she asked again.

"Kentucky"

Anne and Bill Billingsby, Audrey and Ben were seated in a fancy restaurant, one recommended by Churchill Downs, overlooking a large blue grass orchard occupying a large stable and race track. It was one of Bill and Anne's favorite restaurants although they couldn't see the stables, it was about 7 PM and dark as night.

The waitress poured the wine as they looked over their menu.

"Gee, I don't know Dad, are you sure we can afford this place. Everything looks so expensive. $80, $90, $120.00, I'm afraid to order."

"Don't be afraid, remember dinners on me," Bill explained.

"What do you think, Ben, fancy enough?" Audrey looked at Ben seductively.

Audrey was dressed in her burgundy evening gown. Her hair was tucked together in a bun with the combination of a large braid she arranged with her mother's help. Anne wore a modest baby blue skirt suite with an expensive white silk blouse. The two men wore sports jackets fashioned for a formal occasion.

"I couldn't have done it better myself," Ben boasted. "Does the occasion call for such elaborate frivolities?"

Audrey looked at her parents and added, "Actually it does."

"What is the occasion a birthday or anniversary?" he asked.

"Yes I'm being promoted to general manager of a million dollar company," Audrey stated looking at her father for support.

Audrey had been keeping their little secret from Kate and Gene Mayberry but she knew it would be difficult keeping it from Ben. She also knew that soon the cat would be out of the bag anyway and she would have to tell them. She looked at Ben like a cat with a mouse in its mouth trying to hide the truth.

"Seriously?" Ben asked prying.

"Seriously"

"Well then this calls for a toast," Ben proclaimed raising his glass, "Congratulations on your new promotion. I didn't realize I was rubbing elbows with such a powerful business woman."

Bill raised his glass and added, "I'll drink to that."

Chapter 9

Bill walked into Barry's office. The Christmas season was approaching and everybody was beginning to feel in a festive mood. But Bill was not trying to stir up Christmas cheer, he was there for a reason. He drew the papers out of his briefcase and showed them to Barry.

"Sorry to ruin your Christmas old boy but business is business."

Barry briefly read the proposal and pressed the intercom. "Carol get Ed on the phone. Tell him it's important."

Bill got Barry's attention then added, "Barry I'm making Audrey my new assistant manager."

Barry looked at Bill regretfully and felt sorry he didn't go with Audrey to church when he had the chance as his life slipped further away. He thought he heard Christmas Bells but he was not really in the Christmas spirit. He got up, walked past Bill as if in a trance and continued out of his office, past his secretary's desk to the water cooler and grabbed a glass. Filling the glass he took a sip and getting a hold of himself he marched back into his office.

"Bill, I think you're being unreasonable making Audrey your new assistant manager," Barry managed to say trying to grasp the situation before things got out of hand.

"Not at all, I'm completely aware of what I'm doing, "Bill explained. "Why you don't think she's capable?"

"She's got no experience," Barry said. "All she knows how

to do is be a good housewife. She doesn't know anything about the business."

"All that's required of her is to keep inventory. You'll still manage the company."

Bill threw the proposal on Barry's desk and got up to walk out. "Read the law suite Barry," Bill concluded and left.

Jenny was sitting at Audrey's kitchen table making conversation with her older sister as Audrey was making herself something to eat. It was the first day of her new promotion. She was dressed professionally in a grey business suite and Jenny thought she looked exactly like the part. The law suite had been settled privately to protect certain party's and Audrey's divorce had gone through so she was her own boss now. She was free to do what she pleased with her life.

Christmas was a few days away and there was a slight chill in the air as a light snow was falling.

"You look sharp," she exclaimed "If I didn't know it I would be sure you are a business woman."

"Well you know what they say. What comes around goes around." Audrey was being modest but with a cynical twist.

"I still can't believe Barry could have blackmailed the doctor that way. He seemed like such a nice, family type guy," Jenny explained somewhat temperamentally.

"Well you know if there's anything I've learned from all this it's you never judge a book by its cover."

Jenny grabbed Audrey's shoulders and looked her square in the eye. "Just hope you're able to use some of that wisdom on your new job," Jenny stated. "You're going to do just fine." She gave her sister a big hug.

Barry's company was a large manufacturing warehouse in an industrial neighborhood in Louisville. His office was among a number of offices situated at the front of a new modern looking building. The warehouse was in the middle of a large parking lot. Audrey parked her clean white SUV in the parking lot and carried her new briefcase into the front entrance.

Audrey noticed everyone giving her strange looks as she continued to the inventory department. The girl at the desk was pleasant and helpful enough to get out the records for her. She spent about an hour reading the records and duplicating copies. She then spent some time in the payroll department, reading and duplicating records where the girls were also quite helpful. She thought better of disturbing Barry on her first day. 'Better leave well enough alone', she thought.

She was fortunate enough to run into Henry Peterson as she was grabbing a cup of coffee.

"Henry got a minute?" she asked.

"Hi Audrey, sure," he said. He didn't really have a choice but he and Audrey were old friends.

"Dad's made me new assistant manager, Henry, did you know?"

"Everybody knows Audrey," Henry explained.

"I saw Emily yesterday. She was getting a dress repaired when I ran into her," Audrey recollected. "We've got a lot to catch up on."

"Yes I heard what happened to you and Barry," Henry recalled. "I'm sorry Audrey." Henry looked around to see if anyone was listening then whispered, "Things haven't been the same around here."

"Yes well unfortunately life goes on doesn't it?"

"Listen if you're not doing anything some night we'd like to have you and the kids over for dinner," he said.

"I'd like that."

"Merry Christmas Audrey"

"Merry Christmas Henry"

Audrey walked into the lounge later the same day. It was a popular lounge, romantic, quiet, soft lighting, rich cliental. She was meeting Ben for a bite to eat. She entered the ladies room to freshen up before he arrived.

Ben found Audrey seated in a comfortable lounge chair at a table in a corner. "Been waiting long," he asked.

"A few minutes."

"How was your first day?"

"Great…..I guess I have my work cut out for me," Audrey warned.

"You'll catch on. Did you talk to Barry?" Ben asked.

"No"

There was a pause as silence became an issue between them they passed a few moments. The Christmas season was quickly approaching and the two of them had a lot on their minds with the shopping and all. Ben broke the silence.

"Are you giving Barry visiting privileges," Ben asked. Ben seemed to be getting along good with Audrey's children and his concern was understandable.

"I've contacted the doctor and apparently Barry has been keeping his appointments with the psychiatrist," Audrey explained. "I really haven't got any choice."

There was a pause and then another moment of silence.

"Have you thought about what you're going to do about a settlement?" Ben asked.

Audrey looked troubled. "What do you mean?"

"Well usually a woman that is going through a divorce seeks to settle for half of what she came out of the marriage with," Ben was being presumptuous.

"You know Ben. I really don't want anything out of that marriage. I think you know when something is rotten, you know what I mean? I think I've got more than half anyway," Audrey confessed.

The waitress came to take their order.

Audrey and Ben got along well together and eventually after some time he did propose to her. She accepted on condition of a long healthy engagement. The wedding took place in a Presbyterian church. All her friends and family were there enjoying the celebration. Unfortunately Barry wasn't invited.

The End

The West Coast Syndicate

Chapter 1

The halogen halo from the brightly colored lights enhanced the spirit of Christmas in the multilevel shopping center of east Vancouver as the customers travelled up and down on the escalators in Vancouver's lower east side. As the escalators reached the ground floor, a triple layer riser accumulated the remnants of Santa's workshop, with the throne seated in the center, as Santa sat entertaining to their hearts desire on what would have promised to be a special day.

"Can I sit on Santa's knee?", the young eight-year-old girl asked as she tugged on her mother's arm. She wore a red velvet party dress with a white fur coat.

Her mother saw the long line waiting to see Santa and looked annoyed as they were window shopping.

Suddenly, shots fired as people everywhere started running for cover. Shop owners began closing shop, old saint nick directed some of the children to their parents and ran to protect some of the others. The police and armed guards came running in directing the crowd to their exits.

Dedree and Julia, her eight-year-old daughter, could not get out of the exit fast enough.

About forty minutes later, Dedree and Julia were back in their upper middle-class townhouse relaying the story to her husband Henry.

"But we could have been killed" she said as Henry poured

himself a brandy and soda, as Deadree related in detail the events that had occurred at the shopping center that evening. "Relax" Henry said, "You're getting yourself worked up for nothing, it could have been worse." Deadree was in a state of shock.

"But we could have been killed", she stated again.

"Here drink this" Henry handed her the drink.

Julia sat like a little lady on the couch and began fumbling with a ribbon on one of the gifts.

Dedree saw her and screeched, "Not before Christmas". The maid came in and scooped up the little girl.

"Time for bed" she said, taking her off to her bedroom and getting her ready for bed. "Goodnight" the pretty lady said to her daughter, tucking her in after a few minutes.

Lyla the maid said "Goodnight mam" as she removed her gloves and headed for the door. Dedree caught her as she was about to descend the stairs.

"Will you be working Christmas Eve?" she asked. Lyla looked back and smiled,

"If you wish mam," "That pesty man has been calling again" Lyla continued.

Dedree looked surprised, only to keep a reason for suspicion away from Lyla. "Goodnight, Lyla."

Lyla hesitated then didn't give it a second thought and continued towards the exit.

Two plain clothed police detectives and three constables began investigating the Santa Claus that was arrested at the mall the evening in the main police station in Vancouvers east end. His name was Francis Tillbury and he claimed he knew nothing about the mall shooting. Although, the detective would not trust him as we wouldn't even trust his own mother.

"Did you hear or see anything suspicious?" the detective demanded.

"I didn't hear or see anything."

Although he tended to want to agree with the detective, he didn't see anything suspicious. "You're sure?" he said.

"I did see an oddly dressed character with thick black glasses that made his eyes stand out."

"Christmas is here, but we have got all night. Tell us what we want to know, or we'll be here 'till then anyway" said the plain clothed detective. The plain clothed detective took his sports jacket off and threw it on the chair. He wore a white short sleeve shirt and casual slacks.

Mr. Tillbury took off the beard and Santa's cap and loosened his collar as the heat in the room, as well as stale cigarette smoke made the air heavy.

"Well, I did see one suspicious looking character" Francis argued, deciding to agree with them and maybe he'd get out sooner.

"What did he look like?" they asked.

"He was a strange looking character, sort of oddly dressed. You couldn't miss him because he wore large glasses that made his eyes look big."

"Ok, let him go" the detective said, "We've got nothing on him. Just don't leave town." Francis Tillbury walked out of the station. It was dark and a light snow was falling. He stopped at a booth to make a phone call.

"It's all clear," he said to someone on the other end of the line.

"Ok" they said.

It was Wednesday December 19th, 3:30pm, the taxi destination was 250 Parkside Lane. Deadree sat in the backseat relieved that their Christmas shopping was over for another season. She fumbled with a 20-dollar bill as the cab pulled onto Parkside Lane. She handed the bill to the driver and was surprised when the rear door opened, and a hand greeted them to pull her out. She was confused and misunderstood when she saw that it was the man that was pushing his luck trying hard to court her.

"What is it you want?" she demanded, not giving him an opening to try a subtle approach.

"I just want to make sure you and your parcels get safely to the front door" he answered rather abruptly, trying to grab some of the parcels from her hand.

She let him help her to the door and told him to put the parcels on the chair in the lobby. She then struggled with her keys and scrambled to open the door. As she grabbed the rest of her parcels and proceeded into the building, he tried to follow, but she stopped him abruptly stating "I am married."

Although for a middle-aged woman to be offered courtship by a young man was a compliment, deep down she liked the idea and with that she closed the door in his face and walked away.

Two detectives Matthew Bailey and Richard Prichard were doing a statement on Thursday, December 20th instead of enjoying what for most people would be a holiday.

Down the street from the Westview apartments, they sat in an unmarked car, each nursing a lukewarm coffee to keep them awake.

It was 8:00pm. They were looking for suspicious characters coming to or from the high-rise apartment.

A contact known only as Casey was collecting himself in his 12th story penthouse apartment.

He threw on a pair of trousers as the middle-aged prostitute ran her hand over the front of her skirt to clear the wrinkles. She wore a black leopard colored skirt with matching pantyhose. Grabbing her jacket she asked Casey,

"You'll have it ready this week?"

Casey was a heavy-set man dispositioning himself to be an Elvis look alike.

"Yes" he assured her.

Just then the phone rang, and the girl let herself out.

"Yah," Casey answered "Yah that's me. Ok I'll get right on it" and with that he hung up the phone. He quickly dialed a contact.

"It's me," he said. "Get over here quick."

Twenty minutes later a man known as Striker showed up.

"Somebody ratted," he warned as Striker threw his jacket in the closet.

"It doesn't pay to be a rat" Casey explained.

Two hours later Matt and Rick were still watching as they noticed a notorious group of criminals known to the underworld as lynchpins.

Another lynchpin knocked on Casey's apartment door. It was about 10:00pm. Patrick Gemerick, known as Lefty, looked around as he entered hesitating at a discarded scarf that the hooker had previously forgotten, picked it up, and examined it frightfully as if it were a disease then dropped it.

He had another look around hesitating then warned Casey,

"We pay you a lot of money to run this candy factory and we expect to obtain a lucrative return, physically speaking of course" as he looked around again.

"The fact that private information has leaked out only means that we must pull together as a team and eliminate the instigator, and that means we need your help, Casey. We know we can use you to help find the rat, right?"

With that said, he and his boys let themselves out.

Matt and Rick noticed the hooker leave who they immediately recognized and then noticed the crime syndicate boss leave about 10:00pm. After that Matt and Rick called it a night. They hadn't noticed the minor contact Striker leave earlier nor had recognized him as a known criminal.

He was a minor contact in a long line of minor contacts in a criminal racket that ran this illegal drug trafficking region that used Casey as a key lynchpin.

The international port of Vancouver was a key local point in what was known as a harbor for an international drug trafficking ring. It was a contact point to all corners of the globe, starting from Eastern Asia to Central and Middle Europe, and North and South America.

It was December 21st at a posh dinner club in Surry, a suburb of Vancouver.

Patrick (Lefty) Gemerick checked the dinner list at the front desk then checked his watch. Only friends and family were invited, and no one would be permitted past the front door. He noticed his daughter Maria talking with a young hood named Ron.

One of his bodyguards nodded towards as he walked over and introduced himself. He gave his daughter Marie a stern look then asked him what he wanted.

"I just wanted to meet your daughter" he said,

"An introduction" Lefty said, "that's as far as it goes".

He then looked again sternly at Marie, then walked away.

"Oh Daddy," she relented softly.

Then Lefty walked back to the bodyguard, whispered something in his ear, then walked away. The bodyguard then began moving towards the door and began checking the other guests.

The morning after the 21st, the young hood known as

Ron, was discovered. His remains washed up on the beach of English Bay.

The authorities said he was a member of a family of one of the minor contacts said to be employed by "Lefty" Gemerick.

Father Francis lit the Christmas candle as Margaret the organ player began playing Christmas carols one half hour before the Christmas Eve service at St. Alfreds church in Vancouvers lower east side, one block from West View apartments.

One half hour later only a few people filled the pews.

St. Alfreds church was not in the habit of getting church members to come to church. Suddenly a thin girl and her boyfriend walked in.

"Merry Christmas" father proclaimed.

"Merry Christmas" the girl said.

"You're new here, aren't you?" the priest asked, remaining "festive" even though he was disappointed at the turnout.

The neighborhood had a lot of alcoholics and drug addicts.

"A recovering speed freak, Father" she said. "Merry Christmas Father" extending her hand to greet him.

After the service the priest offered to help the young girl as she headed for the door.

"I'm starting a soup kitchen Tuesday and Thursday of each week in the new year, you're welcome to come" he said, "Merry Christmas".

Chapter 2

Friday the 28th of December, 9:30am, the tension was strong at police headquarters in the east side as Matt and Rick sat in Matthew's office, one detective sitting on a desk, legs hanging loosely and the other standing with one elbow leaning on his knee on his office chair. They were both waiting patiently for the chief to brief them on what, if any, was the result of the investigation so far.

"Come in here you two" he shouted through an open door before the two detectives crossed the hall to the chief's office.

Matt and Rick knew this briefing to be of some importance, it being the headquarters desire to rid the chief of crime and drug use that was going on not to mention the illegal trafficking that was occurring under their noses. Vancouver was a tourist town, and it didn't need the reputation as a haven for criminals.

"We have a couple of strong leads," the chief informed them, reading a piece of paper then looking at the rest of it, not looking at the other two officers.

"It seems you two were looking in the right place on the 20th of December" he stammered.

"A contact in the apartment is known to be a reliable key to buying an addicts supply of candy" he concluded.

The two men's reactions were a mix of surprise and relief.

"Rick, I'll put you in charge of that… and Matt, I want

221

you to look up this name, Francis Tillbury" the chief said. "He was there for the mall shooting and is a reliable suspect."

"Any questions?" the chief said. "Good, you start today."

Matthew parked his 1983 Plymouth Reliant just west of Vancouver's China town on a secluded side street and walked over to the busy marketplace. He walked down the main strip and began window shopping. He stopped and paid a street vendor 25 cents for an apple and continued walking, following the address to a secluded side door and found the number.

It said "Back in 15 minutes" so he continued shopping. Fifteen minutes later he tried the address again. Matthew knocked on the door, no answer. He tried the door, it was open.

He walked and looked around. In the main room, Francis was face down on the floor. He checked his pulse. No vital signs.

25 minutes later the place was swarming with police officers, reporters, and paramedics.

"Any clues to his death?' the chief asked.

"Your guess is as good as mine" Matt responded, hesitating, "I guess we'll have to wait for the coroner tests."

One officer walked up reporting, "No frame, no sign of a struggle", he said, "just a clean bullet through the heart."

"Makes it difficult to find clues", the chief said.

That evening Rick Prichard sat out in the front of the penthouse complex on Westview Apartments looking for any suspicious characters.

He noticed one he had seen enter before but did not recognize him from previous arrests. He followed him to an address locally and copied down the street name and numbers. The next day was Sunday.

Monday morning at police headquarters, Richard and Matt used the computer to scan the criminal records to match the address Rick had found after following the suspect.

Modern technology provided information to match a criminal's address or place of residence to his name once a conviction was placed. As luck would have it, they found the suspects name as Albert Leopold, nicknamed "Striker" to his friends.

Leopold had one minor conviction of marijuana procession and worked part time at an off-track gambling club, as a clerk in Eastern Surrey.

The chief approached congratulating the two detectives.

"Well, it appears there was no signs of foul play on Francis Tillbury. I think that he was involved in the mall shootings, but we have no real evidence to prove it. What have you two got?"

"Albert Leopold known as Striker" Richard explained, "Minor convictions of drug procession. Nothing too serious" he concluded.

"We're going to need more evidence" the chief responded.

That evening Matt and Rick sat crouched low in his 1983 Plymouth Reliant a block from the town house on Parkside Lane on a secluded side street.

The next morning Rick slapped Matt to wake him as he noticed Striker waiting out front and looking at his watch.

Soon Deadree and Julia came out to the bus stop and were approached by Striker.

"What is it you want?" she asked after a moment of frustration. She had obviously noticed the man observing them.

"I was hoping we could go for a coffee sometime," he asked. "In the meantime, let me offer you a ride in my car" he said pointing to his souped-up brown Ford Malibu.

She was running a little late, and Deadree wanted to avoid Julia's suspicion, so she said yes.

Matt and Rich had been following up leads, but it was too soon to make any arrests, this time they would need more evidence.

Father Francis folded his prayer mantle and stored it in a drawer. He was taking care of a little business this Tuesday even though from here on in he would be holding his soup kitchen. After the holiday, he was keeping Tuesday and Thursday open. He was determined it was Gods will to clean up the neighborhood.

Today he was volunteering his services in a drug rehabilitation center. This would be a start. In his white collar and everyday street clothes he left his meager lodgings at St. Alfred's church and began walking towards the rehabilitation center on East Hastings Street.

It had been raining earlier but was now drizzle. The girls at the front desk asked if he needed assistance.

"I want to volunteer my services," he said, the girl noticing his white collar.

"Just a moment," she replied, going to report to her superior.

Michael Doughally interviewed him in another room.

"What can I do for you?" he asked.

"I want to volunteer my services," he explained, then told him of his times he'd be available.

Michael asked him if he had experience.

"I can learn" the priest said.

"How about one day a week to start" Michael asked. He then went to a bookshelf and handed him a how-to counselling handbook.

"This will cover most of the details" he said.

Father Francis left thinking "finally I'm making a step in the right direction, now maybe we can finally clean up this neighborhood from illegal drug use."

Matthew Bailey had a few hours off and was checking out the men's clothing at the London Fog on Grandville Square.

Matthew was 5'10" tall, medium build, with dark brown hair and brown eyes. He had a full head of hair that was neatly combed. He wore a light blue jacket, grey slacks, and deer skin loafers.

As he was checking out the clothing, he noticed out of the corner of his eye a popular criminal figure of the underworld.

He had a full head of messy hair, was clean shaven, wore a Calgary Flames jacket, and greenish-blue pants.

He watched as they made a money exchange possibly dealing drugs, and then decided to follow him.

He followed for a while and when he went to his car, Matt was lucky enough to have parked nearby. He followed them to West Vancouver and watched as he went into a dingy bar.

"Scotch single malt" Matt told the bartender.

He then noticed the dealer sitting at a table with two other men where they again exchanged money. They left and went to the back of a white SUV. Matt paid for his drink and left.

He noticed the back of the SUV had 3 or 4 bags that looked like groceries but were probably narcotics. They all climbed into the SUV, so Matt followed them.

After a few moments the realized he was following them and there was a bit of a chase.

West Vancouver is located on a narrow Ridge on the south side of a small mountain so it would be hard with his small vehicle to keep up the chase. The street was tightly laid out and he soon lost them.

Rick Prichard followed the brown Ford Malibu to 250 Parkside Lane on Saturday. He parked down a secluded side street and kept low as he watched.

Striker met Deadree at the front door.

Deadree was an average height 5'6", shoulder length dusty blonde hair, smartly dressed, middle aged lady. She was seemingly attractive, and Striker was a bit of a ladies' man, and was attracted to most women.

Striker had a long trench coat and wore his hair neatly combed.

He led Deadree to his car where they drove to a coffee shop on English Bay. They took a seat overlooking the water.

Richard decided to take a seat nearby to eavesdrop.

"Well now that you've got me out for a coffee, who are you?" she asked him after they sat down.

"A lucky guy" he said, "I work at an off-track betting facility in Surry."

"Oh," she paused. She had a sip of her coffee. "What makes you think I'd be interested" she asked again.

"Oh, dunno" he said, "Just a hunch."

"I'd heard some silly rumor that maybe you're an ex-con?" Richards ears perked up.

"Well, I have been convicted of marijuana possession" he told her.

"Oh," she looked startled and confused.

"Yeh, there you go, I can never pick the right man" she explained, feeling a little nervous.

The soup kitchen was scheduled to open the following Tuesday at 11:30 at St. Alfreds Church.

Father Francis had a small turn out.

The young girl and her boyfriend that attended the Christmas Eve service came for dinner.

"I'm Martha and this is Dan," she explained.

"Yes, you're the girl that said she was an ex-speed addict," Father Francis asked.

"Yes," she confirmed.

"Do you have a place to live?" he asked.

"Yes, but I need groceries" Martha explained, "The pension I get is not always enough."

"We'll see what we can do for you" the priest said.

It was a start. The soup kitchen was a success. Soon they would me coming in off the streets. Maybe they would even get a decent Sunday morning service.

Matt had a lead about a warehouse on the east side near Burrard Inlet. He decided to check it out.

He would remain hidden on a secluded side street and watch who came and went, but first he wanted to see what was inside.

The warehouse was two stories high and there were windows high on the second level. He found a discarded painter's ladder and climbed it that night and looked inside. A box van was being loaded. The contents were bags of white flour. What he did notice after observing for a few minutes was that they were lacing the contents with white powder that was labelled 'sugar'.

"Could be cocaine or heroin" he thought.

He continued his stakeout. His suspicion was confirmed when Matt noticed the man in the Calgary flames jacket enter the warehouse. He knew he was onto something.

It was an overcast morning about a week and a half later. Matt saw the box van leave the warehouse. He followed it to Vancouver International airport and what surprised him was that instead of entering arrivals they entered the freight loading at departures.

At the security gate they asked for dispatch papers, and to Matts surprise they were cleared. The van parked in a loading platform and waited.

Matt parked his vehicle and showed the guard his badge. Matt had to explain that he was investigating a case but was unable to share details. Due to security, Matt was forced to explain himself. The two men weren't at all nervous as they sat and waited for clearance to load their van onto the freight plane to a third world country.

They had two AK-47s strapped behind their front seats and were confident there would be no trouble.

The air traffic controllers waived the driver over. He cleared his papers and was told to begin loading.

As they loaded the bags onto the wagon the two men observed out of the corner of their eye, the K-9 unit checking their load for narcotics. The dogs were trained to sniff out drugs. To Matthews surprise they didn't find any. The two men were relieved as they continued to unload. It was unusual that they were given clearance to unload, but to Matts surprise they were.

Father Francis walked to the rehabilitation drop-in center on east Vancouvers East Hastings Ave.

Mike Dougherty greeted him warmly.

Mike was a burly man in his mid-forties. He had red hair that hadn't seen a comb for 2 or 3 hours. He had a hint of freckles and wore a heavy plaid blue-red checkered cotton shirt and casual greenish-blue slacks.

"So, the handbook didn't scare you away?" he asked.

"No," he paused.

"I think I know what I'm getting into."

"Good, can you work Friday night?"

Father Francis replied "Is that every Friday?"

"Yes"

What to the priest was a faith check, was to the Vancouvers east side a transfusion that would help inoculate the disease the priest thought of drug addiction and crime.

Father Francis wore a dark black suite and a white collar, was exceedingly tall and was thinly built. His hair was still streaked black, but he was prematurely grey with streaks of grey mixed in his hair that was always well kept. He was clean shaven and had a saintly demeaning complexion that gave people the comfort they needed to socialize.

Matt was certain there were drugs in the box van, and he told the chief so. The fright plane was probably flying to Africa and would be making a stopover in Miami for fuel.

It was time to begin making arrests.

Rick laid low in his 1992 Dodge Viper watching Striker as he led Dedree to his brown Ford Malibu on Tuesday afternoon in late February.

They drove to a public school a few minutes away just about time enough to pick up Julia, Dedrees 8-year-old daughter.

It was a cloudy day; the sun was trying to break through but nonetheless was overcast. They waited as the school bell rang, the children began to run out of the school.

Dedree got out of the car and noticed it had begun to rain, as distant sound of the thunder could be heard in the nearby hills.

Julia soon came running with her backpack flying high in the air shouting "Mommy".

Striker got out of the vehicle and raised a hand warning

them that he had heard thunder. Rick suddenly approached and apprehended Striker. "You're under arrest, what you say can and will be used against you in a court of law" Rick said, holding up his badge.

He then thew the handcuffs on him.

Dedree looked stunned. "Can you find a way home mame?" he asked.

"Yes" she said, holding Julia's hand.

Chapter 3

Marie Gemerick finished her shower and threw on a pair of blue slacks and a bright red top and threw herself down to breakfast.

She had a full day ahead of her, having to pick up 7 children and bring them to her daycare center before 9:00am.

"Well, what's on the agenda for today?" her mother asked, placing a bowl of cheerios and two pieces of toast in front of her. She made sure Marie ate a good breakfast.

"I have to pick up 7 children before going to work" she warned her mother proudly. She had recently acquired the daycare center after graduating from a childcare program at the local college and entering the business. She loved children and it was a business she was proud to be in.

Marie was 5'6" tall, a walking beauty. She had brownish-red hair, green eyes and a slim, athletic build. She picked up her red leather purse and heavy light blue winter coat and shouted "Goodbye mom, wish me luck" as she crossed the newly polished hardwood hallway floor and proceeded to the large, varnished twin oak door of her father's 2.5-million-dollar home.

She knew of her father's illegal criminal business. The fact that her friend who had taken an interest in her at the Christmas part and suddenly disappeared had only confirmed her suspicions more, but only gave her all the more reason to "make good" of her life and career working with young children.

Matt had found a lead of the warehouse by following the drug dealer and learning of his where abouts. He then learned crucial information about the suspect that led him to the warehouse.

There was a lead from the man with the Calgary flames jacket to a dealer living in a remote are in West Vancouver, who had been overheard planning another drug deal.

Matt decided to investigate.

He decided this time he would arrest the suspect in the illegal act which means he would have to catch him exchanging money or caught with the drugs on him.

After Albert Leopold, "Striker" was arrested, they found little evidence to convict him, so they had to let him go. This time Matt wanted to make sure of the arrest.

He had stronger evidence as it turns out, and they knew that if he was guilty, it would in turn lead him to other convictions and arrests.

Matt was smart enough to copy the license plate number down when he followed the two vehicles. Once you have the license plate numbers you do a criminal check and can then match the names and possible addresses to the phone or the address. Matt would follow the suspect by doing an undercover check.

As much as Matt believed there were drugs planted on that cargo plane bound for a third world country, he had to be fairly certain that there had been drugs if he was going to follow the plane to Miami where there could be a rendezvous and fuel check. But at least he could gain a list of possible mafia contacts working undercover in the key city to other possible key points in the U.S.

The plan was the Richard Prichard along with three other detectives would surprise the dealer known as "Casey" at the penthouse on Westview apartments in East Vancouver with a 12-gauge shotgun intending to make an arrest.

The west coast was threatening spring, the blossoms peeking through, and the cool weather moving out to lift the rain and bring in more sunshine.

The number of residents in the building, taking the elevator to the 12th floor were scarce as the detectives made themselves ready, properly positioning themselves around the apartment door.

They waited in silence for the right signal from Richard, then burst into the apartment, kicking open the main door.

To their surprise it was unlocked. Someone had been there sooner than them as they heard no movement or stir from anyone in the home.

Casey lay sprawled across a chair looking like he has attempted to make an escape, with a 45 slug in the chest. The contents of the apartment had been sprawled everywhere as if someone had been looking for drugs.

25 minutes later, paramedics, police officers, and reporters scrambled to get an explanation of what had happened.

It was almost two o'clock one Thursday afternoon in early spring as Father Francis turned off the hot plate that was keeping the lunch warm at the soup kitchen at St. Alfred's Church and sat down next to Martha and Dan to briefly socialize.

"Did you get some financial support from where I sent you?" he asked, folding the dish towel and placing it on his knee.

"Yes" Martha assured him, pushing herself away from the table and making herself comfortable next to Dan.

"Is it my imagination or are you gaining weight?" the priest asked.

"Yes I am."

"I'm volunteering as a drug counselor at the drop-in center on East Hastings" the priest informed her.

"Oh"

"If there is anything you two ever need you let me know" he assured her again.

Matt compared the license plate number of the white SUV he followed to West Vancouver with a criminal check with the number and address of the van he followed to the airport and found that the residence of the SUV was indeed correct.

On a bright sunny spring day, he steaked out the residence and followed the white SUV to the B.C ferry that went to Vancouver Island and bought a one-way ticket.

Instead of driving on the ferry he decided not to lose sight of the suspect, he followed him to the car port, and he remained incognito.

It's a 3-hour ferry ride to Vancouver Island and most of the passengers were tourists. Matt decided not to lose him. To his horror about 1.5 hours into the ride he followed him to a public washroom and watched him silently as he sold $800 worth of heroin to an eight-year-old girl.

Matt became furious at the horror and had to decide whether to follow the pusher or arrest the girl. If he arrested the girl, he would lose the suspect, so he decided on the latter.

The ferry docked in Nanaimo and as it made the preparation, Matt watched as the dealer climbed into his white SUV and prepared to leave.

As the ferry was about to unload, Matt quickly displayed

his badge and left a passenger standing in the carport without his vehicle.

"Good morning Marie, I thought I'd like to talk to you this morning. Do you know what time it is?" the medium built young, and attractive, conservatively dressed, middle-aged man asked in an overly submissive, pleasant voice.

"Yes, I have the cheque all filled out, Arthur," Marie assured him.

Marie entered her office in the moderate sized childcare facility she rented from him and grasped the cheque. Before she reached her office Arthur stopped her.

"Some of your fathers' employees already stopped by and paid for the first month. Here is a receipt," he added.

As Arthur left her alone, she looked at him in disbelief. She was shocked.

Matt looked at the gas gauge and was relieved that it was full as he threw the ten-year-old Acura in gear and made a gargantuan effort to follow the white SUV. It would take all his effort not to lose the suspect. Matt followed the SUV continuously until it reached the edge of town. There was just a chance that the suspect didn't have any drugs on him which meant he'd need to patiently wait until he made a proper arrest. It began to boil his blood how an event like this could happen.

It took all he could muster to pull himself together.

Suddenly the van stopped.

The driver went up to a local residence but there was no number or addresses. He then climbed back into his vehicle and pulled into a restaurant down the street.

Matt decided to investigate.

On the front door of the residence, it said "Reverend T.G. Cobbs."

Matt thought it was odd but decided to enter the restaurant anyways. He remained inconspicuous.

After he ordered some food, the man was gone. He then asked the waitress if she knew him.

"He's a friend of the reverend" she warned.

Matt decided he would make the arrest anyway after he returned the Acura to its rightful owner.

"Lefty" alias Patrick Gemerick forced his way into Marie's daycare center the next day after all the children had left to their native habitats.

"How's my little girl today?" he said to Marie in a friendly father-daughter sort of way.

"What do you want" she barked as she showed in her own feminine way she would not be influenced in any way by his affections.

"Now is that some way to talk to someone who has just paid your first month's rent and guaranteed you a steady job?" he scoffed.

"I'm quite capable of paying my own rent and keeping a job" she scoffed.

"Ah common Marie," he insisted, "haven't I brought you up and helped you into this world?"

There was no one else in the room and she decided to say what she liked.

"I'm old enough to take care of myself, I don't need your help anymore" she insisted.

"Well, if that's the way you want it" he warned.

He pointed his finger at her hesitating.

"But you make sure you pay the rent" then he stormed out.

Marie was upset after he stormed out. She knew that was not going to be the end of it.

Father Francis folded the prayer mantle neatly and placed it into the drawer. He then gathered up himself and began his walk. It was about one and a half miles to the rehabilitation center on East Hastings. It would give him time to think.

He had studied the handbook for drug counselling, but he was new at this. It was his first night counselling and he was slightly nervous.

It was April 15th and the blossoms had come and gone leaving a clean, fresh scent in the air as a light rain usually does. Mike Dougherty was there to meet him; it was just before 7:00 PM.

"There's nothing to work about, there's a 24-hour hotline you can call if you run into any problems" he said.

The priest poured himself a coffee as he found himself at last alone.

It was mostly routine for about an hour.

Young kids strung out on some type of drug they needed counselling about and the occasional heroin addict with their methadone substitute administered.

Father Francis did look for opportunities to share Jesus Christ with them.

At the end of the night, he felt he was finally accomplishing something useful towards ridding the city of Vancouver of the epidemic.

Chapter 4

After the Vancouver police arrested the guilty suspects involved with the SUV, a criminal that was by the name of David Lester, Matt decided that a trip to Miami might not be such a bad idea. If he could determine who, how, and what was being shipped he might get enough of this illegal drug trafficking and killing off his contacts.

For Marie Gemerick, the fact that one of the children's parents took the time to communicate other than the normal routine of just dropping off their child and leaving was like receiving something nice as a gift.

"I thought I would help tomorrow by picking up a few of the children and bring them in" she stammered trying to be helpful as well as an all-around nice person.

"Yeah, that would be ok" she answered.

Marie was not her usual self this morning after having it out with her father the day before. The fact that the parent of one of the children noticed it and commented.

"Anything the matter Marie?" she asked hesitating.

"I'm just having a moment about my father, that's all" she confessed, "He seems to think he can run me like one of his bully boys, if he thinks that he's crazy", she reasoned with herself suddenly.

"Thank you" Marie said, "Coffee?"

Richard had some explaining to do back in police headquarters reporting that Casey took a slug to the chest and seeing that someone had already beat him to it. But let the dead bury the dead so to speak. Chances are if somebody wanted Casey dead, Richard wouldn't have got to him in time anyway.

Rick had a lead on an opium den on Grainville street and decided he would check it out. He found the address and learned that the only hours of operation were after 8:00 PM. He knew that he could bust them if he had to but that was not what he wanted. He wasn't interested in a simple marijuana possession charge; he was more interested in the white stuff. He was more interested in the big drug dealers who operated at the top.

The first night was a Saturday and he had to dress the part. He had an old tie-dye t-shirt and picked up a pair of bell bottoms. Then he just threw on an old pair of running shoes. It was busy as he walked in, he tried to find a socially "hip" crowd. He knew sooner or later he'd stumble on to a lead, it was just that he didn't want to find he needed to "indulge". The rooms were fairly ventilated, but he knew from experiencing in his younger days that just breathing the air would take all his concentration to keep a sound level of thinking.

Martha and Dan were walking into the soup kitchen one Thursday morning looking for a warm meal. The kitchen was becoming a success lately. Word of mouth had been working and more and more of the poor local residents were showing up for a free meal. As they ate their lunch Martha asked Father Francis,

"How did your first night of volunteer work go?"

"Very well," he said.

"Did you run into any difficulty?" she asked.

"Not much, I just tell them about the Lord" he said.

"You volunteer?" someone asked, "Where?"

"The drug rehabilitation center on East Hastings."

"You're not afraid of tough ex drug addicts?" the young, disoriented teenager asked.

"I have the Lord on my side," Father Francis added, "they're just people".

It was Monday evening when Richard walked into the opium den on Grainville Street in downtown Vancouver. He hadn't noticed any characters that could have been working for the syndicate. Suddenly in walked three or four suspicious looking characters that in Richard's opinion stood out. He noticed four suspicious characters that sat down and exchanged some money. Then he noticed a suspicious looking package that he carried out onto the boulevard. Richard reached inside his tie-dye shirt and checked his shoulder strap for his snub nosed 38 and then went out onto the boulevard.

One of the suspects wore a bright red spring jacket, the other a navy blue. There was one girl light blonde. The other was dressed casually but had shoulder length brown hair. The two others had a full head of light brown hair. He was determined not to follow too close because if he was discovered following it would break his cover.

Marie and her business partner Sylvia were having lunch in a local restaurant on a rainy Tuesday in April, one and a half months after they opened business together.

"I think it's kind of creepy that he doesn't allow you to pay your own rent," Sylvia started the conversation by saying.

"No, it was just the first month, and I didn't allow him to pay it" Marie answered.

"But don't you think it's kind of creepy having a father who is a gangster?" she asked.

"Sure, but if he thinks he's going to run my life he's sadly mistaken."

"Don't you think it was time to be on your own anyway?" Sylvia asked.

After lunch they both agreed that they would find Marie a suitable apartment.

"Yes, would you help me look for an apartment?"

Sylvia paused, "Yes" she exclaimed.

She would go no further from taking handouts from anyone else, she would run her own life. Sylvia said, "From now on I think it's something you should do."

Striker parked his 1989 Ford Malibu in front of the townhouse at 230 Parkside Lane. He had noticed Dedree and Julia waiting out front and decided it was time to set things right between them. There was a slight drizzle on this Monday morning and was Dedrees normal routine of taking Julia to school. Striker tried to look pleasant as he approached. Dedree wanted to crawl into the nearest crack and hide. She looked perturbed.

"I've got nothing to say to you, if that's what you think?" she warned.

"I'm sorry, Dedree, they didn't have any evidence when they arrested me. I didn't do anything" he confessed to her.

She looked confused, then angry.

"Are you in trouble with the law?" she asked.

"No"

"Well like I said I'm not really sure I know how to pick good guys when it comes to a relationship anyway."

"Can I see you again?" he asked.

She looked at him then looked down, then up.

"She's not getting any younger you know," she thought, in a fit of desperation.

"I'll see you later" Striker added, then quickly left.

Richard followed the possible suspects to a secluded side street off Grainville Avenue where they parked their temporary vehicle. He tried to remain inconspicuous as much as possible. Suddenly he noticed an armed uniformed policeman was writing them a ticket for a parking violation. When the suspects approached, he asked for their license and registration. It was a 1994 Buick and two of the owners began to give themselves up but the guy in the red jacket and the blonde girl began to run. The constable was alone, so Richard ran up to help. They apprehended the two suspects while the constable called for backup. Soon sirens could be heard while Richard began chasing the guy and his girlfriend. He ran back to Granville Street but lost their trail. He knew he had done a good day's work though because he had two of the suspects in custody. They would not only be charged with possession of a stolen vehicle but because he saw them laundering money, he would arrest them with mischief as well. Not only that, but now Richard had a place to go and stretch his legs as well as look for other leads.

After the arrest of David Lester and dealers in West Vancouver, Matt became obsessed with tracking the case involving the syndicate and all the major players involved. To him it was necessary, the fact that an eight-year-old girl and a reverend ministers son made him all the more interested in a "major sting" operation. Even if it meant he'd have to follow them to Miami or Timbuktu or any other place in order to bust them. They knew most of the minor players with their arrest and most of the lynchpins. It would be easy to look up the major drug lords by organizing "stings". Matt was just not sure he could do it by himself.

The chief was making all the necessary arrangements for the trip to Miami, he just wanted to make sure it was necessary. If he could, he would crack some of the major lords here in Vancouver first. Patrick Gemerick had a lot of minor players working under him that used to keep a low profile. In reality no one knew who he was because he had so many lynchpins to rely on. When a major drug lord came to visit, he'd pick them up in a limousine at the airport in Richmond and then take them to a comfortable establishment like the "off track" gambling house in Surry. They would enjoy a comfortable meal and pass the time unnoticed, had his ¾ million-dollar home and his limousine paid for through drug money.

Father Francis entered the rehabilitation center at 6:30 PM on a Friday night in April. The blossoms had come and went, and it was raining slightly. The center was getting a little busier now that daylight savings had arrived. He approached the nighttime volunteer working as a caretaker to let him know he would be working. Joel took him to his office.

"Can I get you a coffee?" he asked.

"Yes, thank you," the priest confirmed to him.

Joel then went about tidying up and watching over the place. They had a pool table and a coffee pot so the members could socialize. About 8:00 PM a middle-aged girl about 36 came in and needed counselling. She was average height, brown hair that looked like it was colored by hand. Her eyes were tired looking, set in deep cavernous looking sockets. She didn't have much color and appeared sickly looking. Her name was Margaret.

"I've been threatened by pushers that give drugs," she confessed weakly, "they won't leave me alone."

Father Francis offered her a bit of spiritual advice then said that he would get involved.

"I'm going to get some people to help" he said. "These criminals can't continue to get away with this."

He comforted her some more then sent her home. He then called the police and said he wanted something done.

Chapter 5

Matt found he had a little unfinished business to attend to after checking into police headquarters. Father Francis wanted something done about Margaret, the girl who had a drug pusher pushing free drugs onto her. Matt decided an animal like that should not get away with it. That along with the 8-year-old heroin addicts. His trip to Miami would have to be postponed for the time being. He could not live with that unless he proved to himself that he had done all he could.

Striker approached Dedree and Julia about a week later and Dedree finally agreed to meet with him for another coffee on her quiet time when Julia was in school. Striker picked Dedree up at 1:30 PM the following day and they went to a secluded shop on Davis Avenue in the greater downtown area. Dedree made it clear that Striker was going to be honest between them otherwise there would be no further meetings. Parked in a shaded parking area in Stanley Park, Striker and Dedree exchanged kisses together until Dedree pushed him off and assumed a dignified disposition then explained it was time to go.

Matt knew the pushers name from what Margaret told Father Francis, and the names of the dealers involved. It was a lead Matt could go on. In the meantime, Richard could strengthen his involvement. They interrogated the suspects already arrested but the king pins in control at the top of the ladder was a greater threat than just doing time for pushing drugs as long as it wasn't murder. Matt and Rick got a lead about a king pin, and they decided to do something about it. It was in a bachelor home on the edge of city limits. There were only a few neighbors, it being a rural district, and at first glance it was quite a masculine establishment.

The door wasn't locked, and it appeared that someone had left it ajar, it being deserted. Whoever had come in had murdered the owner and two of his male guests. There was quite the evidence of struggle because there was furniture and debris scattered everywhere. The name Patrick Gemerick was found with a phone number, who was known to be a gangster and racketeer. It appeared as if they soon would have a list of all the kingpins involved. It would just be a matter of rounding them up.

Patrick Gemerick "Lefty" pulled up to Vancouvers international airport, in Richmond, in a limousine he used as his own private vehicle. He was picking up some syndicate racketeers coming in from other parts of the country. After their arrival he would take them so Surry, a Vancouver suburb, where he would serve them a comfortable dinner at the off-track betting club. As they got underway the driver checked the rearview mirror to see if they were being followed.

When they arrived in Surry there was two or three police cruisers parked in the vicinity. Later there was entertainment and a room at a secluded nightclub (Club 67) and you could be sure there would be mixed company, enough to give them a good time. It was comforting to "Lefty" Gemerick to know that his dealers and lynchpins would not uncover his whereabouts, knowing that if they were caught, they wouldn't live long on the "outside" anyway.

Maude Gemerick was a large slightly overweight, muscular looking woman. She had dry, tired, masculine looking features with long void of features that Lefty wouldn't be interested in sexually. Marie acknowledged good morning to her as she sat down to her breakfast of cold cereal and brown toast. She had to hurry as the business had to be up and running by 9:00 AM.

"I'm going to look at an apartment today, Mama," she confessed modestly trying to be as polite about it as possible.

"Why what's wrong with living here?" Maude demanded, looking concerned.

"I don't want to live here anymore, I just want to be on my own," she protested with annoyance.

"Your father isn't going to like it" Maude stated.

"I don't care," Marie confessed, "I don't want him running my life anymore."

She took a few more bites, and then left for work.

An hour later she and Sylvia were talking quietly over a cup of coffee.

"We'll go see that apartment today, eh?" she warned Sylvia expectantly.

"I'd like to move in before the end of the month" she stated.

"Kind of sudden, isn't it?"

"I don't care, I just want to get out of his life, that's all" Marie stated.

There was a knock on the door.

"Marie Gemerick?" the police officer asked.

"That's me," she told him.

"Is your father Patrick Gemerick?" he continued.

"Yes, why?"

"His name was found at a possible murder scene," he said.

"See, I told you," she looked traumatized.

249

"Is there anything about this you can tell me?" the officer asked.

Marie shook her head. For the next few minutes Sylvia had to calm her down

"I just want to be out of his life," she stated. "He's a gangster and I'm getting a bad reputation" she added.

Just then the new landlord stuck his head in.

"I thought I might find you here, have you looked at the new apartment?"

"This afternoon," she said, "and thank you for your interest" Marie stated.

Marie and her landlord had been hitting it off lately.

"Is she alright?"

"Yes," Sylvia confessed. "She just heard some bad news about her father."

Marie tried to control herself. "You're so kind," she said.

Striker picked up Dedree late Saturday afternoon and Dedree had told Henry she was going to do some shopping and then pick up something to eat on the run. She had left Julia and Henrys dinner in the oven. They checked into a high-class hotel and ordered room service. 25 minutes later the waiter brought cold pheasant, strawberry shortcake, and a bottle of chateau on ice. Dedree insisted they both shower, and then put the do not disturb sign on the door. Their warm embrace soon led to warm kisses and soon Dedree was swooning in pleasure and ecstasy leading them to a sweet release. They both lay and held each other while they talked.

"I told him I was shopping," she confessed.

"That's a good excuse," he added.

"One must be careful you know," Dedree warned him.

Striker remained silent. "What about Julia?"

"She's too young to understand anyway," she added.

"Yeah but…"

"She'll never know."

"But we see her all the time," he said.

"You're her bus driver," she said amusingly.

Striker was quick to change the subject. "Want some cold pheasant?"

They showered and he dropped her off in front of her townhouse about 9:00 PM. It was raining.

The following Tuesday after the reverend had volunteered at the drop-in center, he, Martha, and Dan were having lunch together. Margaret, the girl that had been threatened by the pusher and that Father Francis had confronted at the drop-in center, had found the soup kitchen as the reverend had explained to her. Father Francis had explained how the Lord was going to help her and how she should follow up on her prayers and get further therapy.

"Nice to see you, Margaret" he said. "This is Martha and Dan, the also have been through what you've been through. Have you had your methadone treatment?" he asked.

"Yes" Margaret answered.

"Soon we'll be part of one large family," the reverend explained as he poured her a bowl of soup.

Chapter 6

"Lefty" Gemerick knew the heat was onto him. The detectives Matthew and Richard had done their homework. From reliable resources such as arrests from suspects and word of mouth they had narrowed down who the minor lynchpins and major kingpins were. From computer tracking devices and criminal checks they had a good idea who and what they were dealing with. They knew for instance that there were reliable leads at the opium den or where Lefty took his guests, "Club 67". Matthew had a few personal matters against a few of the "animals" he ran into. Rodger Gibbens who Margaret had described as being dangerous and overbearing needed to be arrested and taught a lesson. She felt this man shouldn't go free. Then there were people like Father Francis who were "led by God" decided to clean up the city for good. Matt and Rick had no problem with that. It would probably do the tourism industry a great favor.

Matt and Rick decided to drop in the opium den for a visit. It was Wednesday night and had been raining most of the day. They dressed in casual mod clothing that would act as a cover for them. The authorities were looking for the Gibbons case and a drug pusher man known as Rodger, but the suspect had been hard to find. Just as the 67 Club was forewarned, a lot of Lefty's lynchpins were forewarned, and they knew how to avoid the authorities. That was caused by word of mouth.

Matt and Rick asked questions, used names, to unravel the truth. Eventually they knew they would get their man. For Matt and Rick, it was like playing some large jig-saw puzzle. "Striker" and Dedree made a date to go for a coffee at a busy local coffee shop.

"I think my maid suspects something, " Dedree explained as they recalled in a quiet corner over a cup of joe.

"Really, how do you know?" her partner asked.

"She mentioned that a stranger was wanting to meet me," she further explained.

"Discourage her," Striker scolded.

"Of course."

A suspicious character approached Striker and handed him some bills. Striker in turn handed him a package. He looked at Dedree and said, "It's some whey powder I picked up at the health food store."

Minutes later two off duty police officers made the arrest. Striker didn't give them Dedrees real name and address. She caught a cab.

Three days later Dedree went to the police station for a visit. They sat facing each other behind a wire screen.

"How could you do this to me?" she scolded.

"I really didn't think I'd get caught," Striker confessed.

"You did this to me. All the low-down tricks," she said.

"I'm sorry."

"I never want to see you again," she warned, and she got up and left.

Matt checked for mail in the lobby of his one-bedroom apartment. Glancing over it he made a mental note then took the elevator to his 10-story apartment. He dropped the mail on the desk and checked his telephone messages. A friend of his was a single mom, separated from her spouse and living alone. He called her occasionally in his off-duty hours or just when he needed someone to talk to. She had left a disturbing message.

"Someone has been calling and threatening over the phone."

She said her 15-year-old daughter had been solicited at her high school. That was odd, he thought. She was an occasional friend who could have found out, unless it was someone who was really wanted to hurt him.

The Gibbon's affair was still unresolved. He had not yet been apprehended. He decided he would have to find out who had been making the phone calls and from where. Then maybe stakeout his girlfriend's daughters high school. He grabbed his keys and headed for the station. He had the chief put a trace on the phone calls.

Matt and Rick nursed a Starbucks coffee for an hour before Carries classes started the following day. Carrie was Lorna's daughter who was also his friend. They would have to come and watch after classes that afternoon as well. As Matt sipped his coffee the thought again occurred to him of the Gibbons affair. Rodger Gibbons, who was the pusher, was a hard nut to crack. He must know a lot of people, but like Lefty, they won't talk. Involvement with this Rodger Gibbons were keeping a low profile as well. If it was him who was threatening Lorna and Carrie, he would probably have a lot of people working for him. It would be for Matt and Rick like answering a large jig-saw puzzle with many extra pieces.

It was a bright and sunny day one Sunday morning in June and the temperature was already at a comfortable 75 degrees.

St. Alfred's church was getting its share of good turnouts for the 10:00AM service.

"Good morning Mrs. Goodwin," the reverend said with a smile greeting a member he hadn't seen in many months.

"It's a lovely day isn't it," he said.

The soup kitchen was also getting favorable turnouts as well. A couple of the church members had volunteered to help, which made many more people interested.

"You seem to be cleaning up our neighborhood" one member exclaimed, making Father Francis' project even more worthwhile. Father Francis knew he was changing lives from the amount of people he was saving. Not just bringing them to Christ, but literally saving lives. Margaret Gordon was just one of the miracles brought about through the service, but Martha and Dan as well. Margaret Gordon had been a safety pin in the Vancouvers police fight with the nations illegal drug syndicate.

From the information from the arrested suspects criminal check to word of mouth and alleged pedophile victims involved, naturally some criminals used phony names, but Lorna's anonymous phone caller had been traced to a phone booth which had been used more than one time. Matt had taken it personally and felt it his responsibility to do something about it. He continued his stakeout at Carries high school as well as have the phone booth under a 24hr surveillance watch. He found nothing. Whoever was trying to hurt her was keeping anonymous as well.Rodger Gibbons of the Gibbons affair was thought to be an assumed name. The criminal check they did on him came up with nothing. The Club 67 that was being used to entertain international guests was discreetly being ignored. Lefty was laying low as well.

"They keep trying to cover their tracks," Matt told the chief.

"It's going to be hard to point the finger on one of these guys."

The department would have to start getting tough.

Max Renfrew has been a second-rate criminal since 1984. He not only was a crack dealer but was an addict himself. His business associates, also crack dealers and users, had been war members serving in Vietnam and had a fair knowledge of the world and what it had to offer. What was useful to Renfrew was that they had a fairly good knowledge of weapons and their use. Later after becoming used to the narcotics trade, he had broadened his horizons by building a machine that made counter-fit money. That and with his friends in the marines, he would be well equipped for the sort of illegal activity he was into. Max kept his money out of circulation by using small change. He didn't want an all-out war with the police and dealing with large bills he felt he was asking for trouble. His associates had smaller people under them. People that used connections as a means of getting their own source of narcotics. This would give him the chance to use his money laundering skills as well.

Renfrew had a million-dollar home at the edge of Vancouver. Large, fenced property controlled by two or three Dobermans. A pool and large spacious living quarters with 10 guest rooms, a butler and four or five maids. He drove a Mercedes sports car paid for with real cash. His contacts with central and south America had to be private and with Patrick Gemericks international drug ring, he had to remain anonymous. He had too many people that depend on his business, and they were steady customers and had been for many years. Small arms, narcotics, and money laundering were about all he could handle while remaining inconspicuous.

Max Renfrew fumbled with the ownership and license papers of his 2010 Mercedes before grabbing his keys and heading for the exit of his multi-million-dollar home. He needed to do a safety check on the car and then change the license plates. As he headed for the exit, he heard the doorbell ring. He had an intercom which was attached to the front gate. He was not used to getting visitors, so it had to be important.

"Yes"

"Max Renfrew?" the intercom asked.

"Yes"

"We'd like to ask you some questions," the voice on the other end answered.

Renfrew answered the door again in a few minutes and was shown police badge and police told him he was under arrest. They had a warrant. The charge was for possession of counterfeit money.

Later at police headquarters, they interrogated Renfrew under intense questioning. Matt and Rick were there. Renfrew with his business haircut slightly styled, his formal blue suit collar messy, and shirt tail hanging with slightly boyish looking features in a state of becoming wimpish.

"Tell you what," Matt proclaimed, carefully, "you give us what we want, and we'll let you off lightly," he hesitated.

Renfrew looked uninterested.

"It may pay for you to listen," Matt related.

"Go on," Renfrew said.

"You help us, and we'll help you."

Father Francis spooned out the second bowl of soup and

put them on a tray with two slices of bread and carried it to Martha and Danny who had just arrived.

"How are you feeling Martha?" he asked inquisitively as they began consuming their dinner. Martha had been straight for about 8 months. It was July and the weather was uncomfortable. Martha looked irresistible.

"I find I still have the desire for a fix," she explained, "it's no picnic."

"Is there anything I can do?" the priest added.

"You've been a great help Father" she said.

Martha and Dan left after lunch and walked to their 1-bedroom apartment as they talked. "The reverend is a bright light," Martha announced.

"Yes, one of the best" Dan commenced to say.

"I guess its people like him who make like a little more bearable," she stated.

"I keep thinking I'd just like to end it all and get a fix."

Dan grabbed her and put his arms around her head and stuck his face close to hers.

"Don't give up," he warned, "you can do it, there are a lot of good things in life."

"Like what?"

"Common, let's get you home."

Dan pushed her shirt from her shoulders later in their private one bedroom. He slowly removed the rest of her clothing and laid in the bed together.

"I'll show you a thing in life," he kissed her passionately then began his foreplay.

Matthew had had enough. When faced with the Gibbons affair and seeing Margaret, almost destroyed, then that not being enough, having two very close friends threatened over the phone he decided that it was time he put an end to the precarious affair once and for all. With the way Patrick Gemerick covered his tracks with his minor lynchpins keeping a low profile, it was grim that the correct perpetrator would be brought justice. He hoped that using Max Renfrew as a guinea pig was the antidote that would bring change to this infectious disease that was ruining the fair city of Vancouver. Police headquarters was a quarry of activity on August 3rd when Matt and Richard interrogated Max Renfrew on what his involvement would be in the arrest of Patrick Gemerick.

" We know you are involved with a couple of war veterans, as well as arms dealers, it that right Max?" the chief asked in a closed, soundproof interrogation room.

"Yes," Max relented.

"And you are involved with many drug dealers, is that correct?"

"Possibly."

"We need you to contact a man named Patrick Gemerick, sometimes known as Lefty, have you heard of him?" the inspector asked.

"Briefly," Max continued.

"Then we need you to set up a time and place so that we can make an arrest, is that clear?"

"Yes."

"You're not to get in any kind of illegal involvement or make and kind of drug deals, understood?" the chief demanded. "You do that and maybe we can lessen some of your sentence."

Matt studied the inspector carefully wasting his expressions. He looked pleased and relieved. Matt and the chief left the room and Matt took the chief aside and warned him.

"I think you should have Max's men covered as well as have extra men covering Lefty, you'll need a good strong force, let's just hope this doesn't backfire" the chief warned.

Chapter 7

Max made an appointment with "Lefty" that was to take place at the multicultural civic center. He was helping in a drug cartel from Columbia, South America. His men were stationed at all the exits. The meeting was to be held in a cocktail lounge, offered inside the building. They would make the arrest after the start of the meeting. Max's appointment with "Lefty" was on Thursday at 2:00 PM. The police force had all the exits to the civic center covered, some of the detectives dressed in disguise as tourists or janitors and security guards so there would be no suspicion of police involvement. "Lefty" would have a few of his men posted guard, but that didn't seem to create concern. Max had a few of his men show up just so as not to cause concern as well. Lefty arrived in a small 30-foot pleasure craft and parked it at the side of the building in the bay for an easy getaway. A police patrol craft was sent to patrol the bay just in case. The men in "Lefty's" pleasure craft had concealed two AK47s under the seat. Most of the arms were small and left concealed.

Sunlight lit the solarium lighting the tall trees and small flowers and shrubs, with the many glass panels delivering the light through illuminated walls of glass, leaving an array of sunlight across the sofas of the cocktail lounge and onto the floor. Max entered and appeared to him as a group of businessmen that could be "Lefty" Gemerick. He extended his hand and asked,"Mr. Gemerick?" "Have a seat," Patrick said extending his hand in that direction. They sat and paused for a moment. Max looked around at the other men.

"My helpers," Lefty confessed.

"Now then, shall we get down to business," both men ignored the handshake.

Just then four police officers showed up, displaying their badges saying "Patrick Gemerick you're under arrest."

"Heads up" one of Lefty's handman shouted, and the shooting began. Everyone ducked. Glass panels were shattered, upholstery was penetrated, and bullets were flying everywhere. Two or three of Lefty's men grabbed him and exited through the side door.

They reached their watercraft and crouched low. His men in the boat covered them with rapid fire from the AK47 as they exited the area as fast as the boat would take them. The police cruiser that was nearby opened fire on them, and the men drew their AK47s. They hit the side of the police cruiser and left holes in the hull. The parole men ducked as Lefty made his narrow escape.

Matt called the airports and had the names checked, but it would be nothing for Lefty to use an assumed name and leave the country. They didn't even need passports to go to the U.S. He then called the coastguard to have their craft followed. He also had Lefty's mother and daughter questioned and watched. Matt knew what he had to do. The coast guard would need to be contacted and the Vancouver international airport as well as the airport in Victoria would have to be contacted. Lefty would try to leave the city if not the country. It would be almost useless though, assuming he would wear a disguise. Assuming he left the country, Matt would have to apologize to Margaret about letting Lefty slip out of their hands.

Lefty's family was notified as to his whereabouts, and the next day Matt was having a coffee with Margaret at St. Alfred's church.

"So, they think he left the country, eh?" Father Francis was curious enough to ask.

"Yes"

"Where do they think he's gone?" he asked again.

"Possibly Miami," Matt explained. "It's a central point to Europe and south America. There are a lot of mafia brothers in Miami also."

Matt looked frustrated and then Father Francis remarked "you have the Lord on your side, Jesus Christ will be your savior."

Matt then looked at Margaret and said "I'm sorry."

"Don't worry, we'll find them."

Matt made sure his friends were taken care of as well. There would be police protection for the girl on her way to school and their phone would be tapped as well. No one would be able to threaten them again.

The buzz at police headquarters the following day was rampant with activity as the apprehension of Lefty was fresh on everyone's minds. The chief, Matt, and Richard were holding a briefing in the chief's office.

"We should be able to find the whereabouts of Lefty in Miami from the minor lynchpins we've arrested here in the city" the chief explained feeling confident in what he recollected.

"What do you mean?" Richard asked the chief to explain further.

"Obviously they'll try to remain in touch with him," he explained. "Someone along the line will have some idea as to his whereabouts."

"That will require some intense interrogation" Richard acknowledged.

"Yes" he paused, "all we want from you Matt is to keep your nose clean while you're there" the chief warned, "the Miami police will help you. You won't be able to apprehend the suspect, we need you to contact the Miami Police."

Matt checked his badge and threw it in the suitcase, then checked the permit for his weapon, a 38 tucked in a shoulder strap, then threw it in the suitcase. He checked the remaining odds and ends like toothbrush, and shaving kit, then zipped the case and left it by the door. His flight was for 10:00am, so he was required to be at the airport by 8:00. He checked the time and finished his black coffee. It was 7:15am. The cab was punctual, and he arrived at the airport at 7:45am, tipping the cab driver he carried his own bag.

Two and a half hours later, he was 1 ½ hours into his flight and he reviewed in his mind what he had to do. They were given instructions that Lefty was staying at the Miami Hilton. He was under care of a mob boss named, Sharky. Lefty was in a foreign country and was under his supervision. Lefty would do the best he could with the remains of his organization and when the "heat" cooled down in Vancouver he would return.

Matt waved down the stewardess and ordered a scotch and soda. Matt reviewed in his mind what he would do once he reached his hotel room. He would check for hidden microphones, then scan the likely casinos, nightclubs, and possible hot spots. More than likely "Lefty" would be lying low, being protected by his peers. It would be difficult finding Lefty because he would be using a phony name as well as staying out of business anyways, so anyone looking for him would have a hard time finding him. Matt sighed, "who knew how long this was going to take… weeks, months."

The west coast syndicate for the most part had been a mistake. The Canadian police department had extracted any foreign gang members from infiltrating Canadian soil, and for certain big drug related gang members were not going to choose Vancouver as their "hot spot" for foreign links such as Asia and South America. More than likely, Lefty would be taken care of and probably retire on some rich corner of the world. Big kingpins had a habit of sticking up for their own. As for Matt, it would all blow over in a few weeks, then he could go home.

Chapter 8

Matthew waited for his luggage at the bag check at the Miami International airport, as he stood waiting, he noticed there were no bags being delivered on the conveyor belt. He noticed an attractive middle-aged woman in a smart blueish-grey shirt-suit. He was tempted to say something but thought better of it. After he gathered his bags, he caught a cab and directed the driver to proceed to the Miami Hilton, taking Ocean Drive as he gazed out the window. After a few minutes he noticed a large lagoon or swamp. He remembered hearing on the news about Flight 92 crashing into this lagoon in 1985. He thought of what his end could be, and then of ending up in some allegators stomach. Then eventually he thought of the sights he was seeing of the popular holiday resort.

The driver took him all the way down Ocean Drive to Osler Street, the popular tourist street along the oceanside of Miami Beach. Tourists were streaming about, all hours of the day. The chief had booked him ahead of time in a modest hotel, but he knew if it suited him, he could make changes in the arrangements. He also learned from the Miami vice (as they were known) that of Lefty's possible whereabouts. Although they were getting cooperation from the local police force, he was not certain they would appreciate arresting someone in another country, which meant he would have to cooperate with the local police.

Matt thought of the words of Father Francis before he left Vancouver, "do with the grace of Jesus Christ." Those were comforting words, and he would need them in the days ahead. He was issued a business phone to keep in touch with his department, and he thought it best to text the chief as he grabbed his room key and headed for his room. It would be comforting to be able to keep in contact if he got into any trouble.

After Matt had a light dinner, there was a few hours of sunlight left, so he decided to rent a car. Then he checked his hotel room for possible bugs, it took him a few minutes. He then relaxed and poured himself stiff Jack Daniels that he picked up at the LCBO. Matt checked his revolver to make sure it was loaded and kept it close just in case. He was sure no one knew he would be there, but knowing all Lefty's followers, he just wasn't sure.

Matts plan for the next morning was to check with the local authorities and let them know he was alive. The flight list for the last 2 or 3 weeks could have been checked, as he thought about the cab driver being the only possible lead to his whereabouts. They could check the flights from Vancouver, but the chances of him getting the red-carpet treatment on entering the city is highly unlikely. But of course, there could be a leak from the police department, that meant Matt would have to be careful who he met and talked to, but he was going to do that anyway.

Marie Gemerick wiped the four-year old's mouth as she undid the bib around his neck that protected the tiny shirt that he wore.

"Now go play with the tractors in the sand box" she

demanded, directing the excited child to the new sand box, part of their new facility that she used as an improvement to the new and larger facility that was a recent upgrade to her new business.

Her business was expanding due to the recent upgrade as well as hiring more helpers. It contained a new swing and playground area, new televisions and DVD players as well as an indoor trampoline.

Marie entered the building and poured herself a cup of coffee, taking silent invoice of the morning activities as she explained to Sylvia her co-owner, "I've been so busy with the things down here that I haven't had time to unpack a thing," she continued, "I'd really like to start decorating the new apartment."

"Did you explain to the detective that you're no longer involved or receiving help from your father?" Sylvia asked.

"I also explained I had no idea what his business was or where to find him," Marie explained, "that part of my life is over, I hope."

Father Francis folded his prayer mantel and placed it in the drawer. He then took an umbrella and began walking toward the drop-in center on East Hastings Street. It was about a twenty-minute walk as if someone were walking quickly. As he walked, he thought of what he had said to Matt before he left Vancouver and flew to Miami.

"Jesus Christ will protect you," then he thought of what he was doing and the lives he had saved. He suddenly became quite satisfied with himself. As he walked, he noticed sleeping in a storefront doorway, a poor beggar that was down and out. He took a five-dollar bill from his pocket and stuck it likewise in the beggar's pocket. He felt he could do anything at all to help just a little bit. It warmed the inside of him, as he continued.

"Lefty", or called Patrick Gemerick, was a small racketeer compared to the larger criminal racketeers in the rest of America. He owned a drug cartel in Vancouver but was only involved in drugs. Other racketeers in Miami, New York, or Las Vegas were not only into drug trafficking but money laundering and prostitution as well. But "Lefty" had contacts and close ties with dealers and cartel owners around and outside the U.S, South America, Europe, Africa, and possibly Turkey. Heroine made from poppy plants were another possibility. So, when the Vancouver City police arrested a suspect carrying 3 bags of crack cocaine on him as he un-boarded a freighter that arrived from Columbia, South America, they made a deal, telling him they would lighten his sentence by giving them valuable information. The street value of three bags of cocaine would be in the triple digits and many of Lefty's contacts would be in touch with him.

Matt woke at 9 o'clock and took the elevator to the main floor where he had a large breakfast of scrambled eggs, sausage, and toast. Although it was late October, the sun was shining, and the air was moist and damp due to the seaside location.

"More coffee?" the waitress asks in a friendly demeanor.

"Yes," Matt relented.

"First time in Miami?" she asked, not being suspicious, just curious.

"Deep sea fishing," Matt stated.

"You'll like that," she concluded.

"Yah, fishing good around here?" he asked.

"The best in the world" she said as she walked way.

Matt heard his cellphone ding like he got a text message. It was Richard, telling him they got some information on Lefty.

'He checked into a room on the west side of Miami, then moved him to a different location. His contact is known as Jigs, probably just a code name' Richard texted.

Matt texted him back, 'keep up the good work, partner'.

"Lefty" was sitting by the poolside of his colleagues three-million-dollar home known as James Bruster, alias "The Spruce Goose" or just "Goose". It was located in Miami's rich suburb neighborhood whom his colleague "Goose" was known for heroin smuggling. The maid handed him a pina colada. She wore a skimpy light blue skirt and a white working blouse. She worked as a house maid as well.

"Thanks Daisy," Lefty said as he gestured to pinch her rear end.

She dodged his attempt. He sipped his drink as the afternoon wore on, enjoying the morning sun.

Lefty and the Goose were waiting for a large shipment of raw heroine to arrive in one of his key Kingpins yachts, a rather large sleeping capacity and a crew of 75. It was supposedly arriving from Turkey.

Matt checked out the address that Lefty was supposed to have met "Jigs" his contact. The landlord claimed he knew nothing which was probably the truth. He continued the first day checking out gambling places or local pool halls asking questions and making inquiries, but to no avail. He spent his nights sifting the local nightclubs.

Each morning the same waitress would ask how the fishing was and if he was enjoying his stay. After a week or two of lying he got to know her a little. She seemed a little distraught, and he picked up on this.

"My son is hanging around some loose characters that seem to be involved in drugs," she confessed. "I think he has a contact arriving by boat."

This was the information he needed.

The next day Matt did some snooping around the local harbor, docks or pier side to look for any suspicious activity related to drug trafficking or buying or selling illegal drugs. It occurred to him that if he told the waitress at the Hilton of what he was doing she might suspect he was a detective, but what he could do was tell her that he would help her son in case he got into trouble. He couldn't do any arresting, but he could give his word that he would protect him.

About a week later she got a little suspicious when he told the same fishing story, so he confessed the news.

"I'm looking for a drug cartel dealer," he told her, "I think he could be related to the shipment that is arriving from Turkey" he said. "I could use any possible leads I can get."

She told him she would let him know.

"Please don't tell anyone where I'm staying" he warned.

"Then in a few days," she said "I can't give you any leads, but I did find out that it was a large yacht that was carrying the drugs, and that it was to land at the state harbor that is south along the coast." She also gave Matt her sons description in case he happened to see him.

Goose, the cartel owner, and Lefty, his temporary boarder or house guest, were sitting around his swimming pool on a routine sunny day, when he got a phone call.

"Yah, good," he related and hung up.

He dialed another number and demanded, "Get ahold of

Cal, yah, just arrived, and let me know if anything changes" then he hung up.

The housekeeper brought Lefty another cocktail. Goose looked at Lefty and warned, "The shipment is in. You'll meet the delivery at the appointed rendezvous. You won't have to worry about cash, the payment will be done beforehand. Is that clear Lefty?"

"Yes."

Lefty had a small job to do for the Goose in exchange for his friendly service. Lefty was to confirm a delivery to the local Mafia. It wasn't a large delivery aside from a few million in white powder, but Lefty thought his resources knew some mob bosses.

Matt swirled his Jack Daniels in the glass as he thought about his next move. He knew what Lefty looked like from the various photos that the detectives had taken on their cellphone on the day he had made his escape from Vancouver. He thought it best to notify the local police. That way once they had rounded up Lefty, he could bargain for his return, for crimes he made in Vancouver.

Suddenly it occurred to Matt he should call his own chief. It was 7:30pm and he poured himself another Jack Daniels, when there was a knock on the door. A message from the front desk. He tipped the porter and the message said "Call the chief."

The next morning Matt drove his rented capri to Miami PD headquarters. At the front desk he explained who he was, and then about "Lefty". He then explained how he found out about the shipment of illegal drugs arriving from Turkey. He had to confirm the arrival, so he offered to volunteer his services, and then let them know of the yacht's arrival. He had little idea it had already arrived. They issued a catamaran and some officers to assist in finding the yacht. They had no trouble finding it and Matt made the phone call. He later found out he would get their total cooperation in apprehending the suspects, providing of course that there really was a "shipment".

Chapter 9

The crew of the yacht unloaded some of the narcotics onto an inboard fiberglass 18-footer and carefully covered the contents in order to unload it nearby to an awaiting truck they would deliver it to the appointed rendezvous. The truck would be driven and followed by Lefty who was to meet them at the rendezvous making sure the delivery was made. The Goose let him out at the delivery truck which he followed in an unmarked vehicle. The loading platform where the 18-footer was docked, was a legal service loading platform as part of the state harbor.

Matt had spent the morning nearby waiting with a pair of binoculars he had luckily packed in his suitcase. As he walked down the harbor, he watched people as they passed hoping to catch a glimpse of Lefty or the waitress's son, who could be an innocent bystander.

Matthew continues along the harbor front looking for Lefty or what his friend described as her son. The sun was shining and from what he could see of the American flag that flew nearby, there was a cool breeze coming from the gulf. He was walking alone, and he had American officers observing nearby. The coast guard was instructed to confiscate the yacht and its crew the moment they were informed. Matt knew he had to catch them red handed with the illegal drugs. They were waiting for Matt to arrest Lefty. The moment they made the arrest the coast guard would be notified. Matt felt he could get his "man".

He could see up the harbor where the 18-footer was unloading as he had observed through his binoculars. He got closer looking around, like a busy tourist until he got close enough to see what was going on. As Matt approached, he noticed a clean-cut gentleman in his mid-forties with a neatly trimmed haircut and a casual suit get out of a limousine and get into an unmarked blue-sedan, the limousine then drove off. Lefty got out and watched as they closed the back door of the truck and began communicating with the workers. Matt gave the word and then the officers surrounded the truck as the 18-footer sailed off.

Matt was sitting in the main headquarters of the Miami police, as the dispatcher took down the information about the captain and arrest of the cartel and its occupants, awaiting the arrival of the patty wagon that would deliver the accused suspects. The officer was calm, with a few workers who had shed their clothing trying to beat the heat, as the ceiling fan rotated, slowly carrying the morning activity that was about to explode.

The rear door slammed open as the suspects were lead in one by one, being led to their awaiting cells. Lefty strode through in handcuffs with a sour look of dissatisfaction on his face and suddenly paused and looked at Matt and the dispatcher.

"Screws," he yelped, "you're arresting a Canadian citizen."

"Good," the dispatcher grinned, "because this detective is from Vancouver, and he's come to take you home."

"They can't charge me for anything, I'm innocent" he said.

"Tell that to the judge," the dispatch warned.

Lefty was charged with three counts of first-degree murder, as well as possession of narcotics. Seeing how Matthew was so eager to come from Canada and arrest him, the U.S feds decided to allow Matt to take him back to Vancouver for the trial and conviction.

The waitress brought Matt his dinner at the Hilton that night, it being the daily special. When he related the events of the day, she thanked him, and then insisted on him staying and doing more activity for her son's drug problem. As he considered how friendly she had become, he asked her out to dinner. He had to take the capri back to the rental lot and pack his few belongings anyway. Later, they laid in his hotel bed, after a heated session of love making and shared a glass of Jack Daniels.

"Do you think they know where you are?" she asked, "I mean the Mafia?"

"No."

"I guess you are quite pleased with yourself?" she noted.

"I'm just glad I got him before he got to your son."

"Why?"

"I guess for the simple reason I don't like seeing 8-year-old girls forced into addiction," Matt explained.

"How will they get Lefty back to Vancouver?" the waitress asked.

Matt explained how they would probably send him in a police escort with his legs shackled and in handcuffs. For Matt, after tonight he would not get much sleep. Probably awake for 48 hours. It was part of the job.

Matt signed the guest list at the soup kitchen at St. Alfred's church in Vancouvers lower east side, in greater Vancouver.

"Hello, Father," he said upon entering.

Martha and Dan were sitting having lunch, Margaret, who was recovering from her drug addiction, and slowly gaining weight.

"You'll be happy to know that the leader of the cartel of the West Coast Syndicate has been apprehended," Matt related, "So now its up to you to keep up the good work, Father."

The End

"Divine Submission"

Julia came from an intelligent family and had several scientific heroes. Some of them Karl Sagan, Albert Einstein, Isaac Newton, her father a retired chemical engineer, and her two valedictorian brothers. Julia was a dual citizen. Due to her American and Canadian citizenship, she couldn't get a student loan to go to school. She decided to take a full-time job making minimum wage. It's hard for a single girl just starting out in the workforce with the cost of car insurance and rent, not to mention food and clothes.

She befriended a man who became successful in the literary world. The world around this man became confused with success and he accidentally took an overdose of sleeping pills. He then called her on the telephone and explained to her that he took an overdose. When she hung up she called the ambulance.

A little while later, he found to his astonishment she was still his friend. In time, she became his best friend.

Julia was a morally sound individual. Not drinking, smoking, or doing drugs. In short, an all-around good person. The bible says "To give one's life for a brother or friend, surprise, surprise, you get your life back."

Julia's father took a part time job as a swim coach for juveniles, for the city they now reside in. Eventually, Julia did the same. She partitioned city call to have a new aqua center built and eventually took over the job full time. Her career went well for a few tears. She was working 24/7 just to make ends meet.

Her parents moved to New Brunswick, and she decided she had enough of being a swim coach. The job itself was becoming too stressful. She decided she was going to move to New Brunswick with her parents. Something happened to her best friend. He lost his sight, he asked her "will you come see me before you move to New Brunswick?" she said she would but unfortunately became too busy with what she was doing and could only keep in touch. She promised him she would come and see him the next time she would visit.

The world was getting wickeder and wickeder. Julia didn't believe in divine healing or miracles, but she wasn't an evil person either. In her heart she believed what was happening to her was very real. She believed in a divine creator but would not admit to it. Her best friend she knew was a believer, but she wasn't aware of the Lord's ways. She was gone for many months and finally went for a visit. He was gone. Although she wanted to see him, she very much missed him. He was her best friend. She would remember him.

"Medical Research"

It was late January. The health complex was modern, but that didn't matter. The world was changing. The plant life was dying, the air was thin, the climate was getting do that one didn't know what the next day would bring. Life was cheap. If you weren't strong and healthy you would soon end up in a facility, similar to life being cheap and plant and animal life were growing scarce, most sickly people were used for experimental services to keep the human race going. Unless you were healthy, you didn't know where your next meal was coming from. Things kept going from bad to worse because the plants and animal needed the air to be clearer to make food.

One level of the facility was the drug experiment program, competent facility because it experimented with the mental state of the civilization. The normal world didn't know what was normal, and it depended on facilities like these to survive. With medical advancements becoming more and more advanced there were older level of medical research as well.

Like cattle, one by one they herded forward for their medications. "that's not my normal dose" one patient said. The patients usually argued with the nurses. Anyway, even though they knew too well that their objections were only futile, they ate what was put before them and did what they were told, or they would face the consequences.

They lived with resistance, like zombies, with the promise of getting well.

Live well, get healthy, and help make normal people and the planet healthy.

"A Success"

There was a young six-year-old named Joey. The other boys in the schoolyard were used to mocking him. He couldn't live like a normal ten-year-old because of the other children constantly made fun of him. It was hard for him to make friends, and he thought he wasn't normal.

Joey was small for his age, thin, fair hair, and blue eyes. His complexion was meek with a boyish demeanor. He was bullied in the schoolyard quite regularly. The children seemed to find pleasure pushing him around.

The schoolyear was coming to an end and Joey like the other boys and girls was looking forward to a fun summer. There were baseball games and times at the beach, and other things that normal boys and girls would do. But Joey wasn't any normal little boy. He decided to tell someone.

One day that summer they were picking teams for baseball. Joeys team was outfield. The opposite team hit a ball towards hum. He didn't throw it home fast enough and the opposite team scored two points.

The following day they went to pick teams again, and they laughed at Joey and left him out. That night at dinner, his parents asked what he had done that day. He explained what happened and that he had a problem. He will be entering puberty soon and he will need to deal with it, his mother said. His parents discussed this later amongst themselves, and three weeks later informed Joey that they had a surprise for him.

That year in late July, Joeys parents took him for a ride. At the edge of the neighborhood was a small farm. To Joeys surprise they showed him a horse. When they told him "if you take care of him, he's yours to keep."

He was ecstatic. Most children didn't have the privilege to own their own horses. He was overjoyed for the rest of the summer taking care of his new friend. He will call her Dolly.

One day in late September, he went to school and told a girl named Sally about his new horse. Sally was impressed that she asked him if she could go see Dolly. They spent the next Saturday afternoon feeding the horse. Sally brought an apple for him to eat.

Sally was medium build, had brown shoulder length hair, green eyes, and a hard rock candy face. She loved animals and usually wore a teddy bear sweater.

Sally came to visit every weekend in the next few months. He and Sally became good friends.

Years later, Joey matured and went to high school. He graduated and was getting his yearbook signed when he ran into Sally. They had been out of touch. But he asked her to sign his yearbook. He told her he was having a hard time getting people to sign it. She signed it ''To a special friend''.

He decided to take horsemanship in college. He was small and meek in high school too. He was still having trouble making friends, but this would not let him down. He knew he was built like a jockey and someday he would be famous.

The years passed and Sally ran across his name in a newspaper. His name came into attention when he began working for a millionaire as a jockey. She ran down to the local racetrack to see if she could run into him. She found Joey working in his trainer's stall. They had a lot to catch up on. It took a few minutes in conversation. She decided to get his picture on the horse. And concluded, ''After all these years, you are now a winner!''

CPSIA information can be obtained
at www.ICGtesting.com
Printed in the USA
LVHW071224110623
749398LV00007B/9